THE HAUNTING OF WILLOW HOUSE

ANTHONY M. STRONG

**WEST STREET
PUBLISHING**

Also by Anthony M. Strong

The John Decker Thriller Series

What Vengeance Comes

Cold Sanctuary

Crimson Deep

Grendel's Labyrinth

Whitechapel Rising

Black Tide

John Decker Series Prequel

Soul Catcher

The Remnants Series

The Remnants of Yesterday

Standalone Books

The Haunting of Willow House

Crow Song

West Street Publishing

Cover art and interior design by Bad Dog Media, LLC.

ISBN: 978-1942207085

For Sonya - who scares easily

THE HAUNTING OF
WILLOW HOUSE

They say that shadows of deceased ghosts
Do haunt the houses and the graves about,
Of such whose life's lamp went untimely out,
Delighting still in their forsaken hosts.

Joshua Sylvester
English Poet

Prologue

December 1958

SOMETHING WAS WRONG. Very wrong.

This single thought lingered in Father Christopher Halloran's mind as he steered his cherry red 1952 Plymouth along the narrow country road a few miles west of Salem, Massachusetts. He drove with the reserve of a man who wished he were tucked up in bed rather than outside on a cold and wintry New England evening, but none-the-less, he drove.

Halloran hunched forward, his hands gripping the wheel so tight his knuckles drained of blood. He loathed driving after sunset, and more so when the weather was inclement. Any other time, a storm such as this would have tempered his desire to venture out, but not so on this occasion. The nagging feeling that things were not right had bothered him for days, and finally, unable to dispel the quiet doubt, he resigned himself to this journey.

Grimacing, he stared into the snow-laden darkness beyond the windshield, his eyes searching for the gnarled oak that stood at the edge of the trail leading to Willow Farm.

For a moment, he wondered if he might have gone too far and missed the landmark entirely. But then, as he was about to turn around, he saw it loom out of the night like a wraith, limbs twisted and bent upon themselves. The oak was a grim sight, devoid of life since the summer of forty-eight when a mighty bolt of lightning had cleaved the tree almost in two.

He threw the steering wheel hard to the right and touched the brakes, feeling the back of the car slip on the icy road. It threatened to careen into the tree, but then he wrestled the heavy vehicle under control again, and was soon heading up the narrow dirt trail toward a faint glimmer of lights beyond the fallow fields.

By the time he pulled up in front of the farmhouse, he was cold and tired, but at least his trip was not to be in vain. Frank Walker's white Oldsmobile, the same one he drove to church every Sunday morning, stood like a silent sentinel near the old barn. The glow from within the farmhouse, once a barely perceptible flicker, spilled onto the driveway through half parted curtains.

Father Halloran opened his door and climbed from the driver's seat, gasping at the sudden cold that drilled into his bones. He hitched his coat collar up against the wind, blinking away snowflakes that drifted under his glasses and into his eyes, and slammed the car door.

For a while he stood still, stared up at the old house, and then trudged toward the front entrance, gripping the brass knocker and letting it fall three times. He listened to the dull thud of his knocks reverberate through the hallway beyond and waited.

At first, he saw no sign of life within the dwelling, but soon the sound of a drawn latch greeted his ears.

The door creaked open.

The woman who stood inside seemed surprised.

"Father Halloran, what brings you all the way up here?"

Her accent carried the hard edge of a born and bred Boston New Englander.

"Well now, Mrs. Walker, I was just passing by and thought I would stop in and say hello." Halloran's own Irish accent, unchanged by his years across the Atlantic, stood in stark contrast.

"Really?" Mrs. Walker glanced past the priest, toward the Plymouth, which was already catching a gentle cover of snow despite the fading warmth from the engine. "You thought you'd drive up here in a blizzard, on a whim?"

"Well, yes. The Lord requires that I tend my flock regardless of circumstance." Father Halloran smiled, his eyes straying beyond the doorway into the house. "How is Mr. Walker?"

"Bullheaded, as ever."

"I see." Halloran paused, weighing his words. "I didn't notice him at mass last week."

"He's had a sniffle. Waking at the crack of dawn every day, tending to the farm in weather such as this, it takes a toll." She shifted her stance. "It's nothing to worry about. He'll be fit as a fiddle in a day or two, you mark my words."

"That's good to hear." Halloran nodded. "I am well aware of the ills of foul weather. May I step inside for a moment, Mrs. Walker?"

"What?"

"May I come in?" Halloran rubbed his hands together. "I won't keep you, I promise, but it will be much better to talk in the warm."

"Of course. Where are my manners, keeping a man such as yourself outside on a night like this?" Mrs. Walker said, but even so, she did not move to allow him passage until the priest mounted the front steps.

"That's better." Halloran brushed the melting snow from his coat and pushed the door closed. That done, he spoke again. "I have to tell you Mrs. Walker, I am a little concerned."

"Really? Why is that?" She raised an eyebrow.

"Like I said, your husband, Frank, was not at church on Sunday, and neither was young Thomas. You came alone."

"Thomas?"

"Yes."

"Why would you be concerned with him?"

"Your son is one of my best altar boys, Mrs. Walker. He was absent on Sunday, along with your husband, and he missed practice today. May I inquire, is he sick also?"

"It's that time of year." Mrs. Walker said by way of explanation. She wiped her hands on her apron. "There's always something going around."

"Indeed, there is." Halloran agreed. "Have you called the doctor out?"

"The doctor? Now why would I do that?" Mrs. Walker took a step backward, toward the stairs. "I haven't lived on this earth for forty-six years not to know how to deal with a common cold. Besides, he's almost back to himself. By tomorrow he'll be tearing around the house getting into all sorts of trouble."

"Now that's good to hear. I am sure he will." Father Halloran nodded. "May I see him then?"

"Now?"

"Why yes. I'm sure he would appreciate a visit, given that he's been cooped up for so long. Just a few words, that's all."

"He's sleeping. Poor thing was tired out."

"Well, that's a shame," Halloran said. "And Frank?"

"He's down at the cow barn, checking on the livestock. The joys of the farm."

"A dedicated man if ever there was one." Halloran glanced around the hallway, his eyes settling on the coat rack, and the row of winter garments hanging there. "I can wait for him, if you don't mind."

"He just left. He'll probably be a while. You should get back to town before the blizzard really kicks in."

"I see." Halloran rubbed his chin. "You are probably right."

"You wouldn't want to get stuck up here, now, would you?"

"No indeed. I would not." Father Halloran took a step toward the door.

He reached toward the handle.

Somewhere above, a thud.

Halloran paused, his eyes drifting upward, toward the second floor.

"That would be Thomas." Mrs. Walker turned her head toward the stairs, then back to the priest. "You see, I told you he was fine."

"And wide awake apparently," Father Halloran said, turning to the stairs. "Maybe I will go up and say hello after all."

"No." Mrs. Walker scuttled backward, positioning herself between the priest and the stairs. "I'm not sure that is a good idea. He needs his rest."

"Of course. You know best, I'm sure." Halloran cast a glance past the woman. "Will I see him this Sunday?"

"If he is back to himself, I'm sure you will."

"Good." Halloran turned back toward the door.

Thud.

The sound was louder this time. It echoed in the hallway.

Halloran spun on his heel and fixed the farmer's wife with a questioning stare. "Are you absolutely sure Thomas is alright?"

"Of course, what sort of a question is that?" There was an edge to her voice, a slight tremble. "Everything is just dandy."

Thud.

Halloran's gaze shot upward. "I think I should go up and see him."

"I can't allow that." Mrs. Walker positioned herself at the foot of the stairs.

"It's not a request, Mrs. Walker." Halloran advanced toward the farmer's wife, and taking her firmly by the shoulders, moved her aside and mounted the stairs.

It was dark on the second floor. A subtle musty scent hung in the air, pushing at the priest's nose.

Halloran paused for a moment to allow his eyes to adjust, and then picked his way along the landing toward the furthest door, under which a thin sliver of pale light was visible.

This was surely the boy's room.

Mrs. Walker was climbing the stairs, the old treads creaking with each footfall.

She appeared on the landing; eyes wild.

"Father Halloran, I implore you, let things be."

"I'll just poke my head in and say hello to the boy." Halloran took the doorknob and turned it, his heart quickening as he pushed inward.

Thomas Walker lay on the bed, shirtless. Deep welts crisscrossed his torso, angry and red. His usually combed hair was disheveled and wild. His arms and legs were outstretched to the four corners of the mattress.

For a moment Halloran could see no reason for this unusual repose, but then he noticed the cords wound around the boys wrists and ankles.

The boy lifted his head, arching upward to see who had entered the room, and as he did so, the headboard pulled forward away from the wall. Unable to maintain the pose, he fell back, the headboard slamming into the wall with a resounding thud.

"Sweet Jesus." The priest muttered the words under his breath, barely able to comprehend what he was seeing.

"Father Halloran?" Thomas's voice was reedy, hoarse. "Don't let her hurt me again."

"I won't, son." The priest wondered when the boy had last taken a drink. He thought about fetching him some water, but there were more urgent things to attend to. He moved toward the foot of the bed, intent upon untying the knots that kept Thomas restrained, but then he felt a presence to his rear.

He turned, a cold dread enveloping him.

"I asked you not to come up here." Mrs. Walker filled the doorway. "I didn't want you to see Thomas like this."

"Like what Mrs. Walker?" The priest fought to keep his voice calm and steady. "Lashed to his bed? Scared to death and beaten?"

"You don't understand."

"Then tell me. What possible reason could there be for this insanity?" Halloran asked.

"The devil." The farmer's wife said the words as if that was all the explanation the situation warranted.

"I'm sorry?" Halloran shook his head. "The devil you say?"

"It's inside of him, living with him. Lucifer has claimed his soul. My Thomas is possessed."

"Mrs. Walker, that is preposterous." Father Halloran backed up until his legs hit the bed. "Why would you think something like that?"

"I was told as much."

"Who told you?" The priest glanced toward Thomas. "The boy himself?"

"No. Not the boy."

"Then who?" Halloran pressed. "Did Frank put you up to this?"

"No."

"Then I confess, I am at a loss." Halloran took a handkerchief from his pocket and mopped his brow, feeling warm despite the chill in the air. "Who could have told you such things?"

"The voice in the walls. It speaks to me," Mrs. Walker replied. "It talks at night, when everyone else is sleeping."

"Mrs. Walker, you are not making a lick of sense," The priest said. "What does Frank have to say about all of this?"

"He didn't believe me." Mrs. Walker ran her tongue across her lips. "He said I'm tired, that I'm hearing things."

"Well thank goodness for that. The voice of reason." Halloran motioned toward the bed. "Now why don't we release the boy and wait for Frank to get back from the barn, and then we can have a chat about this, just the three of us."

"Frank isn't coming back from the barn."

"And why is that?" Halloran asked the question even though he feared the answer, and because Mrs. Walker carried something in her hand that he had failed to notice previously. A heavy wrought iron poker.

"Frank didn't think we should help Thomas. He wanted to take him away. But the voice in the walls knew what to do."

"Did it indeed?" Halloran stepped away from the bed, sensing a change of atmosphere in the room. He moved toward the door, praying that the farmer's wife would step aside. He could come back later with the sheriff. "In that case, I think I'll be off if it's all the same with you. I've taken up too much of your time already, and the weather is growing worse."

"You're just like Frank." Mrs. Walker shook her head. "I'm so sorry, may god forgive me, but I need to protect my boy." And with that she shot forward, the poker leading the way.

Halloran stumbled backwards, desperate to escape the charging woman. He bumped into the far wall, his back against the window. And even though there was nowhere else to go, he kept on anyway, because if he didn't, the sharp end of the poker would find him.

The window held firm for a few seconds, enough time for

Halloran to realize what was going to happen, and then gave way with a sharp pop.

As the priest tumbled backwards through the opening, and fell toward the unforgiving, frozen ground below, he saw Mrs. Walker watching from the shattered window, a cruel smile upon her face.

For Sale

Colonial Era Farmhouse set on 5+ Acres
Don't miss this unique opportunity.
1690's farmhouse on 5 acres.
Parcel includes pristine woodland and brook.
With a little TLC this historic home can be brought back to its
former glory.
Two dairy barns and several other structures on site.

Chapter 1

Present Day

THERE WAS a steady drizzle the day that Andrew Whelan and his family made the journey from Boston to the dilapidated farmhouse nestled on a swath of land between the Massachusetts towns of Danvers and Salem. Jake was ten years old, and had, so far, been about as good as any boy that age can be when riding in the back of a car. Sarah, now almost three-quarters through her teen years, sat up front with her father. It was better that way. There was less chance of an altercation, which meant there was less chance that Andrew would have to pull over to the side of the road and give them the kind of tongue lashing their mother used to handle.

Sarah was the first to speak, as they left the city and drove north through Saugus, and then Lynn Woods, before cutting across south of I-95 in the direction of Peabody.

"Tell me again why we have to move here?" she asked, staring out of the passenger seat window, watching the New England scenery roll by. "It's not fair."

"You know why." Andrew glanced sideways. If he was hoping to connect with his daughter, he was disappointed.

Her eyes never strayed from the passing fields. "We've been over this a million times."

"That doesn't mean I have to agree to it." She played with the top of her black shirt. It matched the black skirt and black boots, not to mention the hair, which used to be brown. That was before. Now she shunned color like it was some mortal enemy. "I liked our house in Boston."

"So did I, Sarah, but we all need a new start."

"Mom would never have dragged us out into the country like this."

"We're not in the country," Andrew said, not bothering to mention that a move out of Boston was something he and Jennifer had discussed on numerous occasions. It would make no difference. "Salem is only a few miles to the south. There are all sorts of things to do. There's even a mall."

"So?"

"You like malls."

"I don't like drafty old farmhouses." She shifted in her seat, turning from the passing scenery, and glared at him. "I don't like starting a new school in my senior year."

"I'm sorry. I know we decided to make the move after you graduated, but that was before-"

"I know what I did. You don't have to bring it up again," Sarah said. "It was stupid. I get it. I didn't really mean to go through with it. I didn't intend to take that many pills."

"I know."

"So why are you punishing me?" Sarah asked. "It's not like you're any better."

"I never said I was. I've made my mistakes. But this move, it's good for us."

"Good for you."

"All of us. And I'm not punishing you," Andrew said. "This house came up out of the blue, and it was too good a deal to turn down. I don't know why you won't let this go."

"I was just saying, Mom would never-"

"Dammit, Sarah." He felt the anger rise like a black wave, an unfamiliar beast that had lurked inside of him ever since the accident. He did his best to contain it, but sometimes, especially when he was thinking about Jennifer, the monster reared its head. "Your mother's not here. She's gone, okay?"

"I know that." Sarah shrank back, alarmed by the sudden outburst.

"I miss mom." Jake spoke up from the back seat. "I wish she was here."

"I know you do." Andrew said, his voice softer now, the anger ebbing away as quickly as it had come. "We all wish she was here."

"Is mom in heaven?" This was a question Jake had asked on numerous occasions over the past year, yet despite receiving the same answer each time, he still insisted on asking again.

"Of course she is." Andrew wondered if it was a coping mechanism. He had talked about it with a grief counselor a few months back when Jake was struggling to understand what had happened. The counselor didn't think it was anything worth worrying about, so Andrew let it be, and answered with the same calm reassurances each time. "There's no doubt about it."

"For goodness sake, dad." Sarah shot him a withering look. "When are you going to stop with this?"

"Drop it, Sarah." Andrew was in no mood to deal with his daughter's petulance. "Not now."

"Then when, Dad?" Sarah pressed. "When are you going to tell him the truth?"

"What truth?" Jake scooted up and put his head between the front seats, his eyes wide.

"There's no such thing as heaven," Sarah said, glaring at her father when she spoke. "There's no heaven, and there's no hell. It's all made up so that stupid people feel better about death."

"It is?" Jake looked between his sister and father. "So what happens when we die?"

"There's nothing. It's just blackness, for ever and ever."

"Jesus Sarah, do you have to be so mean?" At that moment Andrew felt like slamming on the brakes and leaving his daughter on the side of the road. Instead, he took a deep breath. "This isn't helping."

"I wasn't trying to help." Her gaze returned to the landscape beyond the car. "I'm allowed to have an opinion."

"Yes, you are," Andrew said. "But sometimes it would be nice if you kept it to yourself."

"Whatever." She shrugged and sank back into the seat. "How much further is it anyway?"

"Not far. A few miles." Andrew glanced at Jake, who had retreated to the back seat once more, pulling his legs up and pressing himself into the door. "Hey sport, you want to help your dad out?"

"Sure." He didn't sound convinced.

"There's a tree we need to find, a big old oak with twisted branches. When we see that, we are there. Can you look out for it?"

"How will I know when I see it?"

"Oh, you'll know. It's an ugly old thing. You can't miss it."

"Okay."

"That's my boy. It'll be on the right hand side. Yell when you see it." Andrew's eyes drifted to the rearview mirror. He was pleased to see Jake scoot across to the right side of the car and peer out of the window, craning his neck to see frontward.

A few minutes later, as the car meandered down a narrow road barely wide enough to avoid the foliage on the banks scraping the sides of the vehicle, Jake pointed, an excited tremble in his voice. "I see it. I see it."

"Good job." Andrew had seen it too, a misshapen contorted mass of dead limbs attached to a great swollen trunk that had been split in two, the cleft running almost half way down.

"Can we get that thing taken down?" Sarah asked. "It gives me the creeps."

"I think that chopping trees down will be pretty low on our list of priorities." He slowed the car and turned off the road, past the oak, and onto a dirt trail that ran to a large white farmhouse with a gray slate tile roof. To the left and right were overgrown fields, beyond which stood a line of Hemlock and Maple, marking the edge of the woods. "Wouldn't you rather get the house in shape, so that we can be warm and cozy in our new home?"

"I'd rather be in our old home, which was already warm and cozy," Sarah replied, never missing an opportunity to show her displeasure. At least the hard edge was gone from her voice. She leaned forward, looking through the windshield as they approached the house.

"We're here now, so you might as well make the most of it." Andrew swung the car around in the driveway and came to a stop near a barn that stood several feet distant from the main building. He nodded toward the old wooden structure. "I was thinking we could turn this into a garage. What do you think?"

"I think it will fall down on the car and then we'll be stuck up here when winter comes." Sarah pulled on her door handle and hopped out of the car.

She looked up at the house, grimacing when she saw the fading, chipped paint peeling from the wood siding, and the way the gutters hung, just a little askew. The windows looked like they hadn't been cleaned in years, and one, she noticed, had a crack running from top to bottom.

Andrew climbed out and waited for Jake, who insisted upon collecting his game console and headphones, and then joined his daughter. "Well, what's the verdict on our new digs?"

She looked sideways toward him, narrowing her eyes, but didn't answer.

"Come on. You could try to be a little enthusiastic." Andrew nudged her.

"I'm here, aren't I?" She shrugged. "Isn't that enough?"

"I guess it's the best I'm going to get." Andrew pushed a hand into his pocket and produced a key on a silver heart shaped fob. "Who's ready to go inside?"

Chapter 2

THE INTERIOR of the house was no better than the exterior. Sarah looked around in disappointment. They had closed on the property two months ago, and since then it had undergone some much-needed repairs. The hole in the roof was patched, and the floorboards, those that were too rotten to save, had been replaced with carefully matched modern stand-ins. But the pervasive odor of musty abandon still hung in the air, and the walls were still the same faded cream she remembered from her only previous visit, when they had driven up to view the place for the first time.

"I thought you said things had been fixed?" Sarah said, not bothering to hide her distress.

"I said the major stuff had been taken care of, and it has." Her dad replied. "I know there's still a lot to do, but we couldn't afford to have the workmen do everything."

"Great."

"Hey, at least the house is livable now, which is more than could be said about it the last time you were here."

"I was hoping for a little better than livable." Sarah cast her eyes toward the staircase. The railings were the same dirty brown varnish that she remembered from before, worn in places to reveal the paler wood underneath. A floral runner dropped from stair to stair like a patterned waterfall, the fabric threadbare. Above that, the second-floor landing was a dark mystery. She wondered what new disappointments waited for her up there.

They walked through each room, stopping every so often to inspect some repair or other. Sarah tagged along behind, wrinkling her nose when they came upon a dead mouse laying in the middle of the empty dining room.

"Yuck." She took a step backwards. "You really expect me to live under these conditions?"

"It's just a mouse Sarah."

"It's completely gross."

"This is an old house," her father said. "He probably won't be the last one we see."

"Great. Now I have to deal with rodents on top of everything else?"

"You'll survive." Andrew crossed the room and disappeared into the kitchen, returning with a dustpan and broom. He swept the mouse up and went back to the kitchen. When he rejoined them, there was a smile on his face. "See, all better now."

"Not really." Sarah could feel her throat tightening, and for a moment she thought she would be sick. "I hate mice."

"Hey, I have a surprise for you," her father said, no doubt trying to take her mind off the deceased rodent.

"What is it?" A germ of hope sparked within her. Maybe he was going to say she could stay with her friend, Becca, back in Boston. That way she wouldn't have to start at a new school. It was a suggestion she had made several times over the past few months, not that it had done any good.

"You have to see," Andrew said, and nodded toward the entryway. "It's upstairs."

"Oh." Her heart fell.

"Come on, I guarantee you will like it."

"Fine," She said, less enthusiastic than when she thought there might be a reprieve from living in the moldy old farmhouse.

"You want to join us, champ?" Her father turned his attention to Jake, who was wandering around the entranceway peering through doors.

"Where are you going?"

"Upstairs."

"Nah." He shook his head. "I want to explore down here. Maybe there will be another mouse."

"Ew." Sarah let out a snort of disgust.

"So, can I explore?" Jake looked at his father, an expectant look upon his face.

"Alright." Andrew tousled Jake's hair.

"Stop that." Jake squirmed.

Sarah derived a little satisfaction from the annoyed look on her brother's face.

"Don't go outside, and don't touch anything, especially dead mice. You understand?" Andrew gave Jake his best *I'm serious about this* look.

"I get it." Jake nodded, no doubt pleased to be able to explore on his own. "I won't touch any dead mice."

"Or any other dead things you come across."

"Fine." Jake drew the word out, a mischievous grin plastered across his face.

"It's just the two of us then." Andrew said. "Come on."

He led Sarah from the dining room, back into the hallway, and up the stairs. He flicked a light switch, the single bare bulb ineffective against the gloom.

The second floor did nothing to dispel Sarah's opinion of the old farmhouse. The musty, dank odor from below was worse here, and the weak light made everything look drab and depressing. Five doors led off the short corridor, two on the right, one to their left, and one at the end. The closest door was a bathroom. Sarah could see the claw foot tub through the opening. The others must be bedrooms. She wondered which one would be hers. She hoped it wouldn't stink as bad as the rest of the house. She guessed that it would.

"No one's lived here for a very long time," her father said, reading his daughter's mind. "The smell will go away once we open everything up and get some air through the place."

"I hope so." Sarah lingered near the top of the stairs, unwilling to venture any further than necessary. "So what's this big surprise?"

"Come on." Andrew took off, the barest hint of a smile upon his face. At the end of the hallway he turned left and disappeared from sight. His voice drifted back on the stale air. "What are you waiting for?"

"Hang on." She padded down the corridor toward the spot where her father had vanished, and was surprised to discover that the corridor turned at right angles, leading to a second staircase. This one was narrower than the main stairs, with bare wood treads and smooth plaster walls. It rose steeply to a narrow door at the top, which stood open, spilling light downward. Andrew Whelan stood in the doorframe, waiting.

"Hurry up. We don't have all day."

"Stop nagging me." Sarah said, climbing the stairs as fast as she dared. At the top she stopped, surprised.

In front of her was a huge room spanning the whole width of the house. It had sloping ceilings following the roofline, and two large dormer windows. Unlike the rooms downstairs, this one was bright and wore a coat of fresh paint.

"Well?" Her father was grinning.

"What is this?" She wondered how this space looked so new. Had her father paid the workmen to do all this?

Andrew paused a moment, his eyes sparkling, and then he answered her. "It's your new bedroom of course. What do you think?"

Chapter 3

JAKE WATCHED his sister and father leave the room and head to the stairs. When he heard them climbing toward the second floor, the treads groaning and creaking as they went, he wandered into the kitchen, stopping at the yellow refrigerator that looked like it should be in a museum. It even had chrome on the door handle, now worn and peeling. He pulled on the door, wondering if there would be any old, moldy food to go along with the ancient fridge, but there was nothing inside except a box of bicarbonate of soda, which sat on a shelf, lonely and abandoned. He wondered who had put it there, and why. It seemed a strange thing to put in such a place.

Shrugging, he closed the fridge and carried on through the rest of the kitchen, opening cupboards and drawers, but found little of any interest.

At the other end of the kitchen was a door with four glass panes. He approached it and looked out, pressing his face to the glass, but the panes were so caked in grime he could barely see outside. What he could see, though, was that this door led to the rear of the house, judging by the weak sunlight that filtered through the dirt. He reached down and gripped the doorknob, turning it despite his father's explicit instructions not to venture outside. But a little peek couldn't hurt, and he would make sure not to stray too far. Besides, if he were quick no one would be any the wiser.

He turned the knob and pushed, but the door did not budge. Perplexed, he tried again, but still it remained firmly closed.

Then he noticed the bolt.

It was set high upon the door, and it was drawn across.

Jake reached up, his fingers outstretched, but he could not reach it, even when he stood on tiptoe.

He tried again, pushing himself as tall as he could. The tips of his fingers brushed the bolt, but not enough to get a grip, and in the end he slumped back down, disappointed. Whatever was beyond the door's grimy glass panels would have to wait for another day.

That didn't mean he was done.

There must be plenty more to see in the old house.

He retreated from the kitchen, and across the dining room to the hallway.

He heard voices above, on the next upper floor.

Ignoring them, Jake padded down the hallway toward the back of the house. Surely there was more to discover here.

And then the creak came.

It was soft. Gentle.

Jake stopped, looked around for the source.

And then he found it.

Under the stairs, set into a recess, was a narrow door.

And it was open a crack.

Jake narrowed his eyes, peered at the door. His grandparents house had one just like this, set under the stairs in the same way.

It was the basement.

Jake approached the door and stood there, torn. It didn't seem like the kind of place his father would approve of him going, but who knew what awesome treasures lay in wait, right beneath his feet?

His breathing quickened in excitement.

Who cared if he got caught. It was worth it.

Jake pulled the door wide.

The space beyond was dark, but he could see enough to confirm that it was indeed the basement. Wooden steps fell away into obscurity.

There was a light switch on the wall.

He flicked it on.

Pale light illuminated the room below.

But even so, most of the basement was out of view.

He placed a foot on the top stair, testing it. When nothing happened, when he didn't crash through into the unknown pit below, he tried the next, and the next, until he was halfway down.

Now he could see old boxes, part of a bicycle.

He wondered what was in the boxes. He hurried down a couple more steps, eager to find out.

And then he heard the ringing.

It sounded like the ringtone on his fathers cell phone.

Jake stopped and listened.

It came again, a shrill clanging ring.

Had his dad come back downstairs?

Was he looking for Jake at that very moment?

Boy, would he be in for it if he was caught snooping down here.

Jake turned and hurried back up to the ground floor, turning off the light and pushing the door closed.

No harm, no foul.

There was no sign of either his dad or Sarah. He had gotten away with it.

The ring came again, quick and urgent.

It was coming from the living room, the only place on the

ground floor Jake hadn't been yet. He crossed the hallway, following the sound.

The living room was large. Exposed beams ran across the ceiling, and on the far wall, surrounded by built in bookcases, was a wide fireplace, with a stone chimney. The air felt stale and old, and a musty odor pushed at his nostrils.

He paused and waited for the ringing to repeat, but it didn't.

And then he saw the telephone, sitting alone on a shelf next to the fireplace.

It seemed to call out to him.

It urged him to come closer.

He realized that the ringing had come from there. It was not his father's cell phone. It was this phone.

He peered at it, inching closer.

The unit looked old. The plastic was yellowed and dull. Instead of buttons, there was a rotary dial with numbers inside round holes. And the handset was huge, much larger than a modern phone.

He stared at it, fascinated by the strange squat shape and the curly knotted cord that ran from the handset and into the base of the device.

He touched the dial, his finger slipping into the hole above the number one. When he moved his finger the dial spun around clockwise with a clicking sound, and then sprang back when he released it.

He put his finger in the next hole and did the same thing.

Again it rotated back when released.

He reached out to turn the dial a third time, but then paused, remembering his father's words. He was under strict orders not to touch anything.

He glanced over his shoulder, toward the hallway, but there was no sign of his father or sister.

He turned his attention back to the telephone.

He'd only ever seen one other like this, at his grandparent's house in Maine. It was the same shape, but that one had plastic push buttons arranged in a square on the face, rather than the strange wheel.

A sudden memory popped into his head.

It was the previous summer, a few weeks before everything changed.

He was sitting in the back of the blue VW Bug that his mother loved so much. The top was down and it was a glorious summer day. The kind only New England can deliver. They followed the coast from Boston, just the two of them. Sarah was too cool to visit her grandparents, she would rather hang out in Harvard Square with her friends, and dad was always working, tapping away on his laptop, or away on some book tour or other. He supposed it was cool to have a novelist for a father, at least that was what people told him, but to Jake it seemed dull.

They weaved through picturesque seaside towns like Kittery, and Ogunquit, where they stopped to pick up taffy, which he chewed all the way to Portland. It was something they had done every year for as long as he could remember. You couldn't pass through Ogunquit without getting taffy. That was the rule.

When they arrived at Gramps and Granma's house there was blueberry pie, freshly made with berries picked that day in the back yard, and vanilla ice cream.

That was another tradition. Blueberry pie.

Except now it was nothing but a memory.

There would be no more trips up the coast in that Bug, and no more days sitting on the wide back porch with a slice of pie.

It wasn't fair.

His eyes grew puffy and red.

He wiped them with the back of his hand, grateful that Sarah was not around to see his moment of weakness.

Jake sniffed and turned away, no longer interested in the

old telephone, or exploring the rest of the house. That happened sometimes when he thought of his mother.

He slouched back toward the hallway.

The phone rang again.

Jake froze.

The ring repeated, shrill, loud.

He did a one-eighty and stood there, staring.

The ring came a third time.

Jake walked back toward the phone.

Should he answer?

It seemed wrong not too.

The ring came a fourth time, demanding to be heeded.

Jake reached forward, his hand shaking, and gripped the receiver. He lifted it to his ear.

Swirling static hissed from the earpiece.

"Hello?" The word bounced back at him, through the earpiece. "Is anybody there?"

Static buzzed and popped, fading in and out.

"Hello?" He repeated, the word swallowed up in the white noise.

And then, for a brief second, Jake thought he heard a voice. It was low and muted, barely audible above the static, but it was there.

"I can't understand you." He wondered if he should fetch his father. Maybe it was important. Dad was always on the phone with his agent, a small round-faced man who smelled of garlic and called him *the squirt*.

"Jake." The word floated out of the static, still faint, but clear this time.

Jake sucked in a startled gasp.

"Hello?"

"Jake." His name again, the voice scratchy, far away. He almost slammed the receiver down, but the voice didn't sound scary, in fact, it almost sounded familiar. It must be dad's agent, or maybe someone from the school.

"Can I help you?" he asked.
The static roiled and hissed.
The voice stayed silent.
And then, without warning, there was a click.
The line went dead.

Chapter 4

SARAH STOOD in attic doorway and looked around in wonder, forgetting, if only for a brief moment, that she was supposed to be annoyed.

"This is mine?" She asked, her eyes wide.

"Every last inch of it," Andrew said. "I had the workmen tidy it up, sand the floors, and slap on a coat of paint, so everything is clean and shiny. No mice in sight."

"What's the catch?" Sarah narrowed her eyes.

"No catch," her father replied. "I thought you might appreciate a little more space than you had in Boston."

"This doesn't mean I like the house any more than I did ten minutes ago." Sarah tried to sound disinterested and failed.

"I'm not asking you to like it," Andrew said. "But I would like you to give things a try here, for all of our sakes."

"Ah." Sarah nodded. "So this is a bribe."

"I prefer to think of it as a loving gesture."

"What about Jake?" she asked.

"You're worried about your brother now?" Andrew said. "Don't be. There's a perfectly good bedroom on the second floor. It's not as big as this, but you'll go off to college in a year or so. His turn will come."

"I'm not worried." Sarah was quick to rectify the misunderstanding. "I don't want the little brat whining about it, that's all."

"I see," Her father said. "Silly me."

"Is there a bathroom up here?" Sarah nodded toward a door at the far end of the room.

"No. That's a walk-in closet." Her father shook his head. "You will have to use the bathroom on the second floor, along with the rest of us, at least for now."

"There's only one bathroom?" Sarah pulled a face.

"It's an old house," Andrew replied. "Maybe in a few months we can see about putting another one in, but until then we share. That's just the way it is."

"Please tell me there's a shower at least." Sarah could feel her world crashing around her. She wondered if she could run away and go back to Boston, and hide out in their old house until it sold. That was a stupid idea though. The brownstone would be the first place her father would look.

"There is a shower." Andrew laughed. "And hot water too."

"Are you making fun of me?"

"Not at all," Andrew said. "I would never do such a thing." He put his arm around Sarah and gave her a gentle hug.

Sarah suffered the act of affection as best she could, then, unable to suffer any more, pulled away. She walked to the closest gable window and looked out. From her vantage point high above the ground, she could see a long expanse of grass that sloped to sprawling woods. To the right was a meandering track that led to several structures, barns of some kind, and beyond that, overgrown open fields, bounded by yet more trees. She leaned against the wall. "Do we own all of this?"

"Pretty much." Andrew joined her at the window.

"There's about five acres. The farm used to be much bigger, hundreds of acres, but it all got sold off over the years, so I'm told." He pointed toward the barns. "Those buildings back there, they used to house cows."

"Can we get some cows then?"

"And who's going to look after them?" Andrew glanced at her. "You?"

"Maybe."

"Are you going to get up at 5am every day to milk them, even on weekends?"

"What?"

"Cows need to be milked twice daily, come rain or shine - or snow for that matter," Andrew said. "I can't even get you to load the dishwasher."

"Meh. Maybe I'll get a cat instead." Sarah looked sideways at her father. She bit her bottom lip. A minute passed, and then she spoke again. "I'm sorry for giving you such a hard time."

"What's this? I don't believe it." Andrew feigned shock. "You are actually apologizing for something?"

"Hey, don't tease me," Sarah said. She took a deep breath. "I know how hard it's been since mom died, and I realize I've put you through a lot..."

"You can say that again," Andrew interrupted.

"But I'm going to try and do better, okay?" She turned away from the window. "I'm still not happy about being here though."

"I know," Andrew said. "Let's just take it one day at a time, okay?"

Sarah was about to answer, but before she could get a word out, she heard heavy footsteps pounding up the attic stairs.

A moment later Jake exploded into the room, his eyes alight.

"What's going on, sport?" Andrew looked down at his son, surprised. "Did you find another mouse?"

"No." Jake blurted the word.

"Then what's all the rush?"

"There was a phone in one of the rooms." Jake said, the words tumbling into each other as they exited his mouth. "It rang."

"Like a cell phone?"

"No. Not like that." Jake shook his head. "An old time phone, like the one at Gramps house. I was playing with it and it rang."

"Are you sure?"

"Uh huh." Jake shook his head, his hair flopping up and down as he did so.

"Well, that is odd." Andrew scratched his head. "Maybe it was a wrong number. I wouldn't worry about it."

"Why would the phone still be connected?" Sarah asked. "Hasn't his place been empty since the eighties?"

"It sure has," Andrew answered. "Who knows? Maybe it's an oversight on the part of the telephone company. Stranger things have happened."

"Are you sure it was a wrong number?" Jake asked.

"I can't see what else it could be."

"But…" Jake barely got one word out before he was interrupted by the beep of a horn.

"That must be the moving truck," Andrew said, standing. "Who wants to go bring in some boxes?"

"Not me," Sarah said. "Isn't that why we paid a moving company?"

"But if we all chip in it will get done that much quicker."

"What do I get if I help?" Sarah asked.

"Really?" Andrew said, "Isn't giving you this bedroom enough?"

"Not for that kind of work."

"How about I order us a nice big pizza for dinner," Andrew countered, taking off toward the stairs.

"That's more like it." Sarah followed behind. "Breadsticks, too."

"You drive a hard bargain. Pizza and breadsticks it is."

"Can it be pepperoni?" Jake asked. "I like pepperoni the most."

"Sure. Whatever you want," Andrew said. "Unless the queen has any objection."

"Nope," Sarah replied, grinning at the queen reference even though she didn't want to. "Pepperoni works for me."

"That's settled then," Andrew said. "But not until we get our things inside the house."

Chapter 5

THEY WORKED FOR FIVE HOURS, hauling furniture and boxes into the house, and by the time the truck was empty, the contents of their Boston brownstone was in its new home.

Andrew supervised the unloading of the big stuff, allowing the movers to handle it, but that still left the smaller items. Piles of boxes were stacked in each room ready to be unpacked. But that could wait. First up was the promised, and long overdue, pizza.

Andrew made the call, and thirty minutes later they were chewing slices of thin crust topped with melted cheese and pepperoni.

They ate in silence, too hungry for conversation. Usually there would be a few slices left, which would go in the fridge to be consumed cold the next day, but not this time. An hour after they sat down, the pizza box was empty.

Sarah sat back in her chair, sipping coke from a red plastic cup. She glanced toward the boxes stacked in the kitchen. "Do we have to unpack those tonight?"

"No," Andrew said. "I think it can wait until tomorrow."

"Awesome." Sarah said. She turned toward the door. "I'm going upstairs."

Chapter 6

ANDREW WATCHED his daughter flee the room. A moment later he heard the thump of her footsteps as she ran up the stairs in the direction of the attic. It seemed that having such a large, private space to call home had overcome her objections about the move, at least for now. Tomorrow she might be back to her sulky, pouting ways, but tonight he would claim a small victory.

He picked up the pizza box and dropped it in the trash, then turned to Jake.

"You want to help me in the living room?"

"Doing what?"

"There's a lot to put away. Might as well get started on it."

"Okay."

Together they opened boxes, and filled the shelves with books. Andrew had always loved reading, and owned an extensive collection of hardbacks, many of which were first editions. Several were signed. He had spent countless hours sitting in the leather chair near the front bay window at the brownstone, reading these tomes. Jennifer would joke that he kept the bookstore in business single-handed, and he suspected that it even if that was not true, he was surely one of their best customers.

He smiled when he thought of her, standing in the front room, complaining about all the space his books took up. But at the same time a dull ache throbbed inside of him. He wondered what she would think of the old farmhouse. Moving out of the city was something they had talked about on several occasions, but it had never happened. There were always too many obstacles. The kids were in school and they didn't want to uproot them. His writing career – he'd had three bestsellers already and was working on a fourth – meant he had to be close to his agent. So they stayed where they were and fantasized once in a while about their haven in the country, over a glass of chardonnay.

But after her death, the old priorities didn't matter anymore. Andrew felt increasingly lonely despite the crowded huddle of people in the city, and he could feel the children becoming withdrawn and distant. The idea to move them out of Boston was already in his head when he got a call from the school. Sarah had been found unresponsive in a bathroom. They were rushing her to the ER. After that he knew what must be done.

"Dad?"

Jake's voice drew Andrew back to the present. He looked down. "Yes."

"There's only one place left." Jake looked toward the shelf with the telephone on it, a pile of books in his hands.

Andrew walked over to the shelf. "So this is the infamous ringing phone, huh?"

"It did ring," Jake said, indignant.

"I believe you." Andrew picked up the receiver and held it to his ear. "There's no dial tone. Maybe you jostled the bells and it just sounded like it was ringing. These old phones have real bells in them."

"Really?"

"Yup. They have two of them, with a ringer in the middle that vibrates and hits them when someone calls."

"That's neat," Jake said. "so it didn't really ring?"

"I don't see how it could."

"But I heard stuff on the other end. There was a voice."

Andrew picked the phone up, tracing the cord to a wall socket. He pressed down on the plastic tab and unhooked the handset. "It was still plugged in. There might have been some power going to it. Maybe that's what you heard."

"I don't know." Jake looked happier despite his caution.

"Tell you what." Andrew wrapped the cord around the phone. "I'll put this out by the trash, and that will take care of it. Problem solved."

"You don't have to." Jake eyed the handset.

"What else are we going to do with it? It's too old to use, even if we had a land line, which we don't."

"Can I keep it? It reminds me of Gramps phone."

"If you're sure."

Jake nodded, his eyes wide. "I am."

"Okay then." Andrew unhooked the other end of the wire from the back of the unit and handed the telephone over, placing it into his son's waiting arms. "It's all yours."

"Awesome." Jake inspected his new prized possession. "Can I put it in my room?"

"Sure."

"Right now?"

"You don't want to help me with the rest of this first?" Andrew motioned to the partially unpacked boxes.

"Nope." Jake shook his head. "I want to see my room."

"It is getting late." Andrew glanced at his watch. "Maybe we should go upstairs."

"Sweet." Jake grinned. "Is my room as big as Sarah's?"

"Not quite," Andrew replied, wondering if he was about to have a tantrum on his hands.

"That's okay. She can have the attic," Jake said, shrugging.

"It's creepy up there anyway. The ceiling slopes and those stairs are dark."

"That's very adult of you."

"I know." Jake turned, the telephone still in his arms, and walked toward the front of the house. "Can I see my room now?"

Chapter 7

THE HOUSE WAS dark and silent.

Sarah lay in bed and looked up at the ceiling. She always found it hard to fall asleep in new places. Tonight should have been different, after a day spent unloading, and then a whole evening of putting her room to rights. The delivery guys had set up her bed, and carried the nightstands, chair, and dresser up both flights of stairs, but there was still a lot to do. She unpacked clothes, hanging them in the walk-in closet, which proved to be larger than she expected, taking up the whole back wall of the room. She hung posters on the walls, the room finally feeling a little more like home with each one that went up, and then put the sheets and comforter on her bed. There was still a lot to unpack, but she had made a good start.

Despite all that, she still could not sleep.

She lay there in the blackness, the only light a faint glow from the nightlight plugged in on the other side of the room. It was not much, but it cast enough illumination to make her feel comfortable.

At first she heard her father moving around down below. After that the only sound was the faint rustle of wind through the trees outside her window, and the occasional creak as the house settled.

She closed her eyes and pretended that she was back in her old room in Boston. Tomorrow was Sunday, and that meant they would go to brunch in Back Bay. After that they would take a stroll along the Charles River, or spend the afternoon browsing the upscale stores on Newbury Street. The shopping trips all but stopped after mom died, but the brunch ritual remained, if only because it reminded them all of happier times.

But they weren't in Boston, and there would be no Sunday morning omelets or waffles, no walks along the Charles, or anything else for that matter.

Sarah rolled over onto her side and looked at the glowing alarm clock display.

It was 2 a.m.

She entertained the idea of getting up and finding the book she'd been reading, but it was buried in one of the boxes stacked along the wall, the ones she had not unpacked yet. It seemed like a lot of effort to start rummaging through them at this time of night.

Her laptop wasn't packed though. That was sitting on the dresser. Not that it did her much good. The internet was not turned on yet, and wouldn't be for a couple more days. That meant she couldn't stream her favorite shows, or email Becca. Besides, the room was cold, and she didn't feel like moving.

Instead she pulled the covers up so that they were all the way to her chin and lay there, her mind wandering back to those happy times of waffles and walks, and then, just when she thought she would never sleep again, the tiredness overcame her.

Chapter 8

ANDREW CHOSE the room at the top of the stairs to be his writing den. It was the smallest of the three bedrooms, and the one that needed the most renovation. But it was also the furthest from the kid's rooms, which meant less disruptions.

In the brownstone he did his writing in a cramped third floor box room with a window overlooking Beacon Street. Down the road was Boston Common. Sometimes, when he was stuck, needed inspiration, he would take a stroll through the park. There, in an oasis flanked by cramped roads, tourists and locals sprawled on the grass, reading or listening to music through small white ear buds.

Not here though.

In this house he had all the solitude he could ever want. Except that peace and quiet wasn't what Andrew needed. What he needed were the words to start flowing again. He was three months late on delivering his fourth novel, and only half way through. Everything ground to a halt the day they laid Jennifer in the ground. He knew exactly which page he was working on when that happened, because it was the same page that was on his screen when he got the news that she had gone off the road. He hadn't written a single word since.

Actually that was not true.

He had written lots of words, but none of them were any good. They mocked him, each one a small betrayal. And all the time that voice nagged inside his head.

You're nothing without her.

It ate at him, consuming his soul until there was only one place left to go, and he went there without a fight. It was a dim, dark hell with a population of one. It wasn't until after Sarah's incident that he was able to crawl back out of the pit of despair he'd created for himself. She needed him. Jake needed him.

What they all needed was a collective reset.

So here they were.

Maybe now he would be able to finish the damn book, hand it off to his agent, and never think about it again.

He took his laptop from its case and set it upon the oak writing desk that he'd bought in an antique store in Connecticut. All three bestsellers had been written at this desk. Now it would serve as the pallbearer for his fourth.

He turned to the boxes marked *office*, and opened the nearest one. Inside were books, papers, and several legal pads full of jotted notes. He scooped them up and deposited everything on a shelf near the window. He arranged them by height, the tallest volumes first, down through the smallest, and leaned a couple of volumes at an angle to hold everything up.

There were other things in the box. A two hundred year old iron quill stand made in the north of England that once belonged to his grandfather. For decades it sat on the desk next to the old man's reading chair, stacked with pens of varying shapes and sizes, including a big, bulbous fat one in the wider space at the top. It had always fascinated Andrew. He didn't know why. After his grandfather died it was the one thing he took.

And then there was the bottle of vodka.

It lay in the bottom of the box, taunting him.

During the bad times, those dark days, he wasn't adverse to a little self medication. At first it was a quick nip here and there, just to get the creative juices flowing. Or maybe to help him forget.

It did neither.

That didn't stop him from persisting in the vain hope that something would change. Except that wasn't the real reason. While it might not help him forget, it took the edge off. One shot became two, then three. Before long he was polishing off half a bottle on a good day.

Never in front of the kids though.

But late at night, when the lights were out and he was in his writing room… Well, all bets were off.

Until Sarah tried to follow her mother to the grave.

He hadn't taken a drop since.

Not that his drinking had anything to do with what happened, at least, not directly. But he had a revelation that day. He realized that they were all broken, and if he didn't take action, they might not all make it.

Andrew left the bottle where it was and closed the box. Why had he even packed it? For old times sake? In case of emergency? Who knew. Tomorrow he would consign it to the garbage.

He flopped down in front of the desk and opened up the laptop. The screen blinked to life.

He pulled up the book, scrolled to the last of it.

And there was that blank page.

The cursor taunted him, dared him to write something. Anything.

Andrew's fingers brushed against the keyboard. He pecked at a key, then another. The progress was slow, hesitant, but it was movement in the right direction.

Letters became words, and words morphed into sentences. He wrote in a trance, barely thinking.

An hour later three new pages stared back at him.

Were they good pages?

Hardly.

They were clunky, disjointed.

Three pages of crap.

Disappointment washed over him.

He leaned back in the chair and glanced toward the window, and the dark night beyond. This house was supposed to be a clean slate, a chance to put the past behind him and start the process of moving on. He'd battled for his family, almost lost his daughter, barely saved his own sanity. And still he could not write a damn thing.

Andrew slammed the laptop closed.

His eyes settled on the bottle of vodka.

It stood behind the computer, waiting for him like a lost lover.

Shouldn't it still be in the box?

He thought back, tracing his movements. He was sure he had not removed the vodka bottle.

Yet here it was.

He leaned forward, extended his hand. Traced a finger down the side of the smooth glass, following the tantalizing curve from neck to base. It felt cold under his touch.

There was a shot glass waiting there too.

Had that even *been* in the box?

Who cared.

It was good medicine.

His hand closed around the bottle. He dragged it forward across the desk. Stared at it.

The liquor whispered to him.

It seduced him.

Come on, it said. *What could it hurt, just one drink?* And his mind played along. The part of him that yearned for the slow, steady intoxication, considered it. The kids were in bed, sleeping. It was well past midnight. The witching hour. Why not let the vodka cast a spell on him?

Screw it.

Andrew grasped the bottle and twisted the cap off.

He took the shot glass and filled it. Placed the bottle back on the table.

He lifted the glass, smelled the subtle alcohol fumes, like an old friend.

I've missed you.

The words rolled into his head as he put the glass to his mouth, tasted the first drops of liquor as they touched his lips.

And then he remembered where he was, and why they had moved here. This wasn't much of a turnaround. Here he was, about to get toasted. And why? Because the words didn't flow like they used to? Or was it because he still missed Jennifer so much it hurt, and nothing had really changed? Boston or not, the pain was still there. He wondered if it would always be.

But he was better than this. He didn't need to drink to control it. Not now. Not ever again.

He gripped the bottle, emptied the shot glass back into it, and stood. The bathroom was across the hall.

It only took a moment to pour the contents of the bottle into the sink, the clear liquid swirling away.

There. No more temptation.

Andrew dropped the empty bottle into the wastebasket. He would throw it in the trashcan tomorrow. Right now though, he was going to bed. The book could wait. It wasn't as if he'd write anything worth a damn anyhow.

Chapter 9

SARAH'S EYES SNAPPED OPEN.

The alarm clock read 4.15 a.m.

She looked around, wondering what had roused her.

And then she realized.

It was dark.

Too dark. In fact, it was pitch black.

The nightlight, which had bathed the room in a soft yellow glow only a few hours earlier, was no longer working. Had the bulb blown?

A lump caught in her throat. For a moment she was overcome with an unreasoning panic. She'd hated the dark ever since childhood, always sleeping with a light of some sort. She lay still, holding the covers up, waiting for the paralyzing fear to pass. After all, there was a lamp right next to her, on the nightstand. All she needed to do was reach out and turn it on.

Except that now she realized something else.

There was someone in the room with her.

She could hear their soft, light footsteps crossing the room.

A prickle of fear ran through her.

She wanted to scream.

Only nothing came out.

Instead she lay there, frozen with fear.

Her eyes searched the blackness for any sign of movement, but it was no use. All she could see were the vague outlines of the two long windows under the gables.

The hairs on the back of her neck stood on end. She let out a small whimper.

And then the footsteps repeated, louder this time.

She had the unnerving thought that the owner of those footfalls was right next to the bed, leaning over her, watching her.

That was too much. Willing herself to move, Sarah rolled over and reached for the lamp.

Her fingers found the switch.

The room was bathed in soft light.

She sat up and looked around, heart beating so fast she thought it might push through her chest.

The room was empty.

There was no skulking intruder at the end of the bed, no stranger waiting to pounce.

She was alone.

But how could that be? She was so sure there was someone in the room. Was it possible that she imagined the footsteps? Maybe it was some kind of waking dream, a fragment of something that lingered when she awoke, finding its way, for a brief time, into the real world.

And then she remembered the nightlight.

She swung her legs off the bed, slipping out from under the warm safety of the comforter, and padded across the room.

Some nightlights had sensors that turned them on when the room grew dark, and off again at sunrise. Not this one. It was of the sort that had a small switch on the front, enabling it to be operated at will.

And the switch was in the off position.

This was no blown bulb. It was a deliberate act, which

meant that the footsteps were not her imagination. Someone had been in the room with her.

She turned and backed up toward the wall.

Her eyes searched the attic.

Nothing appeared out of place. Boxes waited to be unpacked. The laptop rested on her dresser, the power light glowing a dull orange.

None of this gave her any comfort.

And then she noticed the closet door.

It was cracked open, just an inch.

Had she left it like that?

She could not remember, but it was possible. On the other hand, someone might be lurking in there right then, watching her from the narrow slit between the door and the frame.

That thought made her blood run cold.

She wanted to scream, to run from the room and never come back. And then it dawned on her, like a divine revelation.

Jake.

Her brother knew how much she hated the dark.

He must have snuck up to scare her. It was the only thing that made any sense.

The little shit.

Was he hiding in the closet, waiting to jump out, arms waving?

Well she would show him.

Sarah edged toward the closet. A tingling fear crept up her spine.

She reached out, took the door handle in her hand and pulled.

The door swung outward with a groan.

The room beyond was cloaked in darkness.

She reached toward the light switch on the wall next to the door, her fingers groping for it until she found it.

She flicked it up.

The closet exploded with light.

She blinked against the sudden glare.

When her eyes adjusted and she saw that the space was empty.

That didn't mean he wasn't in here, hiding.

Like behind the row of clothes hanging on the rod along the back wall.

She ducked down and peered beneath them, looking for his legs.

Nothing.

Sarah let out a sigh of relief and turned back toward the door. Just in time to see it swing inward toward her, and click closed.

She stood there in mute horror, unable to make a sound despite the shriek that ached to find its way from her throat. Her breath came in short, ragged gasps.

From the other side of the door there was the sound of retreating footsteps.

She struggled to regain her composure. The little brat had gotten to her after all. Where had he been hiding? Under the bed? Behind the boxes?

It didn't matter.

The important thing was that she didn't let him win.

She swung the closet door open, and then hesitated.

The room beyond seemed different somehow. Darker than before. It was as if the air had grown dense, cloying. The light didn't reach into the corners now. The darkness was fighting for control of the room. She didn't want to step out into it. Somewhere, deep down, she had the feeling that something lurked there, unseen.

Watching.

Waiting.

But that was ridiculous. What was she thinking?

And every second she lingered, Jake was making good his escape.

Pushing the strange thoughts from her mind, willing them down, she stepped out into the bedroom, and hurried in the direction of the stairs.

She had expected to see Jake below her, but the staircase was empty. He must have all but run down.

Never mind that. He wasn't going to escape that easily.

She started down, one hand flat against the wall to keep her steady on the steep and unfamiliar staircase. When she arrived at the landing below she paused, gathering her fury for the rant she was about to unleash.

Jake's room was the closest door.

She knew it was his because she'd heard them earlier, discussing the best place for the bed, and where to stash his toys.

She took the knob and threw the door open, ready to give him hell, except that when she looked inside, something made her hold back.

The bedroom was swathed in darkness, the only light a pale silhouette of the window cast across the wood floor. Jake's bed stood opposite the door, the covers spilling over the edges. The boy shaped lump beneath them told her that he was there, and the heavy snores that emanated from his direction told her that either he was fast asleep, or he was a great actor.

She wasn't sure which.

She stepped into the room, intent upon confronting him, but then she paused.

He really seemed to be out to the world.

But that was not possible.

If Jake was asleep, who switched off her nightlight and closed her in the closet?

Who's footsteps had she heard?

It must be her brother. It certainly wasn't her father, and he was the only other person in the house. But Jake couldn't have gotten back to his room, jumped into bed, and fell asleep so quickly.

It was impossible.

He was faking, he must be.

But what good did it do to cause a ruckus in the middle of the night? Jake would howl and wail, and then her father would appear, mad at being woken in such a manner. Maybe he would decide she wasn't mature enough, and take the attic room away from her. Maybe he would even give the attic to Jake.

She didn't want that.

No.

It was better to withdraw, let Jake think he had won, at least until morning. There would be plenty of time to get the truth out of him.

Her mind made up, Sarah backed out of the room and pulled the door shut, then turned back toward the attic stairs.

As she started to climb, making her way back to the attic bedroom, she thought she heard a faint chuckle drift up from below.

Dammit Jake, she thought, not bothering to turn around, not willing to give him the satisfaction, don't push your luck.

Chapter 10

SARAH AWOKE to three sharp knocks on her bedroom door.

She opened her eyes and rolled over, noting that it was gone ten a.m. She still felt tired, but that was hardly surprising since she had spent half the night either laying awake, or being the victim of Jake's stupid pranks.

The knocking came again.

"What?" She squinted in the harsh morning light pouring through the double gabled windows. She would need either blinds or curtains, otherwise mornings would be untenable.

"We have no food in the house." Her father's voice came through the closed door. "We're going into town for breakfast."

"Okay." She wondered if he meant Danvers or Salem. "Which town?"

"You got it."

"Huh?" Sarah didn't understand his answer.

"Witch town," Andrew said. "Salem."

She groaned, choosing to ignore her father's lame play on words. "Fine. I'll be down in a minute."

"Don't be long. More than ten minutes and we leave without you."

"I won't." She forced herself from the bed, wincing when her feet touched the cold floor. That was another thing she needed – a rug to put next to the bed.

Her father was going back down the stairs. She could hear the treads creak as he went, despite the closed door. Funny, she thought, they didn't creak like that last night when Jake ran down them. Maybe it was because her brother was so much lighter, or perhaps he went so fast they didn't have time to creak. She pushed the thought from her mind and went to the closet, pulling out a black t-shirt with the neck cut so it fell off the shoulder, and a pair of tight Black skinny jeans. The tee was one of her favorites. She'd worn it so many times that the hemline had frayed, and the black dye had faded to a color approximating dark gray. To finish off, she took a silver chain with an amethyst attached, and slipped it around her neck.

When she arrived downstairs, the others were already outside, next to the car. She could feel her father inspecting her clothing, and even if he thought it less than suitable, he kept quiet. After spending six months complaining about her attire, it seemed he'd given up, consigning the conversation to the realm of lost causes.

"Shotgun." She eyed the front seat.

"Too late." Jake beamed from ear to ear. "I already called it."

"Not fair. I wasn't here."

"That's not how shotgun works," Jake informed her. "Only the driver has to be present."

"But…" Sarah could feel the anger welling up inside. She took a deep breath, deciding that it was not worth the hassle. That didn't mean she couldn't appeal to the voice of reason. She turned to her father. "Jake's too young for the front seat."

"Lighten up Sarah." Her father pressed the key fob, unlocking the car. "It's only a short drive. Besides, Jake called it, fair and square."

"See." Jake had that look upon his face, the one he used when he wanted to make it clear that he was the winner.

"Whatever." She pulled the back door open and climbed in, tugging on the seat belt. "The back's more comfortable anyway."

THE RIDE to town was short. She was surprised how close to civilization they actually were. In the farmhouse, surrounded by fields and woodland, it felt like they might be living at the end of the earth, but that was not the case, and soon she began to harbor a hope that the Sunday tradition of brunch was not to be consigned to the past.

The restaurant was small.

Sarah sat wedged into one side of a booth that could have benefitted from a few extra inches of legroom, while her father and brother took up position across the table. She ordered pancakes with maple syrup, not something she usually allowed herself, especially since the jeans were already too tight, but today she needed them. She would have liked a side of sausages to go with the sweet flapjacks, but that was going a bit too far, so she watched Jake consume his with an envy barely contained.

After they ate, while her father drank a third cup of coffee, she turned her attention to Jake. "How did you sleep last night?"

"Fine." He looked at her with narrowed eyes.

"Are you sure about that?" She watched him take a sip of orange juice. "Did you do a little sleepwalking?"

"What are you talking about?" Jake seemed genuinely clueless, but she wasn't buying it.

"You know what I'm talking about."

"No, I don't." He stuck his chin out and wrinkled his nose, scrunching his face up in mock confusion. "You're weird."

"The nightlight." There, she had said it, tipped her hand.

Now there could be no misunderstanding, not that he could have missed the accusation anyway.

"Huh?" Jake ran a finger across his plate, collecting up some stray maple syrup, and putting his finger to his mouth, to lick the gooey liquid off.

"Stop that." Andrew gave his son a withering look. "You know better."

"Sorry." Jake grinned and rubbed his hand with the napkin.

"Well?" Sarah asked, frustrated. Her father had gotten Jake off track, distracted him from the real issue.

"Well what?" Jake was still playing the innocent.

"You know very well what." She glared at him. "You snuck into my room last night and turned off the nightlight. You know how much I hate the dark."

"I did not." Jake's eyes flew wide.

"I heard you. You woke me up walking around. What were you doing you little creep, going through my stuff?"

"I thought you said the nightlight was off?"

"It was."

"So how could I be going through your stuff in the dark?" He leaned on the table. "I don't have x-ray vision."

"I don't think x-ray vision would help you very much." Despite Jake's gaff, he made a good point. It was amazing that he was even able to navigate the unfamiliar room without bumping into furniture, let alone nose through her things.

"I wasn't in your room." Jake finished the last of his juice. "I only got up once to pee."

"I don't believe you." Sarah was not willing to let him get away with it. "How else did my light get turned off?"

"I don't know." Jake shrugged.

"Maybe you just forgot to turn it on before you went to bed, Pickle," Her dad said.

"I didn't. It was on when I went to bed," Sarah replied. " And don't call me Pickle."

"Sorry. You used to like it."

"When I was ten." She had gotten the nickname as a kid, due to her extreme dislike of the cucumber based condiment. She could not remember exactly what had prompted the first use of the affectionate moniker, but in recent years it had become an embarrassment. "I'm an adult now."

"Sorry," Her father said. "It's hard to remember that you are an adult when you're arguing with your brother."

"I wasn't arguing." Sarah felt frustrated. "I was asking him why he turned off my light."

"It sounded like an argument from where I was sitting."

"Well maybe he shouldn't go sneaking around my room."

"I didn't." Jake protested his innocence yet again. "I swear."

"See?" Andrew glanced between his kids. "Jake says he didn't do it."

"I don't believe him."

"And I don't care," Andrew said, pulling a couple of twenty dollar bills from his wallet and dropping them on the table beside the check. "You've been in a bad mood for days. Stop taking it out on your brother. It isn't his fault that you don't like the new house."

"That's not…"

"I don't want to hear it." Andrew held up a hand, cutting her off. "Let's get out of here, shall we? There's a lot to do today, and not much time to do it."

Chapter 11

JAKE SAT cross legged on the living room floor and watched his father pull cables from a box with the words *Living Room – TV Stuff* wrote upon it in scrawled black marker.

"I'm bored." He spoke the words like a seasoned pro, the nuances of tone and accent on each syllable perfected by years of practice.

"You could go up and put stuff away in your room," dad said, his head now lost behind the TV where he was plugging in cables. "I'm sure there's lots more to unpack."

"Nah." Jake shook his head. "I'll do that later."

"It has to be done sometime."

"I know. I don't want to do it right now." Putting stuff away was no more fun than watching his father grapple with the TV. Jake's eyes drifted to the window. "Can I go outside?"

"I don't believe it." There was mock surprise in his dad's voice. "You never wanted to play outside in Boston."

"There's nothing to do here." Jake moaned. "The internet doesn't work yet, and the game system isn't set up."

"Alright." His father was playing with the remote now. "Don't go near anything you shouldn't, and don't wander too far. Stay close to the house, okay?"

"I will." Jake sprang to his feet and bolted for the hallway. He sped through the dining room and into the kitchen, before remembering about the bolt on the back door.

He wavered, wondering if he should go back and get help, but when he looked up, the bolt was already drawn back.

He opened the door and stepped out, pausing to take in the landscape.

A sloping area of overgrown grass dropped away to a line of trees fifty feet away. An old swing set sat rusty and unloved, the wooden seat almost rotted through. He wondered how long it had been there.

Off to the right, a trail weaved through the grass to a pair of barns. He was sure they were out of bounds, but dad hadn't told him not to go there, so that was the direction he went in.

The barns were in a sorry state. Everything in the house was suffering from some level of decay, but these buildings were the worst.

He approached the nearest one and tugged on the door. It didn't move, but there was enough of a gap to push his head inside.

He brushed away a cobweb that stuck to his face, and waited for his eyes to adjust to the gloom. When they did, he was disappointed to see that the barn was empty except for a stack of lumber laying toward the back. Leaning against the wood was an old, tarnished axe. He took a step forward, the axe a beacon to his curiosity, but then he wavered. There would be all sorts of trouble if he was caught playing with something like that. Better to leave it where it was.

He retreated, closing the barn door, and walked to the other building.

Rows of strange looking metal pens lined each side of the structure. Dad had said that these were cow barns, and he wondered if the enclosures were used to keep the cows in.

Beyond these, at the back, were two metal racks, crowded with an assortment of items.

He stepped into the barn, ignoring the pens, but was disappointed to find that most of the items were mundane. Old tractor parts, a 5LB bag of grass seed, the bottom rotted out and seeds spilling onto the shelf, and a variety of rusting wrenches and other assorted tools he didn't recognize. On the bottom shelf of one rack stood a pair of five gallon gas cans. He recognized them because his dad kept one in the trunk of his car, although that one was red plastic. These were metal, and looked much older.

He reached out, lifted the nearest can. It was heavy. Liquid sloshed when he moved it.

He considered pulling it out, unscrewing the spout to see what was inside, but he couldn't be bothered. What else would be inside a gas can other than gasoline? Besides, he didn't like the barn. The air was thick with a cloying, pungent odor he could not identify. It was sickly. Rotten. It left a nasty taste in the back of his throat.

He turned, losing interest in the junk on the shelves, and made his way back to the door and slipped out into the daylight. He squinted, letting his eyes adjust, and then took off again.

Leaving the barns behind, Jake walked across the lawn, in the shadow of the house. High on the roof line he spied two gable windows. These would be Sarah's room. It was unfair that she got such a big space, while his own room was much smaller.

He stopped at the swing set.

It was even worse up close. He reached out and took hold of the chain holding the swing, pulling back and then letting it go. The whole structure creaked and groaned as it swung, sounding like it was in pain.

He looked down at his hands, at the red coating of rust

that had come away when he touched the chain. He wiped it off on his jeans.

When he looked up again, he was surprised to see a gray and white rabbit sitting a few feet away on the lawn.

It was motionless, large dark eyes observing him.

When he took a step forward, it turned and bounded away, toward the tree line, then paused, looking back at him.

He took another step.

The rabbit hopped a bit further before stopping once more.

Jake stared.

Did it want him to follow it?

He walked forward.

The rabbit followed suit, keeping ahead of him.

It was almost at the trees now. It hesitated one last time, and then disappeared into the undergrowth.

Jake sprinted forward, arriving at the trees in time to see the rabbit resting near a fallen log. When it saw him the animal hopped down and scurried a few feet further.

Jake lingered, glancing back toward the house, his father's words echoing in his mind. When he turned back toward the woods the rabbit was still there.

It watched him, half reared on its hind legs, ears pricked up. And then it turned and hopped between two tall oaks, disappearing from sight.

Jake forgot his dilemma. He moved forward, following the animal into the woods.

It kept ahead of him, weaving in and out of the trees, following the line of an old, overgrown path.

He ran behind, doing his best to keep the furry creature in sight. The few times it did evade him, the rabbit always seemed to pop up again.

And then he came across the brook.

It gurgled and gushed, carving a path through the forest.

The rabbit was several feet ahead, sitting in the middle of the path, eyes fixed upon him. In the canopy above, birds chittered and sang. A chorus of crickets chirped in rhythmic harmony. For a brief moment, Jake felt at one with his surroundings. He wondered if the rabbit had brought him here to see this, experience it. It sounded silly, but the thought persisted.

Jake inched forward, reaching his hand out toward the animal, knowing that it would let him pet it. Because they shared a bond that only nature could forge.

Then, before Jake knew what was happening, the bunny launched sideways out of sight.

"Wait." Jake called out in desperation, even though he knew, deep down, that it was pointless.

He ran forward, veering off at the spot where the animal had disappeared.

Up ahead something pushed through the undergrowth, rustling leaves.

Jake followed the sound, eager to catch up with his newfound friend, but this time the rabbit wasn't making things so easy. In the end he came to a halt, his breathing labored.

Where had the animal gone?

He took a few steps forward, his eyes scanning the brush, but it was no use. The rabbit had abandoned him.

A deep sense of loneliness descended up him. He missed his furry little friend.

At that moment, a sudden quiet had descended upon the forest, almost as if a switch had been turned off. The birds were no longer singing in the trees, the crickets had ceased their chirping. Even the trees were still, the rustle of leaves in the breeze chilling by its absence.

The silence was eerie.

Jake froze, confused.

He might have been raised in the city, but it didn't take a born and bred woodsman to know that something was amiss. The air hung like an oppressive blanket, thick and stale. It reminded him of the atmosphere in the barn. There was a trace of the same festering rot.

Jake didn't want to be here anymore.

He looked around, panicked. Nothing looked right. He couldn't see the house, or the back yard. He was not even on a path anymore.

He was lost.

But how could that be?

Surely he hadn't strayed that far into the forest? One glance around told him he had. Tall trees jostled for space on all sides, stretching as far as he could see. They closed in around him, their branches reaching out, choking off the sunlight.

It was cold too. Right where he was standing the air was freezing, which was strange for a summer day.

A creeping fear engulfed him.

He didn't want to be in the woods anymore.

Except that he had no idea how to get out.

And then he remembered the brook. He could still hear the gurgle of water somewhere off to his left. In fact, it was the only thing that hadn't gone quiet.

He took a deep breath, ignoring the voice inside his head that told him to run fast and run far, and started in the direction of the sound. He pushed through wild bushes, stepped over a large boulder, and a few moments later came upon the stream.

He almost fainted with relief. It should be easy to follow this back until he gained his bearings.

Only something wasn't right.

The water, which should have been crystal clear, was not. Ribbons of bright red weaved along in the current, dancing around rocks like streamers in the wind.

His eyes wandered, following the strange red ribbons back upstream.

Fear pricked at the back of his neck.

Something lay on the ground ahead, half submerged in the water.

Something small and round and furry.

Jake moved closer, his pulse racing.

He looked down, furrowing his brow.

At first, he didn't comprehend what he was looking at, but then he saw a big round eye staring back at him, and a pair of long ears. Below that, nothing but ragged, torn flesh.

Jake stumbled backwards, horrified.

Now he knew what had made the stream run red, and he knew what lay at the water's edge.

It was the rabbit, or rather, the poor creature's head, and it looked like it had been ripped clean off.

He felt his stomach churn, tasted the half digested pancakes his throat, hot and acidic. He swallowed, desperate not to throw up. Not here, not next to the savaged bunny.

He backed up, tearing his eyes away from the grisly sight. And then he came upon the rest of the unfortunate animal.

Caught between the lower limbs of a sprawling red oak, was the rabbit's body. It hung there like a limp, dead sack, the fur matted and slick with dark, crimson blood.

He froze.

A cold, hard dread settled in the pit of his stomach.

He didn't want to be here anymore, but he could not will his legs to work. It was as if the fear had hijacked his body, and was intent upon forcing him to stay there, eyes locked upon the mutilated animal.

A tear forced its way from the corner of his eye and ran down his cheek. He lifted a hand to wipe it away.

A twig snapped.

Jake drew in a sharp breath, held it.

There came a rustle of leaves, then another sharp snap of splintering wood.

Jake felt the scream a moment before it erupted.

More rustling.

Jake's legs decided to work.

He turned and fled.

He ran faster than he ever had before, salty tears streaming down his face.

Branches clawed at his face and arms, tearing into him. He barreled forward, giving little heed to the thorns that snagged his clothing, not caring where he was running, so long as it was away from that dreadful dead thing, and whatever had killed it.

His foot snagged on a root.

He tumbled forward, the impact with the ground knocking the air from him in a mighty whoosh.

Something moved off to his left, pushing through the foliage, gaining on him.

Jake struggled to his feet. Whatever killed the rabbit was coming after him.

A branch gave way with a crack.

Jake took off again, ignoring the pain from his fall.

Behind him, getting closer, the unseen pursuer crashed along. It was right there now, by his side, yet still he saw nothing. He braced himself for whatever was about to come shooting out of the brush and rip into him.

And then, by some miracle, the trees parted and thinned, and there was the house, as serene and quiet and normal as it had been before, when the rabbit was still alive.

Jake's lungs burned, and his legs felt like lead, but even so he didn't let up until he was at the back door. He flung it wide, and sped through the house, wailing and sobbing as he went. He ran like a mad thing, driven by blind panic, consumed by the horrific sight in the woods, and didn't stop until his father appeared, a worried look upon his face, and scooped him up, and comforted him, and made everything better.

Chapter 12

ANDREW WAS FINISHING up in the living room when Jake came running in, tears running down his cheeks and a distressed look upon his face.

"Whatever is going on?" He moved to meet his son, who fell into his arms, his body wracked with sobs. "Did you hurt yourself?"

"No." Jake mumbled the words.

"Then what?" Andrew gave Jake a quick once over anyway, just to make sure. When he saw the scratches on the boy's face and arms he pressed further. "I thought you said you didn't hurt yourself? How did you get those marks?"

"I was in the woods." Jake sniffed and rubbed his eyes.

"I told you not to stray too far from the house. You certainly shouldn't have been wandering in the woods."

"I know." Jake looked up, his face red and streaked. "I'm sorry."

"That still doesn't explain the scratches, or what you were doing out there in the first place." Andrew should have been mad, but it was hard when his son was in such a distressed state.

"What's going on?" Sarah appeared in the doorway. She clutched her phone in one hand. No doubt she had been texting instead of getting her belongings unpacked. Andrew could guess who she was texting too, her best friend, Becca. "Is he okay?"

"That's what I'm trying to find out." Andrew could worry about Sarah's slacking later. Right now he was more concerned with Jake. He looked down at his son. "Well?"

"There was a rabbit. I followed it. It went into the woods. It looked like Mister Carrots."

"It did huh?" Andrew knew Mister Carrots well. It was the pet rabbit his class had when Jake was in elementary school. They had looked after it one summer, and for years afterward Jake pestered for one of his own.

"Uh huh." Jake had stopped crying now. "I just wanted to see where it lived, and I got lost."

"That's why I didn't want you going into the woods on your own." Andrew knelt and met his son's gaze. "But there's no reason to be upset. You found your way back. You're here now."

"Something killed the rabbit."

"What?" Andrew's relief turned to concern.

"I couldn't find it, and then when I saw it again it was dead. Something had killed it. It's head was in the water, and it's body in a tree," Jake's bottom lip trembled. For a moment it looked like he might start to cry again, but then he composed himself. "There was lots of blood."

"Did you see any other animals?"

"No." Jake shook his head. "But something chased me. I could hear it in the woods behind me."

"It was probably a fox," Sarah said.

"It was?" Jake looked up at her.

"Yep." Andrew agreed. "We're not in the big city now. There are all sorts of animals out there. These things happen."

"I don't want them to." Jake looked desperate. "Why did the bunny die?"

"Everything dies," Sarah said. "Even you."

"That's not helping." Andrew glared at her.

"It's the truth…"

"Enough." Andrew wished his daughter would go back to the way she was before the accident, before the black clothing and churlish attitude. He missed the bright happy kid she used to be.

"I want the bunny to be alive again." Jake sniffed.

"I know you do." Andrew wondered if he shouldn't have told Jake to stay indoors. But it was no use second guessing himself now. All he could do was distract his son from the situation, and he thought he knew how to do it. "I tell you what, why don't we go and get ice cream?"

"Really?" Jake perked up. "Ice cream?"

"Sure. There's a place I know that serves the biggest cones you've ever seen, as big as your head." Andrew stood up. "How about it, sport?"

"Can we go right now?"

"I don't see why not." Andrew studied his son. "Change that shirt first though, you have dirt and leaves all over it."

Jake looked down, as if he was surprised at the state of his attire despite the frantic flight through the woods. "Do I have to?" He said the words with an exasperation that made it clear he viewed the endeavor of swapping shirts to be a pointless delay.

"If you want ice cream," Andrew said. "Now hurry up."

"Alright." Jake took off in the direction of the stairs.

Andrew watched him go. To Sarah, he said, "We'll talk about this later."

Chapter 13

SARAH SAT ON HER BED, her phone in hand.

It was dark outside and the house was still. Jake was already in bed. Her father had set up his office in the smallest of the three bedrooms on the second floor, and retreated there earlier in the evening to catch up on his work. Not before he'd laid into her though, telling her to cut out the attitude, that they were all hurting, and she wasn't helping things.

Becca was on speed dial.

The only person in the world who still understood her.

She lifted the phone to her ear, listening to it ring a few times, and then her friend's chirpy voice came on the line.

"I thought you'd forgotten about me."

"Sorry. I've been busy," Sarah lied. They had been inseparable since the third grade, always hanging out at one house or the other. Recently that had changed. After her mother's accident, Sarah felt alone, isolated. Nothing mattered anymore. She withdrew into herself, finding it hard to enjoy the things she previously had. Then came the suicide attempt, a bottle of pills in a school bathroom. Becca found her, saved her life, but even so, the feeling that she was adrift in an endless sea of solitude persisted. They still talked, still saw each other, but it was not the same as before, and they both knew it. So Sarah lied when Becca asked where she'd been. "Dad's had me working since we got here."

"That sucks," Becca said. "How are things?"

"Dreadful," Sarah replied. This much was the truth. "The house is disgusting, I hate it here, Jake's being a real pain. To top it off, dad has been giving me a hard time again."

"Sorry. Want to tell me about it?"

"God yes. More than anything." If there was one thing Becca was good at, it was listening. Sarah unloaded, telling her about the house, and how she wished she were back in Boston, and Jake. When she recounted the strange incident with the nightlight, Becca listened in silence, her breath growing heavy as the story unfolded.

When it was over there was a moment's silence before Becca spoke again.

"Wow. Creepy. You must have been terrified," Becca said. "Are you sure it was Jake?"

"Of course it was. Who else could it have been?"

"You said he was sleeping."

"Or faking it."

"Unless there was someone else in the room with you, and it wasn't Jake at all."

"Stop that. You'll give me nightmares."

"Maybe it was a ghost," Becca said. "That house is really old, and you're just down the road from Salem. Practically haunting central."

"You know I don't believe in that stuff."

"Then explain the closet door, the footsteps."

"I've told you, it was my little shit of a brother."

"You should do something to him. Get some revenge," Becca said. "Sounds like he deserves it."

"Nah." An image of Jake earlier in the day, his eyes puffy with tears, entered her head. "He already had the fright of his life this morning. He found a dead rabbit in the woods, with its head cut off or something."

"Gross."

"I know, right?"

"Did you see it?"

"Nope." Sarah was thankful for that. "But I think that it really shook him up."

"That's pretty messed up," Becca said. "Are you sure there isn't something wrong with your new house?"

"Stop it."

"What?"

"You know what," Sarah said. "I won't be able to sleep tonight if you keep this up."

"I thought you didn't believe in ghosts."

"I don't," Sarah replied. "But I still have an imagination."

"Fine." Becca sounded disappointed. She paused, then said, "I saw Tyler today."

"Tyler?" Sarah echoed the word. It sounded foreign, like a distant memory, yet it had only been a three months since she broke things off with him.

"He asked about you."

"So?"

"He misses you," Becca said. "I don't understand why you ended things with him."

"He reminded me of before."

"He's hurting. You should talk to him."

"I'm hurting too."

"I know," Becca said. "But he tried so hard, you shouldn't push him away. He's on your side."

"He doesn't understand." She remembered the way he treated her after the incident with the pills, like she was some fragile, broken thing that needed to be watched over. Their relationship hadn't been the same since her mother's death, but after the suicide attempt a chasm opened between them.

She felt numb inside, and no matter how hard she tried, nothing could change that.

"He wants to understand."

"Can we change the subject?"

"Sarah-"

"Please?"

"Alright. No more talk of Tyler." There was a beat of silence before Becca spoke again. "You know what. I should come up there."

"I don't know."

"Come on." Becca said. "You can push me away all you want, but it won't work."

"I'm not pushing you away."

"We both know that's not true. You've pushed everyone away this past year. It's not good for you." Becca fell silent for a moment. "How about this weekend. I can be there Thursday."

"That soon?"

"Sure."

"Maybe in a few weeks, when-"

"Don't be such a stick in the mud," Becca pleaded. "What else are you going to do? Besides, your dad will be pleased to have me there."

"He will, huh?"

"Sure. He likes me." She laughed. "I'm like the daughter he never had."

"Hey-"

"Alright. Fine. But if I'm there, I can help out with stuff. I'm sure he's snowed under with work after the move."

"That's true," Sarah said.

"And I'll be keeping you busy so you don't bug him."

"What are you, my babysitter?" She couldn't help but smile. Sometimes Becca could still find a sliver of the old Sarah.

"Something like that." Becca said. "What do you say. Please?"

"I'll see what I can do."

"You'll ask your dad?"

"Sure."

"Promise?"

"I said I would, didn't I?"

"Great." Becca squealed with delight. "This is going to be so much fun. I can't wait."

Chapter 14

ANDREW WAS in his newly outfitted office at the top of the stairs when he heard the thump from down below.

He looked up from his laptop.

There was a second, louder thump.

Andrew felt the hairs on the back of his neck stand up. It was late, gone midnight, and the kids should be sleeping. Besides, his door was open, and he would have noticed if either of them had gone downstairs.

That hadn't happened.

He sat still, listening.

A minute passed.

The house was peaceful, silent.

He wondered if it might have been a branch hitting a window. He turned back to the computer screen, tapped out a few more lines, but then there came another noise from below.

Andrew froze.

It sounded like someone had entered the house.

He rose and walked to the landing.

Jake's door was closed.

The corridor was dark. No light spilled from the attic. Sarah must be sleeping also.

He felt a tingle of fear.

Had someone broken in?

He had to investigate.

He searched for something to take with him, a weapon of some sort. If there was an intruder, he didn't want to run into them empty handed.

His eyes settled on the baseball bat he'd owned since he was a kid. It was worn and battered, with a few chips taken out of it. But it held sentimental value. The bat was a link to his childhood. In the old house, it held pride of place on a stand in his study, but he hadn't yet found a spot for it here.

He made his way to the head of the stairs, the heft of the bat comforting in his hand. He paused and listened, eyes examining the darkness below.

And that was when he heard the voices.

They were low and flat, like two people going back and forth at each other. He could not make out the words.

His heart pounded.

He wavered between going to investigate and calling the police.

And then there was something else.

Music.

He stood and listened.

There was a vague familiarity to the tune. At first he could not place it, and then he understood.

This was the theme song to a show he'd watched as a kid. It was the TV.

His thumping heart slowed.

Jake must have snuck past his open door, and was watching the television.

Andrew took the stairs two at a time, bearing down upon the living room, expecting to find his son sitting there cross legged and wide eyed in front of the TV.

Except that the room was empty.

The television babbled away in solitude, the screen casting long, leaping shadows across the floor.

Andrew stopped, alarmed.

"…What are you doing old fellow?" The actor on the TV said, his voice bright and cheery. "Seems like this was all a wild goose chase."

There was a burst of canned laughter.

The camera panned to show another man. "Wild goose chase? There's something here I tell you." He turned and looked directly at the camera, giving Andrew the impression that the actor was talking right at him, which was impossible. "It's with us right now."

Andrew's skin crawled.

He searched for the remote, snatched it up, and stabbed at the power button.

The screen snapped off, silencing the voices.

But why was the TV on in the first place?

He'd used it right around the time that Jake came barreling in, all upset, but only for a few minutes to make sure the cable box was working.

No one had been near the television since.

That was at least nine hours ago.

Had Sarah or Jake been messing with it?

This was the most likely explanation. Either that, or the TV had developed a mind of its own.

It had to be one of the kids.

He dropped the remote onto the coffee table and turned away. He didn't get far before he noticed something else.

It was freezing.

Not cold, but frigid.

He stepped back, toward the TV.

It was warmer here.

But when he returned to the original spot, it was ice cold.

He lifted his arm, could feel where the air grew cool. It was like an invisible wall. He turned a full circle, mapping the edges of the cold spot. It extended about two feet in each direction. A funnel of chilled air sitting in the middle of his living room.

It was weird, and uncomfortable.

He moved out of the cold air, suppressing a shudder, and glanced toward the ceiling. He expected to find an air vent there, but all he saw was smooth plaster. When he stepped forward again, the temperature was normal. It was like the cold spot had never been there.

"Screw this." Andrew turned and made his way to the corridor. He had better things to do than run around chasing cold air. Then he remembered the noises he'd heard. It had sounded like someone coming into the house. The front door was shut and locked. He could see that. But he hadn't checked the back door.

He padded back through the house, cutting across the dining room, to the kitchen.

The back door was closed tight.

Whatever he had heard, it wasn't anyone coming in.

And then his eyes drifted upward, to the bolt.

It was drawn back.

A prickling sensation crept up his spine.

Andrew edged forward, the baseball bat held high.

He reached the midway point of the kitchen, the bat gripped so tight he could feel the grain of the wood under his palm.

At that moment the fridge whirred to life.

He almost dropped the bat before regaining his composure.

Now he noticed other sounds.

The faucet dripped a rhythmic drum beat into the porcelain sink. He would need to replace the washer, or buy a new tap altogether.

A moth flew into the window above the counter, trying in vain to figure out the unseen barrier that stopped it entering the room. Each time it hit the glass panes there was another muffled thunk.

It was amazing how loud a silent house could be.

He felt his heart thumping against his rib cage.

The back door loomed large.

He reached out, gripped the knob, and twisted.

The door swung wide with a drawn out groan.

Andrew peered out into the night.

A gentle breeze blew past him.

Leaves rustled and crickets chirped.

From somewhere far away a lone owl hooted, the sound melancholy and haunting. He spotted a couple of fireflies dancing through the darkness. The swing set rocked back and forth in the wind, the rusty chain letting out a high pitched squeak with each lazy pass.

But apart from that, he was alone.

The back yard was empty.

Andrew closed the door and reached up, drawing the bolt across. Maybe he had left it unlocked earlier. Whatever else he heard must be the building settling. This was an old house, and he wasn't accustomed to its moans and groans yet. He leaned against the door, letting the adrenalin ebb away.

After a while, when his heartbeat had returned to normal, and he'd convinced himself that nothing was amiss, Andrew stepped away from the door, leaning the bat against the wall. He went to the sink and poured himself a glass of water, drinking it down in one gulp. He rinsed the glass and turned to put it on the counter.

A face leered at him through the window in the back door. Dark, piercing eyes stared at him, a gaping mouth stretched into a wide, black grin. The face was just inches from the very door he'd been leaning against moments before.

He let out a cry and staggered backwards.

The glass slipped from his hand and shattered on the hard flagstone floor.

When he looked up again, the face was gone. Now all he saw were swirls of old dirt, and the tangled silk of an abandoned spider's web in one corner. He was still studying the empty window when a voice rang out behind him.

"What are you doing?"

Andrew turned to find his son silhouetted in the doorway. "You should be in bed."

"I heard a noise," Jake said. "It woke me up."

"Sorry about that, son." He could feel his heart thumping still. "Nothing to worry about. I dropped a glass, that's all."

"Oh." Jake looked down, at the floor. "I'm thirsty. Can I have some milk?"

"Sure," Andrew said, "and then it's right back to bed, okay?"

"Alright." Jake nodded.

Andrew took a fresh glass out of the cabinet, and went to the fridge. He filled the glass half way, and handed it to his son.

He watched Jake tip the glass, gulping down the milk, but then his eyes wandered back to the window. Had he really seen a face there, or was it just his mind playing tricks? Regardless, the only thing there now was grime and cobwebs.

Chapter 15

SARAH AWOKE from a deep and dreamless sleep.

She opened her eyes.

Sunlight brightened the room.

It felt late.

She rolled over and looked at her clock.

10 a.m.

She groaned. How had she slept so long? She must have been more tired than she realized. Her eyes flicked toward the nightlight. It was still working. No one had snuck in last night to play tricks. The rabbit incident had put an end to Jake's pranks, at least for now. She decided to go easy on him for the next few days.

Slipping out from under the covers, she pulled on her jeans, found a clean shirt, and then went downstairs, following the smell of bacon that led her to the kitchen.

Her father was at the stove, a spatula in hand.

Jake was at the dining room table, doing a bad job of filling in a coloring book.

Neither looked up when she entered the room.

She went to the fridge and found a carton of juice, poured a glass. After a while she said, "I spoke to Becca last night."

"Huh?" Her father sounded distant, lost in his own head.

"I said, I talked to Becca last night, on the phone."

She narrowed her eyes. "Are you okay?"

"Sorry." Andrew seemed to shake off the funk. "I didn't sleep well. You were saying?"

"Becca?"

"Right. How is she?"

"Good. She wants to come up and visit, stay for a few days." Sarah didn't know if Becca visiting was a good idea, but it might get her father off her back. He thought she was too withdrawn, and had spoken to her about it several times since the pill incident. He'd even taken her to see a shrink, not that it did much good. "What do you think?"

"Once we get the house in order."

"Thursday."

"Sarah-"

"I know. It's too soon. I can tell her to wait if you like."

"No, she should come, it will be good for you." He cracked eggs into a frying pan. "There is a condition though."

"What?"

"I want some help around here, the next few days."

"That's it?"

"Think you can handle it?"

"Sure." She watched her father set up three plates, sliding scrambled eggs and four rashers of bacon onto each. She took one and settled at the kitchen table. "Like what?"

"For a start, you can do the laundry. There's a hamper full already."

"Do we even have a washing machine?" Sarah hadn't seen one. In their old house there was a laundry room off the kitchen, but not here.

"We sure do." Andrew poured a mug of coffee and joined her at the table. "It's in the cellar."

"The cellar." Sarah repeated the words with a shudder. Her grandparents home in Maine had a dark, creepy basement. She had ventured down there twice, and that was enough. "You want me to go into the cellar?"

"It's the only way to get to the washing machine."

"I'll do it," Jake piped up, a grin on his face.

"I don't think so, sport. You still have to put your toys away." Andrew turned to Sarah. "If you want Becca here, that's the deal."

"Fine." Sarah rolled her eyes. "If I must."

"That's the spirit," Andrew said. "The laundry basket is in the bathroom."

Chapter 16

SARAH LINGERED IN THE HALLWAY, cradling the basket of laundry in her arms.

Ahead of her, the cellar door yawned wide. Wooden stairs dropped away into shadow, with only the vaguest hint of what lay beyond visible. She spied a set of old shelves at the foot of the stairs, loaded with paint cans, a couple of moldy boxes. Further in she saw the worn out frame of a bicycle, one wheel missing. A fuse box was attached to the wall, thick wires snaking upward into the rafters. In the far side stood an old hutch with peeling paint.

The cellar did not look inviting.

She stood a moment, wondering whether she really wanted to bother. But what choice did she have? She needed clean clothes, and besides, it was the only way her dad would allow Becca to visit.

Here goes nothing, she thought, testing the top stair with her foot before trusting it with her full weight.

The staircase groaned but held firm.

She moved on to the next step, then the next, peering over the top to gauge her descent.

At the bottom she stopped and looked around.

The cellar occupied the same footprint as the house above, with a compacted dirt floor, rough stone walls, and a cylindrical oil tank resting on a concrete pad. It was painted a dull black and had thick pipes sticking up toward the floorboards above. This was part of the heating system. They would need it come winter when the temperatures would plummet well below freezing.

The ceiling was low, with long trailing cobwebs slung between hefty rafters. The single light bulb affixed between two joists pushed back the darkness, but could not reach the furthest corners. The lone window, a long narrow pane near the top of the far wall, at ground level, was so caked in grime it allowed barely any natural light to penetrate.

The washer and dryer stood at the far end of the room in an alcove flanked on both sides by brick walls.

Sarah groaned.

Why hadn't they put the laundry area closer to the stairs? She had no wish to cross the length of the basement. Who knew how many fat spiders were lurking above her head, or what might scurry away into the shadows. Not to mention that the air was so cold it raised goose bumps on her arms.

She toyed with the idea of turning back, admitting that she was scared, but then she would be teased in relentless fashion, and that would be too much.

So instead she forced herself forward, keeping her head low to avoid the worst of the cobwebs. Even so, a long strand trailed across her face and she almost dropped the basket in her frantic attempt to clear away the sticky gossamer silk. She brushed at her shoulders, worried that she might have dislodged the eight legged occupant of the web. When she didn't find anything her heart rate slowed a little.

At the laundry area she dropped the clothes hamper on the floor. Lifting the washing machine lid she stuffed the contents of the basket inside.

There was a shelf above the washer, made of wood and supported by two rusting brackets. Upon this sat a bright new box of detergent, no doubt placed there by her father. She took it down it and added a scoop to the machine, then closed the lid. She set the machine and waited for the water to start up before turning back to the hamper.

From the direction of the stairs, came the squeal of worn hinges, followed by a reverberating thud.

The cellar door had blown closed.

She was alone and cut off from the rest of the house.

A shudder raced up her spine.

She turned back toward the stairs.

The light bulb flickered once, twice, then went out.

The cellar was plunged in darkness.

The swirling blackness was broken only by a dim rectangle of light that entered through the filthy window. It was not bright enough to see by.

Sarah's breath caught in her throat. She fought a rush of panic.

From somewhere far off in the darkness she heard a faint sound. Was someone in the cellar with her?

"Jake?" She called. "Dammit. Cut it out."

It was just like her crappy brother to do something like this. She imagined him sneaking up to the cellar, reaching in, flicking off the light, and then slamming the door. He was probably standing in the hallway, laughing his ass off right about now.

Except that the door had swung shut *before* the light was extinguished.

A stab of terror clutched at Sarah's heart.

"Jake?" She as trembling now. "Dad?"

Her voice bounced off the cellar walls.

"Help me." The words sounded thin, hollow. There was no way her father or brother would hear her cries unless they were in the hallway. "Anyone?"

But nobody came to her aid.

She was on her own. Unable to see or be heard, she felt like a soul adrift in an endless ocean of nothingness. Like after the overdose, before she woke up.

That thought brought her to the brink of tears.

She fought back a sob.

Something moved in the darkness.

The sob died in Sarah's throat.

She held her breath, listening, waiting.

There it was again. A shuffling, like feet dragging across the bare earth.

The washer clanked and clunked at her back.

Sarah's breath came in short, sharp gasps.

Her eyes darted around, despite the fact that she was pretty much blinded.

The sound came again, closer now.

A light breeze touched her face.

It carried a lingering odor that reminded her of bad breath.

It was almost like someone, or something, was standing right there, inches away. Unmoving.

The air was freezing cold.

Her skin prickled.

She let out a whimper.

The wind came again, caressing her cheek. Rotten. Putrescent.

That was all it took. She took off running, her hands flailing out in front, feeling around in the darkness for the staircase.

Where was it?

Oh god, where was the damn staircase?

And then the washer made one last clunk and stopped.

The sudden silence was worse than anything.

She came to a halt and stood there, her labored breathing much too loud.

Something scratched along the floor. Like nails on a chalkboard, only worse.

Sarah found the will to move again.

She stumbled forward, eyes straining in the blackness.

And then her foot smashed up against something hard.

Jolting pain shot up her leg.

She let out a yelp. Put her hand out to steady herself. Her palm came to rest on a rough hand rail.

The stairs.

She cried with relief.

Up ahead there was a thin crack of light.

The cellar door.

Sarah put a foot on the first step, ignoring the creak of protest. She moved to the next step, then the next, keeping one hand tight on the railing.

The climb seemed endless. She expected to feel icy fingers at any moment, to smell that fetid breath over her shoulder. She quickened her pace, reaching out for the light switch as she neared the top, wanting nothing more than to bathe the cellar in merciful light.

She flicked it up.

Nothing happened.

She jiggled the switch, up and down.

Still no luck.

"Damn." The word came out more like a desperate moan, that a curse. "Why won't this work?"

And then she felt the air stir.

Someone was sneaking up behind her, she was sure.

Sarah gave up the light switch. Turned her attention to the door. She fumbled to find the handle, panic turning to relief when her hand closed over it.

She turned the knob.

Nothing happened.

She tried again, throwing her weight against the stuck door.

And then, just when she was sure the thing in the darkness was going to reach her, the door flew open and Sarah fell forward into bright, wonderful daylight.

Chapter 17

ANDREW TOGGLED the switch to the on position. The neon tube sparked to life, illuminating the basement.

He turned to Sarah.

"See, all working."

"Well it wasn't." Sarah peered past him, a scowl on her face. "I'm not making it up."

"I never said you were." Andrew could hear the washer running the spin cycle. He suspected he would have to transfer the clothes to the dryer. Sarah didn't look like she wanted to venture down into the basement again any time soon. "It's an old house, with old wiring. Maybe there was a short circuit somewhere."

"That's your explanation?" Sarah said. "Wiring?"

"What else could it be?"

"I don't know." Sarah stood with her arms folded across her chest.

"I'll have the electrician come back out and give the wiring a second look. Maybe he missed something." Andrew turned the light off and closed the door.

"The washer turned off too."

"Probably just between wash cycles."

"No. That wasn't it." Sarah protested. "There was someone down there with me."

"That's impossible." Andrew's remembered the night before, the fleeting impression of a face at the window. But that was just his mind playing tricks, wasn't it? "Besides, I thought you didn't believe in ghosts."

"I don't." Sarah's voice rose in pitch. "Who said it was a ghost?"

"There wasn't anyone down there with you. Jake was in the living room, and I was in the kitchen loading the dishwasher."

"I know what I felt," Sarah said. "It wasn't wiring, and it wasn't the washer changing cycles."

"Sarah, what do you want me to do?" Andrew struggled to hold back his frustration. "The basement is empty. There's nothing down there that can harm you."

"You could take me seriously for a start."

"I'm trying, but you don't make it easy."

"Forget about it." Sarah turned and stomped down the hallway toward the front door, slamming it behind her.

Andrew watched her leave with a deepening sense of loss. Her therapist in Boston said it would take some time, but her mental wounds would heal. It wasn't happening fast enough. He was getting tired of waiting. Instead of coming out of herself, Sarah was more withdrawn than ever. He worried that something would happen, a repeat of the incident at school. He'd already lost his wife, if he lost Sarah it would be too much to bear.

"Daddy?" Jake, who had stood silent throughout the exchange, looked up at his father.

"Yes, son?" Andrew struggled to keep the weariness from his voice.

"Should we take Sarah into town for ice cream? She looks sad."

Andrew laughed, despite himself. "I don't think Mint Choc Chip will fix this one, son."

"It makes me feel better." Jake looked up, his eyes wide.

"I know it does," Andrew replied. He wished the solution were as simple as a few scoops.

"Can we get ice cream anyway?"

"Maybe later." Andrew said, his eyes returning to the front door, hoping that Sarah would come back. "But only if you're good."

Chapter 18

ONCE SHE WAS OUTSIDE, Sarah regretted being mad at her father. It wasn't his fault. She would not have believed the story if it had come from her younger brother, so why would she ever think anyone would believe her. And now, in the warm afternoon sunlight, it seemed silly to think that there was something in the basement. Even so, a glimmer of doubt lingered. She could still remember the dragging, shuffling sounds. The shifting air upon her cheek. The slightly rotten, sickly smell that reminded her of death, although she didn't know why.

She hurried away from the house, following the track that led all the way to the road. She had no idea where she was going, but she didn't want to be in that house, not at that moment.

For the first time she took stock of the landscape.

There were fields on both sides, overgrown and unkempt. Beyond that she could see the woods, the tops of the trees visible above the wild grass. At one point she spied another house, the slate roof and double chimneys clearly visible, but it looked a long way off, much too far to reach on foot. Up ahead, further along the trail at the entrance to the property, was the gnarly old tree with clutching, misshapen limbs.

There was something else too.

A shiny blue Mustang turning into the driveway, heading toward the house and kicking up dust as it went.

She came to a halt, watching the vehicle approach.

The car drew closer, but with the sun glinting off the windshield she could not see anyone inside.

Until it came to a stop a few feet away and the drivers side door opened.

A lanky boy climbed out.

"Tyler." She recognized her ex-boyfriend despite the baseball cap shielding his eyes and the black rimmed Oakley's pressed against his face. "What are you doing here?"

"I ran into Becca the other day."

"So?" The sunglasses didn't suit him. They made him look a bit like an enormous two legged insect.

"She got me thinking about you."

"She gave you my new address too, I suppose." Becca hadn't mentioned that little detail on the phone the previous evening.

"It wasn't her fault," Tyler said. "I pried it out of her. I had to practically get down on my hands and knees and beg."

"I would have liked to see that." Sarah felt her mood lighten a little. She tried not to grin.

"You look nice." Tyler said. "Your hair is longer. It suits you."

"Please don't-"

"I've missed you, Sarah." He rounded the door and walked toward her, taking his sunglasses off at the same time.

When she saw his dusty blue eyes, the way his eyelids drooped slightly at the corners, she forgot what had happened, and for an instant, wondered why they had ever broken up.

Except that she could never truly forget, because it was

ingrained in her mind. An indelible stamp seared upon her memory.

He hadn't been the one.

Even though he could see her suffering, even though he knew she had stolen the bottle of prescription sleeping pills, he hadn't been the one.

When she sat in that bathroom cubicle, swallowing those small white capsules, choking them down, she wanted him to save her. Even in that wretched state of mind Sarah still hoped to be saved, because she didn't truly want to die. What she wanted, what she needed, was for the pain to go away. And it had, if only for a while.

But then she was in the hospital. The doctors said she almost died, that they feared she might not wake up. But she knew something they did not.

She had died.

She remembered the cold place, the dark void of nothingness. She also remembered the fear. Even now it stayed with her like a constant companion, lingering.

And then there were the more mundane matters.

She had felt like crap, both physically and mentally. It grew worse when she realized the terrible anguish she had caused her father and Jake. But when she saw Tyler, when he came to visit, all she could think was that he should have been the one to find her. He should have saved her. But he hadn't.

It was all his fault.

All the misery and depression she'd felt since they put her mother's oblong box in the cold, hard ground was because of him.

Even though deep down she knew that it wasn't.

He was a scapegoat, someone to bear the brunt of her pain, because she was so angry that her mother had tried to drive back from Maine on that icy winter evening. Had steered into a tree and died, leaving her behind. He was her sacrificial lamb. He didn't stand a chance.

But seeing him again after so many months, she wasn't so sure. They said absence made the heart grow fonder, but what it really did was dull the knife. She no longer wished to punish him. It didn't seem worth the effort.

She wanted to say that she was sorry. She wanted to let him know that the anger had receded, if only a little. Instead, all she could muster was, "you have a new car."

"Huh?"

"The Mustang."

"Oh, yeah. My dad knew a guy at his work that was selling it off cheap."

"Looks nice. Fast."

"Thanks. It's a pretty sweet ride." He shuffled his feet. The air hung like an invisible barrier between them. After a while he spoke again. "Maybe this was a mistake. I can leave if you want."

"No." She felt her heart quicken. She didn't want that. "Why don't we go for a walk instead."

"Really?" He sounded surprised, but quickly changed tack. "I mean, sure."

"Good." She reached out and took his hand in hers. It was a small gesture, something she had done hundreds of times, but now it seemed like cresting a mountain and looking down the other side. It was a breakthrough.

Tyler stiffened, as if he expected her to realize her mistake and pull away, but then he relaxed. "Where do you want to go?"

"Boston." This was a joke, but not entirely. There was a car sitting there, and the city was less than an hour away. But it would do no good. Her father would find her missing, cause a huge fuss. Maybe even call the cops.

She realized Tyler was looking at her, unsure how to answer. She helped him out. "Why don't I show you around."

They set off toward the side of the house, crossing the back yard in the direction of the trees. There was a trail that

Sarah could see from her bedroom window, and it seemed like a good place to go. It was private, secluded. Best of all, there was no way Jake would be there. He wouldn't be caught dead in the woods after the rabbit incident.

"There hasn't been anyone else." Tyler waited until they were far from the house before speaking again.

"Huh?" It was cooler under the canopy of branches. The trail was narrow. She wondered where it went.

"I haven't dated anyone else. You know, since you…" His voice trailed off.

"Oh." She knew what the rest of that sentence should have been. *Since you dumped me for no good reason and broke my heart.* She felt a pang of regret. "It's okay if you did. I understand."

"I know." Tyler's arm brushed against hers. "But I haven't. Not one single date."

"Me either."

"I felt so bad after…"

"You don't need to explain." Sarah let go of his hand. She slipped an arm around his waist. It felt like old times. "You didn't do anything wrong."

"I suppose." He lapsed into silence.

They continued down the path, ducking under low branches and climbing over a fallen tree trunk, its inside rotted out and hollow. After a while they came to a stream. They found stepping stones and hopped from one to the other, reaching the other side without so much as a splash of water.

The trail meandered deeper into the forest.

"How far does your land go?" Tyler asked.

"I don't know," Sarah replied. "I think there's about five acres."

"Big." He pulled a branch back to allow her to pass.

"I think my dad wanted to make sure I couldn't cause any trouble. This is my private prison."

"He's only doing what he thinks is right," Tyler said. "He was so worried when you…"

"I know." She cut him off, perhaps a little too sharp. "Sorry."

"That's okay."

They kept walking. The trail widened until it opened out into a small clearing surrounded by tall pines. Dragonflies darted in the air, weaving arcs around each other in a complex dance. Crickets chirped. High above, in the branches, Goldfinches and Orioles sang.

But it was the patch of ground in the center of the clearing that caught Sarah's eye.

"That looks like a headstone," said Tyler.

The grave marker was oblong, about three feet tall, and covered in moss. It leaned to the right, a weaving crack running from the apex, almost to the ground.

"Out here?" Sarah walked closer to get a better look.

"What else could it be."

"There's writing on it." Sarah crouched down, tracing the letters with her finger. "The words are hard to make out."

"It's a name," Tyler said. "Martha Ward."

"There's a date too," Sarah said. "1693."

"That's really old."

"Almost as old as the house." Sarah glanced back toward the farm. "I wonder if she lived there?"

"Probably. It's the closest house. They often buried people near their homes in those days." Tyler stood and brushed dirt off his jeans.

"Look at you. Mr. History." Sarah laughed.

"Stop it."

"This place gives me the creeps." Sarah glanced around.

"Are you kidding? You own a graveyard. That's awesome."

"I would hardly call one measly headstone a graveyard," Sarah said.

"It's still cool to have a girlfriend who owns a grave." He shot her a look. "Sorry, I didn't mean that we were…"

"I know." She looked up into his eyes. Something stirred

inside, a long dormant emotion. "I'm not sure what we are right now. I've made a mess of things."

"Nothing that can't be fixed, if you want to."

"I think I'd like that." She took his hands in hers. "It's going to take some time though. I'm not the same person I was before."

"I understand." A shadow fell across his face. "I can wait."

But she didn't want him to wait, not right then. What she wanted was to feel something, anything. She pulled him close, felt his body pressed against hers, and then she kissed him.

Afterward he held her in his arms, one hand stroking the back of her head. Neither one spoke. The crickets chirped. The birds sang. And for the first time since she woke up in the hospital, she didn't hate herself.

Chapter 19

SARAH WATCHED the Mustang drive away and turn onto the main road. For a moment the sun caught the metallic blue paint and it glinted with a sparkling brilliance, and then the car was lost amid the trees.

She lingered, listening to the engine recede until it was nothing more than a distant rumble carried on the breeze, and then even that faded away.

For a while, when Tyler was holding her, she had felt better than she had in a very long time, but now that he was gone the old familiar loneliness returned.

She looked back toward the farmhouse.

It stood stoic amid the lush green landscape, the windows cold black squares that wouldn't allow the sun's rays within.

She shuddered, despite the warm summer air.

The house didn't like her. She sensed it.

And then there was that tree.

The twisted oak at the edge of the property, where the trail met the road. It gave her goose bumps every time they drove past it, which was stupid. It was a piece of dead wood, nothing more.

A sudden urge overtook her. She set off, following the path of Tyler's car.

The tree was worse up close.

The branches reminded her of weaving serpents. They reached out in all directions from a trunk that had pulled itself apart, a deep V shaped chunk missing. The oak looked ancient, and even though the wood was weathered and bare, the limbs devoid of leaves, she sensed that there was still a flicker of life somewhere deep inside of it.

The tree was not ready to concede.

She sensed something else too.

It was a part of this place. Not merely a casual bystander, the result of a lucky acorn landing in the right spot. The oak was one with the house. They were inextricably linked. Yin and yang. Two sides of the same coin. Both were withered, dead things. Yet each was alive and drew energy from the other.

Sarah was pondering this strange intuition, wondering how she arrived to such a thing, when there was a beat of wings overhead.

She looked skyward.

A single black crow settled on the branch above her head.

It studied her with eyes of coal, wings half outstretched.

She backed up a pace or two, alarmed.

The bird let out a single caw, its gaze never straying.

Sarah tensed.

The crow flexed and shuffled its feet, gave a second melancholy cry. Its round, dull eyes bored into her, unwavering in focus.

She fought the urge to turn and run. It was a bird, nothing more. A harmless, stupid bird. Why did it fill her with such dread? She stood her ground, meeting its gaze despite the inexplicable revulsion the animal stirred within her.

And then, without warning, the crow took to the air with a heavy flapping.

It swooped low, almost clipping the top of her head.

Sarah let out a panicked shriek and ducked.

She raised her hands up, expecting to feel the bird's claws snag her hair.

But they didn't.

When she looked again the crow was high above.

It circled, cawing, and then flew toward the house, passing over the roof in the direction of the woods beyond.

Sarah stood a while, her eyes raised to the empty patch of sky where the crow had disappeared. She didn't notice the dirty black clouds that drifted in, blanketing the sky and blocking out the sun. She didn't even notice the way the wind picked up, whipping through the weed choked fields and tugging at the leaves on the trees.

It was only when the first drops of rain fell to earth, bloated and heavy, that she was jolted from her stupor, and made a dash for the house.

Chapter 20

THE RAIN PLAYED a drumbeat on the roof like anxious, tapping fingers, and Willow Farm was about to get its second visitor of the day.

It had been an hour since Sarah made her mad run for the house, reaching the small covered porch and yanking the door open. Andrew was in the kitchen when she entered, her bedraggled form framed by the dining room door. He opened his mouth to speak. Thought better of it. She cast him a sullen glare, hair matted against her shoulders, sodden clothes tight and sticking. Her eyes dared him to say something, anything, and make things worse. When he wouldn't, she turned and stomped off toward her attic lair.

The storm had settled in for the day.

Andrew continued his work, applying a fresh coat of paint to the kitchen walls. Soon the dull dirty cream color would be gone, replaced by a more civilized soft Gray. He should be writing, he knew, but it was easier to deceive himself that this must be done – right now. It made the slacking easier. It gave him permission. It also kept the kids well away, neither wanting to get caught up in such a mundane endeavor.

And then came the chirpy ding dong of the doorbell.

He deposited the paint roller into the tray and passed through the dining room to the front door.

The man standing on the other side wore a black fedora and matching shirt. A white collar circled his neck. His face, carved by decades into a haphazard roadmap of criss-crossing lines, framed a pair of pastel blue eyes that shone under the hat's drenched rim despite the ravages of the years.

Andrew stared at him in surprise.

"Am I calling at a bad time?" The man asked, his voice full and thick despite his age. "I was passing by on the way back to town and thought I would stop and introduce myself. My name is Father Michael Bertram. I'm the parish priest at Our Lady of the Sorrows."

"That's very thoughtful of you, Father."

"Yes indeed. May I come in for a moment?"

"I'm sorry?"

"The rain. May I come in?"

"Of course. Where are my manners." Andrew stepped aside.

"Why thank you. Typical New England. One minute it's dry, the next-"

"So what can I do for you, Father?"

"Oh, nothing. Nothing. Like I said, purely a social call." Bertram scooped his hat from his head and held it across his chest. Water dripped to the floor and pooled. "You're that author fellow are you not? Andrew Whelan."

"Guilty as charged."

"I've read a couple of your books. Most entertaining, if a little grim."

"Are you wanting an autograph?" Andrew asked. "I can sign a book if you have one."

"No. Goodness me." Bertram smiled but his eyes remained cold. "I'm not here to collect a souvenir."

"Then if you don't mind my asking, why *are* you here?"

Andrew was not particularly religious. "Looking to expand your flock perhaps?"

"Mercy no. Nothing like that, I assure you." He looked toward the stairs, his eyes rising to the second floor. Looking back. "How are you settling in, Mr. Whelan?"

"Well enough." Andrew replied.

"I see." Father Bertram scratched his chin. "It must be hard, moving in to a house that has been vacant for so long. There must be a million things to fix. I can't imagine."

"It has its moments." Andrew wondered what the priest wanted.

"Ah, yes. I'm sure it does. I hope the old place has been treating you well, not causing you too much distress."

"No." Andrew sensed that the priest was digging at something. His mind wandered to the night before, the strange incident with the TV. "We're settling in fine, thank you."

"Now that warms my heart to hear. Truly it does." He took a deep breath, let it out slow and long. "I knew the previous occupants of this house. Nice family. Such a shame what happened."

"I don't follow," Andrew said. "The house has been empty for years. You said so yourself."

"Indeed it has. You are correct about that." Bertram nodded. "Time has certainly flown by. I don't know where it goes."

"You mentioned the previous occupants?"

"Oh, yes. The Stevenson's were parishioners. Good people. I got to know them quite well. Spent many an evening at their dining room table breaking bread, so to speak. Goodness. I haven't been back here since…" The priest trailed off, turned toward the dining room.

"Father Bertram?" Andrew reached out, touched the priest's arm.

"Forgive me." He pulled his gaze away, looked toward

Andrew. "I'm an old man. Sometimes my mind draws me back to better days."

"What happened to them, Father?" Andrew's interest was piqued. "Did they move away?"

"Heavens, no. I wish that were the case."

"Then what?" Andrew was not sure he wanted to hear the answer. A sudden dread had overtaken him, a premonition. The house had kept them for itself.

"They died, Mr. Whelan," Bertram said, his voice flat and even. "They all died."

"Oh." Andrew felt vaguely uncomfortable.

"Yes Indeed. It was a tragic accident. Their car had a run in with the old oak down by the road. Slammed into it head on, almost like Mr. Stevenson did so on purpose. Goodness knows how fast they were going, or why. They weren't even wearing seatbelts. Poor Melissa – she was the daughter – got thrown clear through the windshield. She lingered for three days. Never regained consciousness. Well how could she with injuries like that? I gave her the last rights myself."

"That's dreadful." An image of Jennifer wormed into his head. Her car was sliding on the ice slicked road, a final scream caught upon her lips as the front of the vehicle buckled against a tree. He pushed the uninvited thought away, focused on the priest.

"After that the house came into possession of Mr. Stevenson's brother, Eric. He had no interest, was content to let it sit empty all those years. He hated the house, wouldn't set a foot inside. It was like he blamed it for his brother's untimely death." Bertram sighed. "It was only after his own passing that the farm was put up for sale."

"And here we are," Andrew said.

"Here we are indeed."

"It must be a hard thing, for you to come back here, relive something like that," Andrew replied.

"It is, of course." Bertram nodded. "But the good Lord gives us challenges so that we may overcome them."

"Well-"

"Are you truly not a man of faith?" The priest fixed Andrew with those cold blue eyes.

"Not so much, Father." Andrew shrugged off a pang of guilt, a remnant of his upbringing. "You could say, I'm on the fence."

"Well now, that's better than nothing. If you ever fall off, let's hope it's in our direction." Bertram laughed, but somehow it came out mirthless, hollow.

"I'll do my best."

"That's all one can ask."

"I guess so," Andrew said. He nodded toward the kitchen. "Can I get you something, a mug of coffee perhaps."

"No, thank you. I can't stay. Lots to do I'm afraid." The priest took a step toward the door.

"I understand," Andrew said, thankful that the strange old priest wasn't going to outstay his welcome. "Please, feel free to drop by any time."

"That's mighty kind of you." Father Bertram said. He deposited the fedora upon his head and pulled his coat collar around his neck. Before he ventured out into the rain he turned back, his face dark and troubled. "Will you do me a favor, Mr. Whelan?"

"If I can."

"Be careful with the house." He met Andrew's gaze. "Be very careful."

"I'm not sure I follow."

"Places like this, old places, they hold onto things. They take a little bit of each person that lives in them, and they keep it, they feed on it."

"Are you trying to say that-"

"I'm giving you some friendly advice, nothing more." He

tipped his hat. "My door is always open if you need to talk. I pray that you don't, Mr. Whelan. I surely do."

And with that the old priest turned away. He hunched down against the rain, holding the brim of the hat, and hurried toward the waiting car.

Andrew watched him climb in, pull away, and then closed the door.

When he turned toward the hallway, he sensed a presence. He raised his eyes to see Sarah leaning on the second floor railing. He wondered how long she had been there, watching, listening.

"Well, that was odd." He kept his tone light. Heaven knew, he didn't need her any weirder than she already was. "What do you think?"

Sarah stayed mute.

"You want to come down and give me a hand painting the kitchen?" He raised an eyebrow. "I don't bite."

For a while he thought she might actually agree, but then she turned and disappeared in the direction of her room, leaving Andrew alone in the hallway.

Chapter 21

JAKE WAS asleep when the phone rang.

At first he didn't wake up. He was in the VW Bug, riding up to Maine. Everything was great. The sun was high in the sky, and his mother was alive. She laughed and talked and sang along with the radio, just like she always did.

This was the way things should be.

And then there was the noise. A shrill ringing that seemed to push back against the illusion. It came from the radio, it came from the engine. It even seemed to come from the road itself.

Jake put his hands over his ears to block out the sound, scrunching up his face, but it was no good. And then, even though his palms were pressed to the sides of his head, his mother spoke. She took her eyes from the road, fixed her gaze upon him, and she spoke to him.

He heard three little words. No, not so much heard them, as discovered them inside his head. Her mouth moved, but the words didn't arrive via his ears, but rather filled his mind.

It's me, Jake.

He didn't know what she meant. Of course it was her.

Who else would it be? He could see her sitting there, next to him in the car.

And still she was looking at him. She wasn't paying any attention to the road, or the way the car drifted closer and closer to the verge. She didn't care that the steering wheel was slowly turning of its own volition.

She didn't even look back when the car mounted the grass, wheels kicking up chunks of dirt and sod. Not even when the front impacted a tree so hard that Jake felt himself lifting from the seat and careening toward the windshield…

Jake opened his eyes, a terrified scream dying on his lips. His mother's words echoed, as if they had followed him out of the dream.

It's me Jake.

He lay there, the phrase rolling around in his head, still not sure what it meant. If it meant anything at all.

He sat up.

The bedroom was dark. The clock in the shape of a cartoon bear, a Christmas gift from a few years ago, announced that it was after midnight.

The house was quiet.

Except for the old rotary dial phone.

It was on the floor in the corner of the room, where he had abandoned and forgotten it a few days before.

Now it was ringing.

It was disconnected, unplugged.

But even so, it was ringing.

Jake rubbed his eyes and swung his legs off the bed.

He took one step, then another, approaching the telephone as if it were some sort of cornered animal.

Still it rang.

If it kept this up the whole house would be awake.

Jake knelt on the floor and reached out. He knew he should be afraid, but he was not. The phone was his friend. He sensed that.

But only if he answered.

Jake reached out and dragged the unit across the floor-boards until it nestled between his legs, then lifted the receiver.

The shrill ring was cut short.

Silence returned to the room.

"Hello?" Jake could see the cord trailing from the back of the phone. It wasn't plugged into anything.

The same old familiar interference popped and whistled against his ear. Like before, in the living room.

"Who's there?" Jake tried again. The phone had rung. There must be a person on the other end, even if it wasn't actually connected to a wall socket.

Swirling static spewed from the handset.

Jake peered at the receiver, disappointed.

His mother's words popped into his head again.

It's me Jake.

Something connected inside his head. He almost dropped the receiver, the revelation was so sudden. He knew who was on the other end of the phone. He knew why it was so hard to hear them. Phone calls from beyond the grave were not meant to be easy. Talking with the dead was a tricky business, even with the help of a magic telephone.

"Mom?" He spoke into the phone, his voice rising at the end of the word. It repeated, a beat out of synch, in the earpiece. His voice sounded thin and reedy relayed through the small, ageing speaker.

The static buzzed and hissed.

And then a voice came through.

It whispered in his ear.

Jake listened.

Chapter 22

NOTHING.

Four miserable hours sitting in front of the computer screen, and nothing.

Zip.

Zilch.

Not that Andrew hadn't tried. There had been words a plenty, but not a single one was worth the time it took to tap the keys. Delete was Andrew Whelan's best friend these days. That was why he'd spent the afternoon doing other things, avoiding the inevitable confrontation with his laptop. He'd painted the kitchen, telling himself it must be done right there and then. He'd fixed a sticking door handle. He'd even entertained the kooky priest and listened to his stories about the previous inhabitants of Willow House, as the farmhouse had been called since at least the middle of the nineteenth century.

And now he was sitting in the semi-darkness, his writing room lit only by an antique brass desk lamp and the glow of his screen, with midnight fast approaching.

There would be no good words today, he knew that much. Andrew was no fool. He was deluding himself. But better that than think about his agent in New York fuming and waiting for the manuscript that should have been delivered months since. The only reason Andrew still had a publisher was out of deference to his situation. Take all the time you need, they said. Work through the grief. We understand. Except that such sentiments only went so far. Soon things would turn from *poor guy* to *see ya, wouldn't want to be ya*. People would only give so much rope. In the end they let you hang yourself from it.

He leaned back in the chair, rubbed his tired eyes. Glanced toward the window, the night black and stormy beyond the glass. As it always did on evenings like this, his thoughts turned to Jennifer. The bad ones, he had come to call them. Those long hours when the loneliness overwhelmed him and he wondered how he could go on without her. If it wasn't for the kids...

Best not to think about that.

Some ideas were toxic. They festered at the back of your mind, growing, becoming real. Demanding attention. They could overpower that rational voice in your head, pervert it to their own will.

Andrew stood and paced, fighting back the surge of grief that came, unbidden, at such moments. His mind went back to that day, the one when everything changed forever.

It was late afternoon, around four. He was working on the manuscript, typing away in the third floor den. The sound of the city was a distant soundtrack drifting from the street below.

The phone rang.

He didn't recognize the number.

He answered anyway.

And his world crumbled.

Andrew blinked back a tear, wiped it away. The memories of that day were always painful. People said it got better with time, but that was a lie. It didn't get any better, you learned to live with it. The grief was a constant companion, a shadowy figure waiting in the wings, ready to make an entrance at any moment.

An image pushed its way into his head.

Jennifer laying on the cold steel mortuary table, the white cloth pulled back from her face so that he could identify her.

She looked so small. Broken.

By the time the funeral rolled around she would appear as if she were sleeping, but not yet. Now her face still bore the purple and yellow bruises sustained in the crash, a gift from the steering wheel when her head slammed forward.

So much for the airbag.

There was a gash on her left cheek, the skin curled back from a black ragged slit. Her hair was limp, all the volume gone.

Andrew closed his eyes, opened them again.

He took the memory, pushed it back. Forced his mind to other things. Happier things.

Jennifer and the kids at the zoo.

The time they went to Old Orchard Beach, taking the coast road through small Maine towns with postcard views.

Their wedding night.

These things helped, but not enough. It was never enough.

"Shit." He spoke the word aloud. It hung in the air, an affront to the otherwise peaceful house.

Why did you have to leave?

It was not the first time he'd asked that question. A silent plea to a woman who could never answer. If there was an afterlife, the phone lines were down.

I can't do this alone.

Andrew went back to the desk, sat down.

The computer mocked him, the cursor blinking on the white, empty page. He slammed the lid down.

Saw the vodka bottle behind it.

The same one he'd poured away a few nights ago. He knew this because it was the only bottle in the house. His emergency stash. He should have disposed of it in Boston, but instead it had found its way into the writing room boxes. And now it was back again. Even stranger, it was full.

But not quite.

There was a small amount gone from the top.

He knew where that missing liquor was too.

It filled a shot glass next to the bottle.

Where had that come from? He knew he hadn't brought it from the Boston house. Too much temptation. Right now his shot glasses were on a shelf in a thrift store an hour's drive away. He'd taken them there in person, given them to the bored and surly worker at the donation drop.

So why was this one here, tempting him?

It didn't make sense.

He picked up the glass, peered at it.

One swig. That was all it would take. Who cared where the damned glass came from, or how it had gotten filled all on its own. Sometimes you just had to roll with the punches. Don't look a gift horse in the mouth was what his father would have said. Not that the old man knew anything worth a damn. Spent his whole life spouting clichéd metaphors and anecdotes while his career tanked and his wife cheated with the high school football coach. The old man died lonely and depressed.

Like father like son.

Andrew would have chuckled, except that he wasn't in any mood for mirth.

Screw it.

He touched the glass to his lips, felt the alcohol slosh forward. The fumes tickled his nostrils.

His stomach tightened, anticipating a visit from an old friend.

A quick flick of the wrist, that was all it would take to make the pain go away, at least for an hour or two.

It wouldn't be one flick though.

It never was. Not when the bad times came-a-calling.

Andrew didn't care.

He tipped the glass, let the liquid fall into his mouth. And then he poured himself another.

Chapter 23

ANDREW AWOKE SLUMPED in his chair.

At first he wasn't sure of his surroundings, only that this was not the bedroom, and then the memories rushed back to fill in the blanks. At least up until about the sixth shot.

He rubbed his eyes.

His eyelids felt sticky and heavy. His head felt worse.

He leaned forward, resting for a moment while a wave of nausea passed. His stomach let out an angry gurgle. Something nasty, slimy and acidic, rose in his throat and for a split second he thought he would actually vomit. He swallowed, forcing the vodka laced gunk back down.

His father's voice echoed in his head, offering more of the same useless advice.

Better out than in.

Shut up, he thought. The last thing he needed was advice from beyond the grave. Especially from a man who couldn't have cared less about Andrew in the twenty years they shared the same planet. Only it wasn't his father talking, he knew. It was merely his own subconscious making trouble.

Still, the sentiment carried some merit.

He stumbled to his feet and went to the bathroom, pulling

the door closed – the kids did not need to see him in this sorry state – and leaned over the sink.

Except that now the contents of his stomach seemed content to stay right where they were.

He caught sight of himself in the mirror, was shocked to see angry red rims around his bloodshot eyes, the puffy sacs underneath. His skin looked pallid. It sagged, like someone had taken dough and sculpted his features from it.

He looked dreadful.

He turned on the tap, cupped the running water in his hands, and splashed his face. It helped. But what he really wanted was something to drink. He was dehydrated. His mouth furry and dry, lips parched. When he swallowed it felt like shards of glass lined his throat.

There was orange juice in the refrigerator.

The sugar would help clear his head, give him some much needed energy. Plus he might get rid of the sour taste that lingered on his tongue.

He made his way back to the corridor, turned and descended the stairs.

Weak light filtered through the front door pane. It was early, still in that early dawn moment before the sun crested the horizon.

Good.

Plenty of time to recover before anyone else awoke.

He walked to the kitchen, suppressing a yawn. The effort sent a jolt of pain through his tender head. He grimaced, rubbed his forehead, kneading his temples until the tension eased.

In the kitchen, he poured a large glass of juice and took a grateful sip before walking to the living room. He flopped down on the couch, placed the drink on the coffee table.

Whatever had he been thinking? Four months without touching a drop, and then he caved. And why? Because he still could not write. Better to get rolling drunk than face the fact that he might never finish the novel. But there was more to it. No matter how hard he tried, no matter what he did, Jennifer was always there at the back of his mind. More than anything, the booze made the pain go away, took the edge off. And really wasn't that all he wanted, to forget about the accident, and his dead wife? To pretend none of it had happened. If he never wrote another word worth reading, he could live with it. Never seeing Jennifer again, now that was a different matter.

He settled back into the soft cushions, closed his eyes. The pain in his head ebbed, faded to a dull background throb. He knew he should go back upstairs. There was a soft bed waiting for him, and he could get a few hours in before Sarah and Jake woke up, but the couch felt so good. He sighed and stretched out, lifted his legs up and let them hang off the end.

And then the atmosphere in the room changed.

At first he was aware of it only as a vague, seeping chill. He pushed deeper into the couch, huddling his arms across his chest. When it got too cold for even that, he opened his eyes, and was surprised to see a faint mist in the air each time he exhaled. How cold did it have to get for his breath to cause condensation? He didn't know, but it shouldn't be happening in his living room in the middle of summer.

He swung his legs from the couch, sat up.

It was practically winter in his living room.

If he was outside he would have expected to see snow drifting down.

A memory stirred. This was not the first time the temperature in this room had taken a nose dive. He'd encountered a similar cold spot a few nights before, had chalked it up to the quirks of an old house. He wasn't sure this could be so easily dismissed.

It was then that he noticed the glass of juice.

It looked odd, but how he could not fathom.

He reached out, touched the glass, and was surprised to find it frigid under his fingers.

Peering closer, Andrew pushed the glass an inch or two across the table. The liquid didn't move, even when he picked it up, held it upside down.

The juice was now a frozen chunk of colored ice.

He put the glass down, contemplated this for a moment. It was impossible, but there it was, in front of him.

And then, as he sat there observing the solid glass of juice, something else pushed at the edge of his perception. A feeling that he was not alone. Overwhelming. Terrifying.

A prickle of fear ran up his spine.

Andrew glanced around, saw nothing at first. Then his gaze came to rest on the bookshelves lining the back wall, and the dark figure that lurked there, hiding in the gloom.

His heart skipped a beat.

The figure stood with its back to him, concealed within the shadows. Yet even so, Andrew could make out the gentle curves that only a woman possessed. At first he hoped it might be Sarah, but he knew it was not.

He stood up, took a step closer, his heart beating fast.

There was something about the figure. He did not know why, but it looked familiar.

And then he understood.

"Jennifer." The word tumbled from his mouth before he even stopped to think.

The figure remained swathed in shadow.

"Jennifer, is that you?" He edged closer, knowing it could not be Jennifer. Yet he hoped that it was. She had felt his pain, witnessed his suffering, and had come back to him.

He was halfway across the room now, his pulse racing.

The figure moved.

It turned to face him, stepped from the shadows, and in that instant Andrew knew that whatever he was sharing the room with, it most certainly was not his dead wife.

The face that stared back at him had been beautiful once, but now it was desiccated, the skin stretched tight over ancient bones. Her lips were pulled back in a vicious snarl, showing rotten brown teeth. But it was the eyes that alarmed Andrew the most. They were not there. Instead two black, empty sockets glared at him.

Andrew felt a wave of disgust.

The uninvited visitor raised a bony arm. Her lips curled back over those hideous, foul teeth.

He stumbled backwards, a scream forcing its way up. The sofa was right behind him. He crashed back. The force of his fall lifted the couch up on two legs, threatening to tip over before it settled back with a dull thud.

He struggled to regain his feet, but his legs felt like they were mired in tar, heavy and useless.

He raised his arms to shield himself from whatever was about to happen next, waited for the inevitable scrape of long, raking fingernails...

ANDREW JOLTED AWAKE.

He was still on the couch. The room was empty. He lifted a hand to his forehead, wiped away a bead of sweat. His heart still pounded in his chest.

He took a couple of deep breaths, letting them out slow and long, until the terror subsided.

It had all been a dream.

He must have fallen asleep on the couch, still half inebriated. He almost laughed out loud, relieved that the dreadful apparition was nothing more than a figment of his fevered imagination.

And yet it felt so real.

Her face. Those dead, dark eye sockets. They were burned into his memory. He had the feeling that if he closed his eyes again she would be there, waiting.

Which meant no more sleep for him, at least not until the dream had faded.

He leaned forward, scooped up the glass of orange juice. The sugar would keep him alert. Keep the nightmare at bay.

He lifted the glass.

Something bobbed up in the liquid, something cold and hard. It bumped against his lips.

He pulled the glass away and looked down, was surprised to see a lump of frozen juice floating in the drink.

Andrew stared at the chunk of inexplicably solid juice, his mind straining to make sense of it. Then he stood, went to the kitchen, and emptied the glass into the sink, watching the liquid swirl down the drain until all that was left was the frozen core. This he stuffed down the disposal, and ran it until nothing was left.

Chapter 24

AT 2 O'CLOCK in the afternoon Sarah lay on her bed, feet propped up on the pillows, her head hanging off the foot of the mattress. She looked up at the ceiling, eyes following a hairline crack in the plaster until it reached the wall above her closet. The ceiling was new, barely two months old, but the house was not. When she showed her father the crack he said it was nothing to worry about. She wasn't sure she believed that. It felt like the house was rejecting the renovations. There were times, when the lights were off and everyone was in bed, that the building made unusual creaking sounds. It groaned and complained, almost like it was a living entity. They said houses remembered the people that had lived in them, soaking up emotions, gaining energy from the events that took place there. Good or bad. If that was the case, she was sure some nasty things had taken place in this one. It had that kind of an aura. Not that she believed in stuff like that, but even so, the house had a way of getting under the skin.

Sarah's attention strayed from the crack.

She was bored.

Restless.

She got up and and went to the window.

It was pouring outside, the raindrops hitting the roof in a soothing pitter-patter. The downpour hadn't let up since yesterday afternoon when she had gotten drenched.

She peered through the water-streaked window.

The landscape was flat and gray, as if the torrent had washed all the color away. It felt like she was living in a black and white world, an old movie from days gone by.

It was depressing.

Sarah turned her back on the window.

How was she going to occupy herself?

They still had no internet. There was some sort of issue with the line and it would be at least a few more days.

But the TV worked.

There must be something worth watching.

That meant going downstairs, where she might be conscripted into helping paint a wall, or unpack a box. Worst of all, her dad might ask her to go down to the cellar again, load more laundry in the washing machine. That thought filled her with dread. The memories of the last basement visit still made her squirm inside.

She shuddered.

There was no way she was ever stepping foot in the cellar again, even if it meant walking around in dirty clothes for the next year.

On the other hand, she couldn't hide out in her bedroom forever, and the house was quiet, still. Maybe her father was writing, something he hadn't been putting much effort into of late. He thought she didn't notice, but she did. She also knew why. Sometimes she wondered if he would ever write again.

Sarah went to the bedroom door, opened it. She padded down the narrow stairs to the second floor. She was passing Jake's room, when she heard a low murmur from beyond his door.

She froze.

Jake was talking, the words low and muted.

Sarah lingered at the door, listening. Who was Jake speaking too? She knew he didn't have any friends in the area, there hadn't been time to make any, and besides, the conversation seemed one sided.

The door was open a crack, but not enough to see in.

Her curiosity got the better of her.

She gave it a push.

The door swung inward.

Jake sat cross-legged in the middle of the room, an old rotary dial telephone in front of him. He held the receiver up to his ear. He was so enthralled by the antiquated device that he didn't even look up when Sarah entered the room.

He mumbled into the handset, ignorant of the fact that he was no longer alone. There was something about the way he chatted that made her hair stand on end. It was too serious, not the boyish make believe that a child his age should be engaged in. She got the feeling that he truly believed he was talking to someone.

"Jake?" She stepped closer.

He didn't look up.

"What are you doing?" The room was cold. More than that, it was freezing.

"Nothing." Jake glanced up, pulling the handset from his ear.

"Who are you talking to?" Sarah was overcome with the urge to turn and run from the room.

"I can't tell you." He shuffled forward, nearer to the cradle.

"Sure you can," Sarah said. Her stomach clenched, she forced herself to stay put despite the growing sense that something was wrong.

"Nu huh." He shook his head.

"Why can't you tell me?"

"I'm not allowed." He looked down at the receiver. "It's a secret."

"Why aren't you allowed?" Sarah's eyes wandered to the untethered cord and followed it across the floor. It reminded her of a snake, the way it twisted and turned - A wire snake with a plastic plug for a head.

"You need to go now," Jake said, his eyes narrow.

"I do huh?" She shivered, hugging her arms across her chest for warmth. Why was it so cold in this room? It didn't make sense. "Is that what your friend on the telephone wants?"

He nodded. "She wants you to leave."

"Why don't you give me that phone so that she can tell me so herself."

"She doesn't want to talk to you."

"Who Jake?" Sarah said. "Who doesn't want to talk to me?"

But Jake was done. He lifted the phone back up to his ear. He listened, his eyes never straying from Sarah, and then murmured a reply, lips pressed close to the handset.

Sarah strained to hear, to make out what he was saying, but it was no use.

She thought about snatching the phone from his hand, proving to him, and to herself, that there was no one on the other end. But that would cause a huge ruckus, and it wasn't worth it. So in the end she turned and left the room.

It was warmer in the corridor. Sarah felt the change as soon as she stepped from the room. She turned to look back at Jake, but as she did so the door swung back, slamming shut with enough force that she took an involuntary step backwards. She stood staring at the closed door, her pulse racing. She wondered if there really was someone talking to Jake, someone who didn't want her around, but then she thought better of the notion. It was coincidence, nothing more, an errant draught blowing through an old house.

At least, that's what she told herself. Even so, she could not shake the feeling that something weird had just happened.

Chapter 25

BY THE TIME darkness descended upon her small corner of New England, Sarah had pushed the incident with Jake to the back of her mind. But it was not entirely forgotten. A lingering sense of strangeness tainted the hours after their brief conversation.

Her mind kept returning to the way Jake cradled the handset, talked in hushed tones to an unseen companion on a phone that wouldn't work even if it were plugged in.

She hated this house.

It felt wrong.

More than anything, she wanted to go back to Boston, where life was normal, familiar. After the incident, while standing in the corridor, she entertained the thought of fetching her father, telling him what she had witnessed, venting her fears. But it would do no good. He knew she didn't want to be here. He was also on guard for any aberrant behavior, thanks in part to the pill incident. One wrong move would send her straight back to the psychiatrist, Doctor Mendelsohn, who would have a theory, and a bunch of meds.

She didn't need that.

So she kept quiet, at least to her father.

But he wasn't the only person she could talk to.

Sarah picked up the cell phone, called the only number she ever dialed these days.

Becca was in high spirits, and their conversation lifted Sarah's own mood. In less that forty-eight hours her friend would be at the farm. The thought of that went a long way to dispelling the feelings of gloom that had wormed their way into Sarah's subconscious mind. Sometimes all one needed was a dose of normal to gain perspective. It also helped that Becca was the voice of reason. Of course it was a draught that slammed the door. So what if Jake had an imaginary friend. He was probably lonely and bored, just like Sarah. Everything had a rational explanation.

By the time Sarah hung up she felt much better, and as the night wore on the uncomfortable feelings dissipated, until she wondered what she had ever been concerned about.

She went to bed tired and looking forward to the days ahead. If she could not go back to Boston, at least a little part of her life in the city could come to her. Nothing was ever as bad as it seemed.

She fell asleep in minutes, and when she dreamed, it was good for once. Her mother and the accident, the bad times, were banned from her mind, and she slept more soundly than she had for months. Until she awoke, wide awake, with the feeling that she was not alone.

Chapter 26

SARAH'S EYES SNAPPED OPEN.

Darkness cloaked the room, the only illumination the dim glow from the nightlight on the far wall. Long shadows crept across the bare wood floors, like reaching, bony fingers.

Her heart was pounding. A thin sheen of sweat clung to her skin. She lay in bed, listening, but the house was calm. The only sound came from the steady tap of rain against the windows, and even that had trailed off to nothing more than a light drizzle. She looked around, unsettled by the sensation that there was someone else in the room with her. Everything was as it should be. Nothing was out of place. So what caused the strange feeling?

You're alone, she told herself, *it's just your imagination.*

If only she could believe that.

She sat up, the covers falling away. The room was full of familiar shapes. The dresser. The nightstand. Her chair tucked into the corner near the window. Except that the chair looked different, as if…

She let out a whimper.

There was a shape sitting there.

A person.

They didn't move, but Sarah could make out the head, bent slightly forward, and the hunch of the shoulders. Two legs dangled from the seat. Two beady eyes glinted, watching her.

She pulled the covers back up, as if the act would prevent the figure in the chair from seeing her. She wanted to scream, but her throat tightened until nothing but a choked sob managed to escape.

The figure in the chair moved, lurching forward.

Sarah found the will to react. She lunged sideways, terrified, and reached for the lamp next to the bed.

The room filled with soft white light.

Sarah slumped back, her eyes on the chair, and almost laughed out loud.

It was a pile of discarded clothes.

Nothing more than a couple of shirts, her coat, and on the floor, where it slipped moments before, a pair of black skinny jeans.

Her heart rate slowed. She was trembling.

The room was empty. Safe.

When she turned the lamp off, the intruder, now legless, reappeared, eyes glinting in the glow of the nightlight. Except it wasn't eyes, it was the metal buttons of her shirt catching the glow of the nightlight.

What's wrong with you, Sarah said under her breath.

But she knew what was wrong.

She was on edge.

There were strange things going on in the house. She could not deny it anymore. Between the frightening incident in the cellar, and the events of the first night, to Jake's new found phone friend. And then there was the grave in the woods. What was up with that?

She slid back down, leaving the light on this time. There was no way she was sleeping in the dark, not tonight. Not after what just happened.

She lay there for a while, eyes wide open, mind replaying all the events of the past few days. When it became obvious sleep was not forthcoming she sat up.

Frustrated, she pulled on a flannel bathrobe. A glass of milk would help her relax. It was an old trick, something her mother taught her. It was to do with a chemical in the milk. Turkey did the same thing .

She padded to the door, opened it, and listened for any noise. It didn't sound like anyone else was awake. She descended the stairs, and crept past Jake's room. Subtle snores filtered through the closed door. Her father's bedroom was dark, but not his writing room at the top of the stairs. a sliver of faint yellow light showed under the door.

It was past midnight. Surely he would not still be awake. But the glow spilling into the corridor indicated that he was. Maybe this was a good thing. He might be writing again. Before the accident he would work well into the night, sometimes staying up until dawn, at which time he would emerge from his den, exhausted, and retreat to the bedroom. He claimed that he got the best writing done when the house was silent, everyone else tucked up in bed. He called it his special time.

That was before.

Since her mother's death the late night sessions had all but stopped. It was as if he blamed the work for what happened. After all, he wasn't in the car with her that day because he was too busy writing. But self pity didn't pay the bills. She was still a teenager, but she wasn't dumb. Sarah knew the previous books royalties would not last forever, especially if he didn't keep publishing. She worried what would happen when the well dried up. Maybe that was part of why he was so insistent on moving them to this dump. Maybe the brownstone in Boston was too expensive for him to keep up on his own. A wave of compassion for her dad washed over her, and she had the sudden urge to walk into the room and hug him tight.

She lingered outside the door, not wanting to disturb him if he really was writing again. She wavered back and forth, and almost continued on without investigating further, but it was too much. She had to know if he was writing.

Sarah gripped the doorknob, the age worn brass cool under her touch, and turned. The door opened inward with a moan. She stepped into the room.

Her dad was sitting at the desk with his back turned. The laptop was open, an empty white rectangle visible on the screen. Her heart fell. He wasn't writing. The open page was blank. So what was he doing?

"Dad?"

He seemed not to notice her. Never moved.

"Hey, dad." She moved closer, extended her hand to touch him on the shoulder. Her fingers brushed his shirt.

Andrew jumped, as if he was surprised that someone was in the room with him. He looked up, the chair swiveling as he did so. "Hi, Pickle."

She ignored the nickname. "What are you doing? It's so late."

"Oh, I was trying to write." He looked back at the screen, at the white expanse of nothingness. "Pretty pathetic, huh."

"At least you're trying." Sarah's eyes drifted past the computer, to the desk, and the open bottle of vodka. A shot glass sat next to it, brimming with the clear liquid. "What's that?"

"Nothing for you to worry about, Pickle." Andrew moved the bottle, twisted the cap back on. He slid the shot glass away.

"I am worried about it." Sarah felt a pang of fear twist in her stomach. "You shouldn't be drinking."

"Sarah-"

"Don't." She shook her head. "You think I didn't know what was going on in Boston, the late nights in your den, the hangovers. I could smell it on you every morning."

"I had no idea." Andrew looked genuinely sheepish. "I got carried away, let it get out of hand. I was finding it hard to deal with things."

"We all were, dad." Sarah felt a tear push at the corner of her eye. "You don't think Jake and I were struggling to deal with it too?"

"I know you were," Andrew said. "That's why I stopped after the pills, when you tried to…"

"So why the bottle?"

"This is different."

"Is it?" She wiped the tear away.

"Yes. I promise." Andrew took her hand in his. "I have it under control."

"How can you say that?" Sarah glared at him. "Sitting here with a full glass in front of you."

"Because it's the truth," Andrew replied. "I haven't drunk any. The glass is still full. See?"

"Then throw it away," Sarah said. "Pour it down the drain right now."

"I can't." Andrew glanced toward the bottle. "It won't let me."

"Then I'll do it." Sarah reached around him, snatched up the bottle by the neck, and turned away.

"Sarah, come on."

"No." Sarah swiveled back toward him, anger flashing in her eyes. "You talk about me coming to terms with what happened, you say I'm not being rational. You want the old Sarah back, the one who didn't think about death all the time, and who thought that life would go on the same forever. Well that person is gone forever, but at least I know what I am, and what I'm not."

"You're right." Andrew shrugged. "I'm not perfect, but you don't understand. You can't get rid of it."

"Watch me." She stomped toward the door, went across the hallway into the bathroom, and upended the bottle.

"It won't let you." Her dad's voice carried from the other room.

"Whatever." Sarah ignored him. She watched the last of the liquor drain down the sink, then crossed back across the hallway, depositing the empty bottle on his desk. "See. All gone."

"For now." A thin smile crossed his lips.

"This is ridiculous." Sarah turned away, not wanting him to see the look of fear on her face. She raced into the hallway, all thought of the milk excursion abandoned. It was only when she reached her bedroom, slammed the door and flopped face down on the bed, that she let go of the pent up emotions. An hour later, after the crying was done, she finally fell asleep.

Chapter 27

ON THURSDAY, two days after the vodka incident, Becca arrived. She pulled up to the house in her bright yellow Toyota, and parked in front of the dilapidated barn. She wasn't even half way to the front door when Sarah opened it and ran out, hugging her friend as if she hadn't seen her in years, not merely a couple weeks.

"I'm so glad you're here," Sarah said, refusing to release Becca.

"Me too." Becca pulled away, saw the strained look on Sarah's face. "Are you okay?"

"No." Sarah's voice trembled. Since discovering her father with the alcohol two nights before, things had been tense. There was an atmosphere in the house. Gone was the hope for a new start. It was Boston all over again, and even if her dad had not consumed any vodka since she found him nursing the bottle, it felt as if there was an uneasy truce that might be broken at any moment. The few conversations she had engaged in with her father had been brief and stilted, as if each was trying to figure out where to go next. It filled her with dread, and she didn't know what to do.

"Tell me everything." Becca hitched her backpack high on

her shoulder and took Sarah's hand, leading her toward the house. "You will feel better."

And Sarah did.

As soon as they reached the third floor attic room she unloaded all her frustrations and fears. She told Becca about the weird events in the cellar, Jake's odd behavior, and about Tyler's visit. And finally, catching her father engrossed in a bottle of vodka.

Becca sat on the bed next to her and listened to everything without interrupting. She nodded here and there, and then, when Sarah was finished, was quiet for a moment digesting it all. After a short silence she spoke again. "Sounds like you've really been through it."

"I'm not sure how much longer I can take it here, in this house," Sarah replied. "I feel like things are worse than ever."

"Maybe you should sit down and talk with your dad, tell him how you feel."

"No." Sarah shook her head. "It won't do any good. He's changing. The drinking was a thing of the past, he hadn't touched a drop for months, at least until we got here."

"Are you sure?" Becca asked. "People are good at hiding things like that."

"I'm sure. He kept it well hidden when he was drinking, but I could always tell. He's different when he drinks. Not bad, just more subdued, out of it." Sarah didn't like to think about the months after her mother's death. They were not good, and her father's retreat into the bottle hadn't helped things. That was part of the reason she downed the pills. A cry for attention was what the psychiatrist called it, and maybe it was. "I can't explain it Becca, but things feel…" She struggled to find the right word. "They feel off."

"You've been through hell in the last year, give it time."

"No. It's not time I need. It's the house. I can feel it."

"The house?" Becca raised an eyebrow.

"I know it sounds crazy, but I swear, there's something

wrong with this house. There are cold spots, not always in the same place either. And I've heard things, seen things."

"The cellar."

"Not only that. My nightlight turned off all by itself. There were footsteps. The other night, I was sure there was someone in the room, watching me."

"So what are you saying, the house is haunted?"

"I don't know." Sarah shrugged. "Maybe."

"I thought you didn't believe in that kind of thing."

"I don't. That's the frustrating part. But it's happening anyway."

"Are you sure you're not imagining it?"

"I'm not." Sarah paused, chewed her lip, and then took her friend's hand in her own. "Can I tell you something?"

"Of course, always. You know that you can."

"There was something in the darkness."

"I don't follow. What darkness? Here at the house?"

"No. When I was in the hospital, after I swallowed the pills. Before I woke up."

"You remember that?"

"I think so. It was so dark, like I couldn't even see my hand in front of my face. And it was empty. A vast nothingness that stretched in all directions, even up and down."

"You were dreaming."

"I don't think so. It didn't feel like a dream. It was real, and there was something living in the darkness. Something terrible. I didn't see it, just sensed it, waiting for me to die. Whatever it was, I could actually smell the rot and corruption."

"Okay, now you're spooking me," Becca said. "You're making this up, right?"

"I wish I was," Sarah replied. "And I'm scared that it followed me. What if that thing from the darkness is here, in this house? What if it's mad that I lived?"

"You're talking nonsense."

"You don't know that."

"I know that there aren't monsters waiting in the darkness for us to die."

"What other explanation is there for what's been happening?" Sarah said. "I'm scared Becca."

"Then maybe we should do something about it."

"How?"

"With this." Becca reached into her bag and pulled out a flat folded wooden board with two brass hinges. She opened it up on the bed to reveal a semicircle of letters, A through Z, and underneath, the numbers 1 through 9. On the left side of the board was stenciled the word YES, and on the other, the word NO. In the middle was a printed GOODBYE in large, ornate type. Delicate scrollwork framed the entire thing.

"Is that what I think it is?"

"You bet. I found it in a store in Salem a few years ago. Neat huh? I've played with it a few times at parties. Got some pretty creepy results. After we spoke on the phone, I thought it would be the perfect thing to bring up here." She grinned. "And it's a good thing I did. We can get some answers."

"No way. Absolutely not."

"Come on. Don't you want to know?"

"Yes, but not like that." Sarah eyed the board. "What if it makes things worse?"

"Do you trust me?" Becca raised an eyebrow.

"You know that I do." Sarah felt as if she was being boxed into a corner, but she didn't have the energy to fight back.

"Good. We'll do it tonight after your dad and brother are asleep." Becca picked up the Board, closed it, and slid it back into her pack. "Now why don't you show me to the kitchen. I'm starving."

Chapter 28

AT 9 O'CLOCK in the evening Andrew made sure that Jake was tucked up in bed. As had been the case over the past few evenings, the boy was playing with the old telephone, which had become something of an obsession for him, and begged for just a few minutes more. Like all boys, he resisted bedtime, and would have tried to negotiate his way out of sleep even if it were three hours later. Andrew was having none of it, and after a quick trip to the bathroom to brush his teeth, Jake settled down, leaving Andrew free for the rest of the evening.

He turned out Jake's light, pulled the door almost closed, but not quite – that way he would know if his son slipped back out of bed and turned the light on – and went down the hallway in the direction of his writing room.

From above, on the third floor, he could hear Sarah and Becca talking. The girl had arrived earlier that day. Not that he would even have known she was in the house were it not for her brief presence at dinner. The girls grabbed slices of pizza (a household staple given Andrew's lack of cooking skills) and were gone again before he knew it.

Now they were in Sarah's room conversing in hushed whispers, punctuated by the occasional giggle. Heaven knew what they were talking about, but he could guess. Boys. Not that it mattered. Sarah had been so depressed lately. She needed Becca more than she realized, and it was good to hear her laughing for once, even if it might prove to be short lived. If he was being honest with himself, Andrew knew that part of that depression was his fault. The drinking in Boston had gotten out of hand. He hadn't realized she was even aware of it, but like all drunks, he had been deluding himself. Now she had caught him nursing a bottle here, at the new house, something he had sworn he would not allow to occur. He hadn't even intended to start drinking again. It just happened, thanks in part to the strange availability of liquor. It was hard to quit drinking when the bottle never got empty. A rational Andrew would have questioned this turn of events, but it didn't bother him. Who cared where the booze came from as long as it did its job, and boy, did it do that. Just a couple shots and some of the pain went away. it might not be a magic bullet, but it sure came close.

Andrew slipped into the den, closed the door behind him. This time he turned the latch, making sure it was locked. The last thing he wanted was Sarah barging in again. This was nothing to do with her. He was the adult. She was a kid. She didn't understand.

Andrew went to his desk, sat down.

When he touched a key, the laptop sprang to life. Maybe this time he would get some writing done. But deep down he already knew the answer.

He turned his attention from the computer.

The bottle was back, as usual. So was the shot glass, full to the brim and waiting for him as if some celestial bartender had snuck in and prepared it.

There you are boss, just what the doctor ordered.

The voice in Andrew's head coaxed him, urged him on.

You'll feel so much better with a little medicine inside of you.

The voice validated the need. It gave him permission.

Andrew took the shot glass, observed it for a moment, and then sank it in one before slamming the glass back on the desk. The liquor warmed him as it went down. He felt the alcohol hit his stomach. The guilt eased a little. Another one would ease it more.

He glanced down.

The glass was full again. The celestial bartender never disappointed. He picked it up, lifted it to his lips – without pause this time – and took it back in one fluid gulp.

Chapter 29

IT WAS after eleven when Becca pulled the old wooden board out again. She placed it on the bed, opened it, and reached into her bag, bringing out a worn teardrop shaped planchette with three tiny ball shaped feet. She laid the pointer on the board, between the words YES and NO, then sat back.

"We're really going to do this?" Sarah asked, worried.

"Why not." Becca grinned. "Don't tell me you're scared."

"No." Sarah shook her head. "Of course not, but aren't these things dangerous?"

"Only if I hit you over the head with it," Becca said. "Don't be so nervous."

"I'll try." Sarah wished Becca hadn't brought the board, then she would not be in this situation. "How do we do it?"

"Really? You don't know?" Becca scoffed. "What kind of a Goth are you?"

"The kind that doesn't hold séances and talk to the dead."

"Until now," Becca said. "Tonight we make you a real Goth."

"I thought the point of this was to find out what was wrong with the house, not initiate me as a real Goth."

"Two birds with one stone," Becca said, matter-of-factly. "Now concentrate. If you don't take it seriously this won't work."

"Fine. What do I do?" Sarah thought she knew how to do it, had seen boards used on TV shows and in the movies, but this felt different, more personal. If they were really going to try and talk to the spirits, she wanted to do it right.

"It's easy. All you do is touch it with your index and middle fingers like this. Don't press down, just touch it." Becca placed her fingertips on the planchette. "And then we ask questions. Actually, I ask the questions. You just provide energy and listen."

"Suits me." Sarah looked at the board. "Want to get this over with?"

"Okay. Come closer." Becca motioned to her to scoot forward on the bed. "Sit with your knees under you, like you are kneeling."

"Like this?" Sarah adjusted herself.

"Perfect." Becca did the same, moving close so that their knees touched. She picked up the board and placed it between them, resting on their legs. "We both need to be in contact with the board. There's more psychic energy that way."

"This is silly." Sarah thought about hopping off the bed, refusing to play along, but instead she placed her fingers on the planchette next to Becca's, gingerly brushing the top of the cool wood pointer.

"Now clear your mind." Becca took a deep breath. "Relax and think positive thoughts."

Sarah closed her eyes, took two large lungful's of air. When she felt ready, she opened them again. "Good to go." She smiled, although she felt a tingle of apprehension.

"Whatever happens, don't lift your fingers from the pointer," warned Becca.

"Got it."

"And if things get out of hand, we move the planchette down to GOODBYE to end the session."

"I thought you said this was safe?"

"It is, if you follow the rules."

"I'm having second thoughts. There's enough weirdness in the house already, without making it worse."

"Do what I say, let me ask the questions, and everything will be fine." Becca fixed Sarah with a long stare. "Now be quiet."

"But…"

"Shhh." Becca took another breath, then spoke in a clear, loud voice, her fingers hovering on the pointer. "Spirits. Come to us, be with us in this safe place."

She waited a moment, then spoke again, seeming to direct the question into the empty space above Sarah's head. "Is there a spirit here with us?"

The planchette didn't move.

"Is there anyone there?"

Sarah suppressed a giggle.

Becca shot her a withering look before continuing. "I ask again. Is there anyone there that wishes to converse?"

Still nothing.

"Spirit, come to us."

The planchette might as well have been glued to the board.

"I implore you, talk with us."

"This is lame." Sarah went to lift her fingers from the pointer.

"Don't." Becca's gaze snapped back down. "Keep your fingers where they are."

"This isn't working," Sarah said, but even so, she kept touching the pointer. "It's a waste of time."

"Give it a while. Sometimes the spirits need to find us."

"Fine." Sarah slumped back. "But hurry up, I'm getting bored."

"This is serious," Becca scolded. "Now pay attention." She looked down at the board. "I ask one more time, is there anybody there?"

For a few seconds nothing happened, then, just as Becca was about to speak again, the planchette moved.

The movement was subtle, slight at first, then it slid sideways to the word YES.

Sarah looked at the pointer with wide eyes. "Crap. Did you do that?"

"Oh my god. There's a spirit here." Becca's face lit up. She grinned. "This is awesome."

"You're full of shit. There's no way that moved on its own."

"I swear to god, I didn't move it," Becca said. "We should ask something else."

"Like what?"

"Like this," Becca said. "Are you dead?"

The pointer moved back to the center of the board, stopped, went back to YES.

"Oh, crap." Sarah felt the knot in her stomach tighten.

"Did you live in this house?"

YES.

Becca glanced at Sarah. "Did you die in this house?"

The pointer snaked across the board. NO.

"Where did you die?" Becca's voice trembled.

The pointer shuffled across the board. T-R-E-E.

"What does that mean?" Sarah said, doing her best to keep the fear from her voice. "Tree?"

"Beats me." Becca focused on the planchette again. "When did you die?"

1-6-9-3.

"How did you die?"

T-R-E-E. The planchette picked the letters out one by one.

"I don't like this," Sarah said. "If it isn't you moving the pointer, then whatever we're speaking too shouldn't be here."

"So, let's ask why it is still here."

"No." Sarah shook her head. "I'm not sure I want to find out."

"We've come this far," Becca said. Then to nobody in particular, "Why are you here?"

The planchette drifted to the middle of the board, then back up to the row of letters.

An answer formed.

U-N-R-E-S-T

"What does that mean?"

I-N-O-C-N-T

"Huh?" Sarah was confused. "That's not a word."

"Innocent." Becca looked pleased with herself. "Are you saying you are innocent?"

YES.

"What were you accused of?" Becca asked.

The planchette drifted to the middle of the board.

It stayed there.

"What did you do?" She tried again.

The planchette didn't move.

"Why is it not answering?" Sarah asked.

"I don't know." Becca shrugged. "Maybe it doesn't like the question."

"So, ask something else."

"Any ideas?" Becca looked at her friend.

"Ask it for a name." Sarah wasn't sure she wanted to know the identity of the entity they were conversing with, but at the same time she had a feeling it was important.

"Okay." Becca said. "What is your name?"

This time the pointer started to glide across the board. It drifted to the middle of the alphabet, picked out several letters.

M-W-A-R-D.

"Is that your name?"

The planchette stayed where it was, pointing to D.

"Are we missing some letters?" Becca tried again. "Is that your name?"

The planchette drifted to the middle of the board, stopped there.

"Are you still with us?"

The pointer remained still.

"Are you still there?"

Nothing.

"I think it's gone." Sarah said. She lifted her fingers from the pointer.

"No, put them back." Becca motioned to her. "We have to close the connection. It's very important."

"Sorry." Sarah placed her fingertips hack on the planchette. "I didn't know."

"It's fine," Becca said. She looked down. "Is there anything you wish to say?"

As before, the pointer stayed still.

"Okay. We're going to go now. I'd like to say goodbye."

The planchette moved again, slower this time. It crawled across the board, heading down until it reached the word GOODBYE. It stopped.

The two girls sat there for a while, their fingers still on the pointer, and then, after a minute had passed, Becca spoke in a small voice. "I think it's gone."

"Holy crap." Sarah lifted her hand from the pointer. She could feel the adrenaline rushing through her body. "That was intense."

"Oh my god, it's never worked that well before." Becca looked shocked. "That was freaking scary."

"I told you I didn't want to do it." Sarah wished she'd been more insistent. It was bad enough dealing with the strange things going on, let alone this. "How am I going to sleep after this?"

"Does any of the stuff the board said mean anything to you?"

"No. I don't think so," Sarah replied. But then she remembered something from a few days before. "Actually, it might."

"Well?" Becca said. "Don't keep it to yourself."

"The name. MWARD." Sarah hesitated. It sounded familiar, and she thought she knew why.

"You know something, don't you." Becca closed the board, laid it aside, and shuffled closer to her friend. "Spill it."

"It's better if I show you."

"Let's go." Becca hopped off the bed. "I want to see."

"Right now?"

"Sure," Becca said. "Why not?"

"Because it's out in the woods."

"Mysterious. I'm even more intrigued." She looked excited. "Come on, what's the harm?"

"It's the middle of the night, and we've just spent the last half hour talking with..." She struggled to find the right words. "I don't even know what the hell we just talked with."

"Even more reason to go now."

"How do you figure that?"

"What, are you scared?" Becca taunted.

"No. Of course not." That was a lie.

"I think you are."

"Just drop it. Besides, it's raining." Sarah pushed the board away, happy to put some distance between it and her. "I'll show you first thing in the morning. Promise."

"Come on," Becca pleaded. "It'll be an adventure. Please?"

"You're not going to give up on this, are you?"

"Nope."

"Fine. We'll go, but at the first sign of anything weird, we come back. Deal?"

"Deal."

"Just great." Sarah muttered the words under her breath. The woods were the last place she wanted to be in the dark, but on the other hand, she wanted to confirm her suspicion about the name. To Becca, she said, "how do I let you talk me into these things?"

Chapter 30

"KEEP QUIET." Sarah turned to Becca. "I don't want to wake anyone."

The girls were on the second floor, moving along the hallway. Jake's door was closed. She paused for a moment, listening, but could hear nothing. Further along was her father's room, and then his new den, where she'd found him with the vodka a few nights before. Tonight the writing room light was off, the house silent and sleeping. That was good. She didn't know what she would do if her dad was drowning his sorrows in booze again, especially with Becca there.

They descended the stairs. Sarah told Becca where to avoid, which steps creaked the worst, and soon they were in the kitchen.

Sarah went to the sink, opened the cabinet beneath, and reached in, coming away with two flashlights, one large and hefty, the other smaller, made of molded red plastic.

"Dad put these here in case the power goes out," she explained. "He said a tree branch could take down the line running to the house if the weather gets bad over the winter."

"A regular boy scout," Becca said in a whisper. "Give me one of those."

"Here." Sarah held out the smaller of the two. "Take this."

"Why do I get the crappy one?"

"Because I know where we're going." Sarah said. "Besides, it's my house."

"Fair enough." Becca clicked the flashlight to the on position. The beam of light lit up the dark kitchen.

"Ready?" Sarah activated her own light, went to the back door, drew the bolt back, and stepped out into the night.

It was chilly outside, and wet.

Sarah was glad she had the forethought to bring a coat. The rain hadn't let up for days, and despite the cheery optimism of the weather girl on Channel 16, it didn't look like it would ease up any time soon.

"Where now?" Becca clasped her hands around her torso, pulling her own jacket tight.

"This way." Sarah took off across the grass with Becca following behind. They passed the swing set, which was gently swaying on rusted chains. As it moved, the chains made lingering high-pitched squeals that sent a shudder through Sarah. She was glad to move on, leaving the swing behind.

At the edge of the woods she paused, glanced back toward the house. The only light came from the third floor gables. That meant they had escaped the house undetected. Sarah was both relieved and disappointed at the same time. If they had been caught there would be no choice but to abandon this foolish errand and wait until morning. Now she had no excuse and must continue on, despite her unease.

It was darker after they entered the woods. The trees loomed above them. They closed in overhead, blotting out the sky. Branches reached like gnarled hands onto the trail, threatening to snag their clothing, and a few times Sarah was forced to stop and push foliage out of the way. To make things worse, a faint malodorous scent wafted their way whenever the wind weaved through the woods, as if the entire place was rotting from the inside out. The putrescent smell reminded Sarah of the time they drove past a sewage works in upstate New York. The smell had been so bad her father turned the air conditioning off in an unsuccessful attempt to curb the stink. This odor was nowhere near as pungent, but it was there all the same.

"What's that smell?" Becca wrinkled her nose, voicing what they were both thinking.

"I don't know," Sarah admitted. "Maybe something died nearby, a deer perhaps, or a bear."

"Gross." Becca looked around, as if she expected to see a carcass laying in plain view. "I think I'm going to puke."

"Keep moving. I'm sure it will pass soon," Sarah said. But just to be on the safe side, she breathed through her mouth, and after a while the odor had all but vanished.

They kept on down the trail until they came across the stream Sarah had discovered when she'd been in the woods with Tyler. It was wider than before, and faster, thanks to the unrelenting rain. In early spring, when the winter snows melted, it would be a torrent.

"Tell me we don't have to cross that," Becca said.

"Afraid so."

"That's perfect." Becca glanced down at her running shoes, pristine white with pink bands running along the sides. "I've only had these a week."

"Hey, this was your idea."

"I know."

"We can always turn back," Sarah said.

"Nice try." Becca gave her friend a gentle shove. "Keep moving."

"Alright, alright." Sarah placed her foot on a flat stone that poked a few inches above the water line, then stepped onto another rock. "Follow me, it's not too wide. And be careful, the rocks will be slippery."

"I'm going to be so mad if I get these wet." Becca stepped

onto the first rock, steadied herself, and then hopped across to another, following Sarah until they were both safely on the opposite bank.

"It's not far now." Sarah pointed down the trail. "See that clearing up ahead?"

"About time." Becca hurried to catch up to her friend.

"This was your idea, remember?"

"I know," Becca said. "Doesn't mean I can't complain."

"You're impossible." Sarah covered the last hundred yards at a jog. When they entered the clearing she shone her flashlight across the ground, until the beam found the gravestone.

It was just as she remembered.

"Is that a grave?" Becca came to a halt in the middle of the clearing.

"Yep." Sarah nodded. "Weird, huh?"

"Holy crap. You actually have a grave in your back yard."

"It's not really in my back yard," Sarah said.

"This is your land, right?"

"I think so."

"Then this is your back yard." Becca trained her flashlight on the headstone. "Neat."

"It's not neat. It's creepy," Sarah replied. "There's a dead body down there."

"So what?" Becca shrugged. "There are dead people everywhere. There was a huge cemetery less than two miles from my house."

"You don't have to live next to it though." Sarah knelt down, ran her fingers across the face of the marker. The stone felt rough and cold under her touch. "See this? The name?"

"Martha Ward." Becca leaned close. "That's the same name the board spelled out. MWARD."

"Exactly. And look at the date."

"1693." Becca took a step backwards. "Okay. That's too freaky. Are you sure you weren't pushing the pointer as a joke?"

"No. I swear." Sarah stood up. "Why would I do that?"

"I don't know. Because you want me to think your house is haunted?"

"I'm beginning to believe that it is." This was the first time Sarah had vocalized the vague impressions solidifying in her mind. The admission made her feel queasy.

"Stop it. That's enough. I have to sleep in that..." She never finished the sentence. Instead, she paused, glanced around. "Do you hear that?"

"Hear what?" Sarah asked.

"Some sort of whooshing sound." Becca turned, her eyes searching the woods. "Like something's coming."

"I don't hear it." Sarah strained to listen, and then, to her surprise, she did hear it. A rising thunder, like a great wave was rolling toward them. Except that they were nowhere near water, so...

Just then the leaves stirred and rustled, and a mighty wind blew up out of nowhere. It rampaged through the trees, screaming and complaining. It whipped into the clearing, stripping branches of their foliage and sending twigs and leaves aloft in a crazy dance.

Sarah let out a shriek and raised her arms, shielded herself as the tumultuous gale slammed into her, raged around her.

"Holy shit." That was Becca.

Sarah didn't really hear the words as much as lip read them. She braced herself against the chaos, blinked to clear her eyes as the rain, driven sideways by the wind, almost blinded her.

"What's going on?" Becca staggered backwards, such was the force of the onslaught.

"I don't know." Sarah shouted the words, but no sooner were they out of her mouth than they were snatched away by the maelstrom. "Let's get out of here."

"Look." Becca was pointing at the grave.

The debris, branches and foliage, had spun itself into a

miniature cyclone, tearing around a column of angry air that settled over the grave. The funnel stretched upward, high into the darkness, twisting itself into a corkscrew. Leaves and twigs spiraled up and out of sight.

Sarah struggled to train the flashlight on the odd twister, almost losing her grip as the wind tugged at it, tried to rip it from her grasp. Even with the bright beam of light she could not see the top of the churning shaft. It might as well go on forever.

And there was something else too. The smell was back. Cloying and pungent, reeking of death. It rode the wind, made Sarah want to gag. She felt her stomach heave, felt the bile rise in her throat. She swallowed hard, pushing the sensation back down, desperate not to puke.

From off to her left, Becca let out a scream.

Sarah turned, startled.

Becca, still fighting against the gale, looked pale. Her eyes were wide.

"What is it?" Sarah didn't know if her friend could hear her or not.

"I saw something." Becca was ashen. "A person, standing behind the grave."

"There's no one there." Sarah looked around the clearing but saw nothing.

"We have to leave, right now." Becca gripped Sarah's hand, dragged her backwards.

"Hold up." Sarah stumbled along behind, one arm raised to her face in a desperate attempt to avoid the worst of the barrage.

They pushed back toward the trail.

It felt like they were walking in a hurricane, one step forward, two back, but Sarah didn't care as long as she was putting some distance between them and the grave. She had no idea what Becca had seen, but she knew it couldn't be good. She also knew it was dangerous to stay, although she didn't know how. Maybe it was intuition, a sixth sense, but Sarah had the overwhelming feeling that if they lingered in that place, something awful would happen. It was as if the woods didn't want them there.

"Where's the path?" Becca shielded her face, looked around. "I don't see it."

They had reached the edge of the clearing, but found nothing but a wall of trees and undergrowth. Thick bushes clogged the forest floor, the way forward impassable.

Sarah searched the tree line, but could not find a way out. She battled a rising sense of panic, resisted the urge to run blindly. That would do no good. And then, as the wind threatened to topple her and stray branches flew left and right, she saw a dark gap in the trees. "There." She pointed. "That's the way out."

"Come on." Becca pulled her along. They skirted the edge of the woods, reached the narrow path, and stepped from the clearing.

At once the wind died down.

It was as if they had passed some invisible threshold. Without pause, Becca kept going, running down the path as fast as she could. Sarah struggled to keep up, feeling the first stabs of a stitch in her side. She cast a glance back over her shoulder, toward the clearing, and was surprised to see that everything looked calm and peaceful. Gone was the raging wind, the swirling glut of debris and plant matter. The gravestone stood silent and serene, as if nothing had ever happened.

When they reached the stream Becca slowed. She bent over, chest heaving, and gulped large mouthfuls of air.

"What the hell was that?" Sarah leaned against a tree, her lungs burning.

"I don't know. But I never want to see that gravestone again." There was a strange expression on Becca's face. "We have to keep moving. We need to get to the house."

"What exactly did you see back there?" Sarah followed her friend across the stream, using the same rocks as before.

"I'm not sure." Becca scrambled up the bank, used a tree trunk for support. "A figure. It was only there for a moment, and it was hard to tell what I was looking at with all the crap flying around, but it looked like a woman."

"No way."

"I'm serious." They were on the trail now, leaving the stream far behind. "It was so quick. A glimpse, that's all. But I swear, she looked right at me. There was something about her, so much anger."

"Do you think she was…" Sarah trailed off. She didn't want to finish the sentence, to say what they were both thinking.

"Who knows," Becca said, her voice shaking. "I know one thing though, I'm sure as hell not going back there to find out."

They were at the edge of the woods now. Up ahead, across the grass, was the house. The third floor windows cast rectangles of yellow light onto the lawn. Sarah had never been so pleased to see a building in all her life. She took Becca's hand and led her from the forest, an overwhelming sense of relief passing through her. For a while she thought they would not make it out, that whatever had caused the furious wind would not let them leave. But now, with the house in sight, she knew that they would.

Even so, a cold, dark dread lingered.

There was something evil in the woods behind her house, and even though they had escaped it this time, there was no guarantee that they would be so lucky again.

Chapter 31

JAKE WAS SLEEPING when the girls snuck down from the attic room and made their way along the hallway toward the main staircase. By the time they slipped from the house though, he was wide-awake.

The telephone, which he'd moved to the dresser near his bed for ease of access – he now viewed it as some kind of otherworldly bat phone – gave out a shrill ring, pulling him from his slumber.

He was groggy at first, the noise weaving itself into his lingering dream, but then he recognized the sound, and jumped from the bed.

He lifted the receiver to his ear, grateful that the ringing had not awakened his father, and waited for the familiar voice to whisper to him.

And whisper it did.

He listened with a concentration unusual for a boy of his age, and when the phone had said all that it was going to say, he put the handset back on the cradle and went to the door. He cracked it open, peeked out into the hallway.

Satisfied that the coast was clear, he stepped out, and padded toward his father's writing room. The window there overlooked the back yard, unlike his own window which had a view of the side of the house.

He paused when he reached the den. The light was off, the door closed. It was unlikely his father was inside. Even so, he was careful to keep quiet and only open the door wide enough to pass through before closing it again.

He went to the window, looked out.

Two bright beams of light bobbed across the lawn in the direction of the woods. He couldn't make out the identities of the dark shapes behind the flashlights, but he knew it was his sister and her friend. They had been ensconced in Sarah's attic room for hours. At one point when he needed to pee, he'd stopped at the bottom of the third floor staircase and listened to them talking and laughing, but soon lost interest. He didn't care about girl stuff. Now though, they were on a late night adventure.

He stayed at the window for a few minutes, watching as the girls entered the forest, and then retraced his steps, sneaking back along the hallway. When he neared his room however, he turned left and climbed to the attic.

Sarah's room was big, much larger than his own. He didn't care though. He liked the room at the end of the hallway. It felt welcoming, like he was at home. He didn't know why, but he had the sense that he wasn't the first boy to occupy that space. The third floor room, on the other hand, didn't feel welcoming at all. It had sloping ceilings, and windows that looked like they were cut out of the side of the building.

Jake shuffled over to the bed, circling the blow up mattress that had been inflated ready for Becca to sleep on. He opened the nightstand drawer, peeked inside.

There was nothing interesting, just a lipstick, a few pieces of jewelry, and the diary that Sarah had never bothered to write anything in. He knew this because he'd snooped before, and unless she'd taken up journaling in the last month, all the pages would be blank.

On top of the nightstand was a framed picture of his sister grinning next to a freckle-faced boy with dark hair. This was her boyfriend. In the year prior to their mother's death, Tyler had spent a lot of time at the brownstone. After the accident Jake hardly saw him anymore. That was a shame. He liked Tyler, who always took the time to chat to him. One time Tyler had taken him to Boston Common and they had thrown a football around for a while.

Jake turned away from the photo. He could snoop anytime. Right now there were more important things to do. He was on a mission, and he didn't want to fail.

He glanced around and soon saw what he'd come for.

The Ouija Board was on the bed, half covered by the sheets. Jake perched on the mattress, pulled the board close, and unfolded it. He studied the intricate details of the stenciling, read a couple of the letters aloud. It was an odd looking thing, with the alphabet and numbers printed across the face. It reminded Jake of the posters they put up on the walls in elementary school to teach kids to read, except that he had a feeling this was not some overdone teacher's aid. This felt dark. Ominous.

He wondered what Sarah and Becca had been doing with it. Was the board some kind of game, like Scrabble? He didn't think so. He could ask them about it, but then they would know he'd been up here. Besides, he didn't want to draw any attention to himself, especially since he was about to do something bad.

Jake pushed the board back across the bed, folded the covers back over it so that it looked like it had never been moved, then reached over and snatched up the planchette. He turned it over in his hands. This was what he'd come here for.

He stood up, took one last glance around the room, just to make sure there was no sign that he'd ever even been there, and tiptoed back down the stairs.

When he reached his room, he closed the door, went to

the closet, and leaned in. He pushed a toy truck to the side, reached past a couple of pairs of sneakers, and found what he was looking for. The leather baseball glove he'd used in little league the year before.

He hadn't worn it in months, had lost interest in the game. He didn't put the glove on now either. Instead he pushed the planchette deep down inside of it, and then leaned into the closet, depositing the glove as far back as he could reach. Finally he moved the toy truck back in place, arranged the sneakers over the glove, until it was out of sight.

Mission accomplished.

Jake stood, feeling pleased with himself, and walked over to the bed. He crawled under the covers and pulled them tight around his body, a warm cocoon.

By the time Sarah and Becca returned from the woods, drenched and scared, Jake was already asleep, and dreaming of his mother.

Chapter 32

SARAH LAY in her bed with the covers pulled up to her chin.

Next to her, on the floor on an air mattress, she could hear Becca's gentle breathing. If her friend was awake, she showed no sign of it, but Sarah suspected that she was.

How could either of them sleep after the night's events? She wished she had never agreed to use the Ouija board, or go into the woods in the middle of the night.

It was crazy.

It had almost gotten them killed.

For she had no doubt that whatever they had encountered out in the woods, whatever malevolent energy had summoned up the maelstrom, it was dangerous. She also suspected that something was here too, lurking in the darkest corners of the house, waiting to strike when they least expected it.

She glanced at the clock next to her bed. Two hours had passed since they tumbled into the kitchen, terrified and cold, closing the door and pulling the bolt across, against whatever Becca had seen. For a while they talked in scared whispers. Sarah made them both cocoa and they sat at the table in a kind of nervous disbelief. Sarah felt as though she had gotten punched in the gut. It was one thing to hear a few odd noises or feel like someone was watching you, that stuff could be rationalized, but quite another to encounter the kind of angry energy they had witnessed. She was still shaking when they climbed the stairs, crept to the third floor, and slid into their beds.

Sarah left the light on – neither girl had any desire to sleep in the dark – and for a while they exchanged brief snippets of conversation. But eventually the room fell silent. There was nothing left to say, because no matter how much they analyzed it all, there simply was no rational explanation.

Chapter 33

WHEN SARAH WOKE the next morning she was surprised to find that she had eventually succumbed to a fitful, restless sleep.

She opened her eyes. Yawned.

At first the events of the previous evening were nothing more than a hazy fog, but when she sat up the Ouija Board was there, sitting on the dresser, and everything came flooding back in horrific detail.

She shuddered.

It looked so innocent. A piece of varnished wood with some stuff stenciled upon it. Harmless old wood. Only she knew that it wasn't. Whatever they had contacted the previous evening – and she was starting to believe that it was the spirit of Martha Ward – was not friendly, of that she was sure. She could no longer pretend that all was right at Willow Farm, and that thought terrified Sarah. Was it Martha in the cellar with her? And what about the nightlight? Someone was in the room with her that first night. Sarah didn't even want to think about that. Maybe it was time to have a talk with her father, voice her concerns about the house. But right now there were other, more pressing matters, like the need to pee.

She slipped out of bed, was about to make her way down to second floor bathroom when she noticed Becca's empty sleeping bag. It sat on the floor, atop an inflatable mattress they kept for situations such as this, the zipper open and flap folded back. Becca was standing at the window in her night-gown. She seemed to be looking at something in the yard.

"Hey." Sarah approached her friend. "What are you looking at?"

Becca didn't answer.

Sarah reached out, touched her friend on the shoulder.

Becca jumped, turned around, a startled look upon her face. "Crap, don't do that."

"Sorry," Sarah said. "I didn't mean to scare you."

"Then don't creep up on people."

"What were you looking at?" Sarah peered over her friends shoulder, but could see nothing untoward.

"A bird." Becca turned back to the window. "I woke up and there was this big old bird sitting there, on the window sill. I swear, it was looking right at me."

"Newsflash. We have things like that out here in the coun-try," Sarah said. "You're not in Boston now."

"I know that," Becca said, the indignation in her voice clear. "This was different. It was actually peering in, beak pressed up to the glass. It had this unwavering stare. Ugh. Gives me chills just thinking about it."

"What did this bird look like?" Sarah asked, although she had a feeling she already knew. Could it be the same one that had swooped down at her on the driveway the day Tyler visited? Surely not, but even so, she dreaded the answer.

"Big. Black," Becca replied. "It flew off when I got out of bed. Landed on the old swing set in your back yard."

So it was the blackbird. A lump caught in Sarah's throat. She glanced over Becca's shoulder, fearful of what she would see, but the swing set was empty, much to her relief. "It's not there now. Must have flown away."

"Good riddance." Becca walked over to the bed, sat on the edge. "Listen, about last night-"

"I don't want to talk about it," Sarah said, her stomach churning when she thought about the gravestone.

"I was thinking, we should do some digging, see what we can find out about Martha Ward."

"I don't know. I don't want to cause more problems."

"You won't," Becca said. "There must be historical records at the library in Danvers. Don't you want to know why there's a grave in the woods?"

"Sure, but-"

"Then we need to go to the library, especially since your crappy house doesn't have internet yet."

"Dad said it will be a few more days. The house was empty for years before we bought it, and there's issues with the internet line."

"It's settled then. We'll go to Danvers after breakfast."

"How can you eat after what happened last night?"

"You're not still scared are you?"

"Of course. You were there, are you telling me you're not scared?"

"I don't know." Becca shrugged. "All we really saw was some wind, during a rain storm."

"The board spelled out the name on the grave. It got the date of Martha Ward's death correct. Besides, you said you saw a figure in the clearing, that was nothing to do with the rain."

"I know. But there can't really have been anyone there. Maybe I imagined it."

"You really believe that?"

"I don't know what to believe," Becca admitted. "Which is why I want to find out some more about your resident corpse."

"Okay. We'll go." Sarah knew it was pointless to argue. Besides, it would get her away from Willow Farm for a few hours, and that could only be a good thing. "We'll have to ask my dad first though."

"No problem. I'll ask him. He likes me."

"He tolerates you," Sarah shot back. "We all do."

"Either way, I'll put on my girlish charms." Becca twirled a lock of hair above her forehead. She cocked her head. "He'll be putty in my hands."

Chapter 34

ANDREW WOKE up to a raging headache. He stumbled from the bed and went to the bathroom, found the bottle of painkillers. Downed two.

The evening before was a blur, at least the last part of it. He remembered putting Jake to bed, going to the writing room. The bottle of booze was there, as usual, full to the brim and ready to go. He should take that bottle and open up a bar. He'd make a fortune.

Whelan's — Where the booze never runs low no matter how much you drink.

Only it wasn't a laughing matter.

If Sarah found him with the bottle again she'd have a fit, and rightly so. He had a responsibility to her, and to his son. Which meant that from now on, no more drinking. At least he'd woken up in his own bed this morning, and not slumped over the desk in the den. That was something.

It was not enough.

Andrew went back to the bedroom, sat down and waited for the orchestra in his head to cease their racket, and then got dressed.

Downstairs, he went to the kitchen, gulped down a large

glass of juice, and was making toast – somehow that took the edge off his hangovers – when the girls appeared.

"Hi, Mr. Whelan," Becca said, all smiles.

She leaned against the counter, just a little too close for his liking. He hoped she didn't smell the stale alcohol on his breath. "Hello Becca. How did you sleep? I hope the blow up was comfortable."

"I slept like a dream." She stretched, ran a hand through her hair. "Your new house is neat."

"Thanks." A faint burning smell reached his nose. He remembered his breakfast, looked back toward the toaster oven. The bread was now black and smoking. Dammit.

"Oops. Looks like you will have to start over." Becca reached past him, plucked two more slices of bread from the bag, offered them to him. "Here you are."

"Much appreciated." He tossed the burnt toast, and dropped the fresh slices into the toaster.

"Becca has something to ask you." Sarah said.

"I was getting to that." Becca shot her friend a withering look. She turned back to Andrew. "I was thinking…" Her voice trailed off.

"Yes?" Andrew said, wary. He'd learned from experience that when a teenage girl started to think, it could end in trouble. "Please, continue."

"Would you mind if we went into town for the day?"

"I don't know. I have a lot to do-"

"You wouldn't have to drive us. We'll take my car."

"How long have you had your license?" Andrew knew he shouldn't be worried, but ever since Jennifer died he'd been terrified of letting Sarah ride with anyone but him. God alone knew what he would do when she wanted to take her driving test. She was already old enough, but so far hadn't pressed the issue.

"A few months," Becca said. She sidled closer. "I'll be careful. I promise."

"I don't know."

"I'm a great driver. Call my dad and ask."

"You'll stick to the speed limit?" Andrew narrowed his eyes, tried to give her his stern look. A jab of pain shot through his tender head. He might need a couple more painkillers.

"Of course. You have my word," Becca replied. "We'll even call you when we get there, so you know that we got there safe and sound."

"Alright then." He couldn't think of a good reason not to agree, and besides, it might do Sarah some good to get out of the house for a few hours. She spent so much time on her own.

"Awesome." She grinned.

"What are you going to do in town?" He probably should have asked that before giving permission.

"I don't know," Becca said. "Catch a movie."

"Sounds like fun." Andrew rubbed his forehead. All he wanted was for the girls to go away so that he could get some peace and quiet. "Be home by dark. And drive carefully."

"We will." Becca took Sarah's hand and practically dragged her from the room. As they left, she shouted over her shoulder. "Thanks, Mr. Whelan. You're the best."

"You're welcome." He watched them go, and then, after the front door closed, turned his attention back to the toaster oven. A dark curl of smoke rose from behind the glass door. He'd burned his breakfast again.

Chapter 35

AS SOON AS they were in Becca's car, driving toward the old gnarly oak that stood at the edge of the road where their property ended, Sarah turned to her friend. "You lied to my dad."

"No I didn't." Becca took a right, pulled off the dirt track onto the paved road. "We are going to Danvers."

"I don't mean that. You said we were going to the movies."

"Well duh. Of course I did." Becca made a frustrated huffing sound. "I swear Sarah, sometimes you can be so dense."

"I don't get it. What's the big deal about saying where we're really going?"

"Because if we tell him we're off to the library, he'll think we're up to something."

"No he wouldn't," Sarah said.

"Yes, he would."

"Why?"

"Because no one goes to the library. It's boring, and we're not studying for a test. One mention of that and he'll know we're going to meet boys for sure."

"But we're not meeting boys," Sarah said. "We really are going to the library."

"Exactly." Becca fell silent, as if that was all the explanation that was warranted.

"I don't get you sometimes." Sarah settled back in the seat. "I'm pretty sure there was no need to lie."

"Whatever. It's done now."

"And what about breakfast? I thought we were going to eat before we left." Sarah's stomach grumbled in response. She hadn't expected to feel hungry, but apparently her digestive system had not gotten the message.

"Yuck. Toast?" Becca wrinkled her nose. "No way. I have something better in mind."

"What?"

"Dunkin' donuts. There's one up ahead." Becca was already steering the car toward the drive thru.

"Do we really need to eat donuts?" Sarah said.

"I'm going to pretend I didn't hear that." Becca said, rolling her window down to order. Afterward, with a donut in her hand, she spoke again, between mouthfuls. "Besides, your father didn't look too hot."

"He looked fine to me."

"Trust me. I know," Becca said. "He had a hangover."

"I still don't see the need to lie." Sarah turned away, glanced out of the window as they entered the town of Danvers. She didn't want to believe that her father was hung over, wanted it to be another lie, but deep down she knew it wasn't. She felt trapped, hopeless to stop him sinking back into the despair that had crippled him in Boston. She also hated that Becca had sensed it, so she remained mute until they pulled up outside of the library, a large classic revival building set within several acres of lush parklands. It boasted arched windows and majestic columns bearing a half round portico that gave the whole thing a regal look.

"Come on." Becca hopped from the car, slammed her

door. She waited for Sarah to climb out, then locked the car and took off across the lawn in the direction of the building.

It was cooler inside. The air smelled of lemons and books. Becca went straight up to the information desk and asked where the internet stations were located.

"Reference Department," replied the young woman behind the desk. She twirled her ID badge lanyard around her index finger, then uncurled it again, only to repeat the motion. "You'll need a library card though, and it's an hour limit."

"Here you are." Becca pulled a card from her wallet. She held it out.

The woman took it, swiped it, handed it back. "All set. The Reference Department is to the left past the meeting rooms. Workstation three."

"Super." Becca slid the card back into her wallet. She set off, hardly waiting for Sarah, who hurried to catch up.

"What are we doing?"

"Looking up Martha Ward, of course. The internet seemed the best place to start." Becca turned left toward a bank of computer workstations. Each one had a card attached to the top of the terminal with a number. She made a beeline for workstation three.

"Couldn't we have used our phones to do that?"

"This is easier," Becca replied. "Besides, We can go look around the stores once we're done here."

"Fine. So what are we looking for?"

"Let's start with the name, date and location. Martha Ward, 1693, Massachusetts." Becca brought the search engine up, tapped on the keyboard.

The screen changed to show a list of results. The top one was a link to the University of Virginia. The name Martha Ward was prominent.

"Try that." Sarah pointed.

Becca clicked on the link. "It looks like an online archive

of the Salem Witch Trial documents. There's a record for a Martha Ward." She scrolled down the page. "Crap."

"What?"

"Martha Ward was accused of being a witch," Becca said, wide eyed.

"No way." Sarah peered closer. The screen showed a scan of an old yellowed document. The writing was oxidized, brown, and faint. "Can you read it?"

"I can try. It's not very clear." Becca studied the page, and then began to read. "Martha Ward of Salem Village was brought before us by Joseph Herrick, Constable in Salem, to Answer John Fellows and Joseph Wright of Salem Village Complainants on behalf of their Majesty's against Martha Ward, for suspicion of witchcraft by her committed, according to a warrant dated Salem, March 20th, 1692."

"Oh my god." Sarah shuddered. It was bad enough that she suspected Willow Farm to be haunted, but to find out that there was a victim of the Salem witch trials right in their back yard, that was something else. It scared her, but at the same time she felt sympathy for Martha Ward, who surely did not deserve her fate, whatever that might have been.

"There's more." Becca was still reading. "It says here that Martha Ward denied the charges, but it didn't do any good. She was tried and convicted in the spring of 1693."

"That's the year on the headstone," Sarah said.

"Oh, this isn't good." Becca glanced at Sarah, a worried look on her face.

"What?" Sarah tried to see past her, to the screen. "What have you found?"

"They hung her." Becca was shaking. "They strung her up in an oak tree at the entrance to her property."

"Willow Farm."

"Exactly." Becca was pale. "You don't think the oak they hung her from is the same one that's there now, do you?"

"There aren't any other oak trees close to the road, and it

does look old enough." Sarah felt like crying. Things were going from bad to worse. "Crap."

"At least it explains the grave. Unconsecrated ground."

"Great," Sarah said, her voice flat. "They hung a witch in front of my house."

Chapter 36

IT WAS AFTER MIDNIGHT.

Sarah opened her eyes, roused from her sleep by the padding of feet on the wood floor, the creak of a door. She lay in the darkness, her heart beating fast, but then she remembered that Becca was there, just a few feet away. If things were going to get weird, at least she wasn't alone.

She rolled over, looked down at the inflatable mattress. Becca's sleeping bag was empty. The bedroom door was ajar. It had been closed earlier, when they went to bed. Of that she was sure.

She slipped out from under the covers, went to the door, peeked out. The stairs were dark. There was no sign of Becca.

Sarah put her shoes on, opened the door wide enough to pass through, and made her way to the second floor landing.

She paused, a creeping sense of uneasy coming upon her. Where was Becca?

As if in answer, the sound of the front door opening, the worn hinges squeaking, drifted up from below.

Sarah moved again, taking the stairs as fast as she dared, and hurried to the door. It was closed, but not locked.

She gripped the door handle, unsure if she should go

outside, especially after the events of the previous night. But Becca was already out there, and that made no sense. Taking a deep breath, she turned the knob, and stepped out into the night.

It was cold.

The chill cut into her like a sharply honed knife. She pulled her top tight and looked around. There was no sign of Becca. It wasn't that long since Sarah had heard the door open, so where was she?

Somewhere far away an owl hooted, the call sad and haunting. The wind rustled the leaves, and from some distant location there was the faint sound of a car engine, but then it faded almost as quickly as it came.

Sarah was perplexed.

She walked past the old barn, the one her father wanted to turn into a garage. It leaned a little to the right, and the roof sagged. If outward appearance was anything to go by, the building was a goner. A few feet away stood Becca's car, so wherever she was, it was on foot.

Sarah paused, her eyes searching the darkness.

"Where are you?" She spoke the words under her breath. And then, when she was about to give up, there was a flicker of movement at the periphery of her vision. She turned and watched the figure as it moved away from her. This had to be Becca.

Gravel crunched underfoot as Sarah hurried down the trail. It was much too dark. She wished she had a flashlight, considered going back to fetch one, but dismissed the idea. Becca was ahead of her, and she didn't want to lose her.

The fields on the left and right were nothing more than expanses of empty black nothingness. It made her feel like she was walking through an endless void. She shuddered, remembering her days in the hospital, when she was lost in limbo, comatose. She wished she didn't remember the way it felt, but she did. There was a presence there with her, just out of sight, and she had the overwhelming conviction that it wanted to keep her there. She liked to say that she didn't believe in heaven or hell, but that wasn't entirely true. She did believe, deep down, and she thought she already knew what hell was like. She also wondered if the entity in the house – and she did now think something was there – had latched onto her because she had straddled both worlds already. She was an easy target.

A flash of movement pulled Sarah from her thoughts.

There was someone there. A figure hurrying along the trail. It turned, the face in shadow, but Sarah recognized Becca despite the distance.

Her friend slowed, raised an arm, and beckoned for Sarah to keep going, to follow her.

And then she lost the figure again in the darkness. She could see the low fence skirting the road, the woods on the other side, and the twisted oak, but not Becca.

Sarah picked up the pace, the hairs on the back of her neck standing up. She felt a tingle of apprehension.

She was almost at the end of the driveway now.

She stopped in the shadow of the oak. She looked left, then right. If Becca was on the road she would be visible, but there was no one there. The only other option was the driveway leading back to the house. This too was empty.

So where was she?

Sarah stood there, confused.

How could Becca have vanished?

It didn't make any sense.

And then she heard something. A low, lazy creaking sound from above, in the tree. Sarah looked up, and what she saw filled her with terror.

Becca was in the tree.

She appeared to be hovering between two misshapen branches, her arms drooping. She swayed in the wind, her head bowed, hair falling past her shoulders like a silken waterfall.

At first Sarah could not understand what she was seeing, could make no sense of it, but then she noticed the rope slung over a high branch, followed it down to the noose pulled tight against Becca's neck. And in a flash she understood.

Her friend wasn't hovering.

Becca was dead.

Chapter 37

ANDREW WAS DREAMING ABOUT JENNIFER, and their honeymoon together in San Francisco, when the frantic scream pulled him from his sleep. His eyes snapped open. Instantly alert, he was on his feet in a matter of seconds, and pulling on a pair of pants.

He rushed from the room, almost tripping over himself as he hurried to buckle his belt. In the hallway he went to Jake's bedroom.

Jake was sleeping soundly. The room was dark, silent.

Andrew turned toward the staircase leading to the attic, a knot of fear churning in his stomach. He was half way up when he heard another scream. Only it didn't come from above, it came from below, on the ground floor. He flew down the hallway, took the stairs two at a time and almost ran into Sarah as she came barreling through the front door.

"Whoa. Slow down. What's wrong?" Andrew surveyed her looking for any outward sign of an injury. "Are you hurt?"

"No." Sarah gasped, her face flushed and red. Tears streamed down her cheeks. "Not me."

"Then whatever is the matter?" Andrew took her by the

arm, led her away from the open front door, and pushed it closed. "And what were you doing outside?"

"I followed Becca," Sarah said. "I woke up and she was missing. I heard her go outside and then…"

"Why on earth would she go outside at this hour?" Andrew didn't know what time it was, but he knew it was late. "It's not safe to be wandering-"

"Who cares about that," Sarah blurted. "You're not listening to me."

"So tell me," Andrew said. "But if Becca is outside we need to go and find her."

"There's no point." Sarah's voice rose. She sat on the bottom stair, wiped the tears from her eyes. "Becca is dead."

"What?" Andrew felt light headed all of a sudden. He leaned against the wall. "What do you mean, she's dead?"

"She's hanging in the tree, out by the road. The old oak. There's a noose around her neck, and she's dead." Sarah looked up at Andrew with a look of pure anguish. "I followed her down the driveway. When I got to the tree she was there."

"Show me." Andrew was already pulling on his shoes. He wondered where his cell phone was. "We need to call the police too."

"What's going on?"

Andrew recognized the voice right away. "Becca?"

"Who else would it be?" Becca stood at the top of the stairs, on the landing. Her nightgown hung to her knees. "Why are we calling the police?"

Sarah stood up, watched Becca descend the stairs, a confused look on her face. "How is this possible? You're dead."

"I don't think so. I was sleeping pretty well though, until you guys woke me up."

"You were upstairs all the time?" Andrew asked. "You didn't go outside?"

"Why would I go outside?" Becca said.

Sarah studied her. "You were gone when I woke up. I saw you in the driveway."

"No, you didn't." Becca yawned. "I've been in bed the whole time. Haven't moved."

"But…"

"Okay. Enough of this fooling around." Andrew slipped his shoes back off. He turned to Sarah. "I don't know what you are playing at, what kind of ploy for attention this is, but it had better not happen again."

"It's not a ploy for attention," Sarah protested. "I really did see-"

"How, Sarah?" Andrew asked. "Becca is right here. She's not hanging in a tree. She's not dead. Whatever you think you saw, you didn't."

"I'm telling you, I did." Sarah looked near to tears again. "Come with me. I'll show you."

"Show me what?" Andrew said. "There is nothing to see."

"I'm right here Sarah. I'm fine." Becca placed a gentle hand on her friend's arm. "Why don't you come back to bed?"

"No. I don't want to go back to bed," Sarah said, pulling away. "I'm not making this up. You have to believe me."

"I give up." Andrew shook his head. "For heaven's sake, Sarah. If it's not one thing, it's another with you. I swear, I don't understand you at times."

"But-"

"I'm going back to bed. You can do what you want." Andrew pushed past Sarah, climbed the stairs. "Just do it quietly, please."

Chapter 38

"YOU REALLY THOUGHT I WAS DEAD?" Becca sat perched on the edge of the bed. "Hung in a tree?"

"I swear." Sarah was still shaken up by the ordeal. Even though Becca was here, and clearly very much alive, Sarah couldn't stop replaying the moment she saw the corpse in the tree over and over in her mind. Even now it made her feel numb. "I'm not making this up."

"No one is saying that you are," Becca replied.

"Except for my father."

"He's worried about you."

"He thinks I'm crazy." Sarah swallowed hard, leaned back on the bed. "He hasn't treated me the same since I took the pills."

"Do you blame him?"

"No, not really." This was the truth. It didn't make her feel any better though. "I know I let everyone down."

"You didn't." Becca put a hand on Sarah's arm. "Trust me."

"I wish I could believe that."

"So what was it like," Becca said, steering the conversation back to the night's events.

"What?"

"The body in the tree."

"I don't want to think about it." Sarah wished her friend would let it go. She felt bad enough already, and a little confused. How was it possible that she had thought Becca's bed was empty? Why had she thought Becca was outside? Worst of all, who or what was she following on the driveway?

"Do you think it was the witch?" Becca's eyes were wild. "Maybe she put a spell on you."

"There's no such thing as a witch. Martha Ward was in the wrong place at the wrong time, that's all. She was a victim of mass hysteria."

"And now she's in your back yard," Becca replied. "And haunting your house."

"Stop that," Sarah said, ignoring the tingle of fear that pushed up her spine.

"What do you think she wants?" Becca said.

"How should I know. To drive me insane if tonight is anything to go by."

"We should ask her." Becca was already off the bed.

"No." Sarah knew what Becca was going to suggest. "That's not a good idea."

"Why not?" Becca plucked the Ouija board from off the dresser and brought it back to the bed. "You want answers don't you?"

"Not like that."

"Well, there's no other way." Becca went back to the dresser, then turned to look at Sarah, a confused expression on her face. "Did you move the pointer?"

"No, of course not."

"Well it's not here." Becca hunted around, checking the floor and the bed. "Where could it be?"

"It can't be too hard to find." Sarah scooted off the bed and joined Becca in her hunt.

"Really? Well where is it then?" Becca was on her hands and knees, peering under the bed.

"Forget it. We'll look tomorrow. I'm, tired."

"Don't you want to find out why Martha is still here?"

"I'm not sure that she is," Sarah said. "Honestly, it's possible I am going mad. I know what I saw. You were hanging in a tree. You were dead, a noose around your neck. But here you are, so it must have been a hallucination. Or maybe I was sleepwalking."

"You think you dreamed it?"

"I don't know." Sarah flopped back down on the bed. She felt drained, weary. "But if you really want to find out more about Martha, and the history of this house, I think I know someone who can help."

"Who?" Becca sat on the inflatable bed. "Tell me."

"There was a priest that came around a few days ago. He talked to my dad. I overheard them." Sarah wrapped the blanket around herself in an attempt to get warm. "He was talking about a family that used to live here."

"Wow. Do you know which church he came from?"

"No. But I remember his name. Father Bertram. It shouldn't bee too hard to find him."

"Hang on." Becca was already tapping on her phone. She looked up, a look of satisfaction on her face. "Got it. He's the parish priest at Our Lady of the Sorrows."

"That was fast."

"We should go and see him tomorrow." Becca slipped the phone back in her purse. "What do you say?"

"Tomorrow. Assuming I'm not grounded for what happened tonight." Sarah yawned. She reached out, clicked off the lamp. The room was swathed in darkness, the only illumination coming from the nightlight plugged in under the window. "In the meantime, I'm going to get some sleep. I'm exhausted."

Chapter 39

OUR LADY of the Sorrows stood in a neighborhood of large
Victorians, surrounded by neat manicured lawns and deli-
cately trimmed hedgerows. The building itself was simple,
built of stone, with a small bell tower at one end and at the
other, a white cross on the roof's apex. An arched walkway led
from the side of the church and followed the perimeter of the
property to create a half enclosed courtyard in which was
erected a statue of the Virgin Mary, her arms held open.
Stone benches arranged at intervals along the path offered
views of the blooming flowers that filled a host of flowerbeds
scattered throughout the grounds.

Becca circled the block twice before finding a parking
space on the road near the front of the church, and backing in
with an ease that contradicted the newness of the drivers
license in her wallet.

The car had hardly come to stop before Sarah jumped out
and hurried toward the church's main doors. Becca locked the
car and scurried behind, catching up with Sarah as she
reached the main doors.

It was cold inside the church, despite the glorious day

outside. Slants of sunlight cut through intricate stained glass windows, casting colorful splashes of light upon the tiled floor between the benches. Stone columns rose on each side of the nave, blossoming into intricate twisting sculptures at the point where they met the vaulted ceiling. The air smelled of incense and age, the atmosphere thick and heavy.

Sarah made her way up the center aisle to the crossing, where a pair of transepts, one on each side of the building, separated the rest of the church from the chancel. She stopped short of the altar and stood looking up at the crucifix suspended on the back wall. A sculpture of Christ, hands and feet pierced with nails, painted blood seeping from the wounds, hung from the cross in lifelike detail. His head bowed and ringed with thorns, the sculpture looked like it was peering at them from pain drenched eyes.

"That's a bit too real." Becca drew level, her gaze drawn upward to the crucified Jesus.

Sarah didn't respond.

"Are you okay?" Becca cast a worried glance in her friend's direction.

"The last time I was in a church we were burying my mom." Sarah spoke the words in a hushed voice. "I remember sitting in the front row, looking up at the cross on the wall, focusing on the figure there, because I couldn't bear to look at the casket."

"That was a hard day for everyone." Becca put an arm around Sarah, gave her a light hug. "I was so worried about you. I still am."

"All I could think was how unfair it all was. That if there really were a god he would never have let a thing like that happen. He would have saved her. Wouldn't he?"

"I don't know," Becca admitted. She fell silent for a beat, then spoke again. "Look, if this is too much right now, if you're overwhelmed, we can leave and come back another day."

"No. This is important. We'll find Father Bertram and see what he knows." Sarah pulled her eyes from the crucifix. She turned back toward the aisle. "I want to know what went on in my house."

"It doesn't look like he's around." Becca glanced around. "Shouldn't he be here if the church is unlocked?"

"I have no idea." Sarah shrugged. "Don't they always leave churches open?"

"Beats me." Becca made her way back down the aisle toward the doors. "We should have called ahead, made sure he was actually at home."

"Maybe," Sarah agreed. "I assumed he would be here."

She followed Becca toward the back of the church, unsure what to do next. She had almost reached the doors when a deep voice echoed down the aisle.

"Can I help you?"

The girls turned, surprised by the sound.

Father Bertram stood on the altar steps. He was dressed in black, his shirt open at the top, white collar missing.

He clearly wasn't expecting visitors.

The aging priest descended the steps and met them in the aisle. "If you're looking for the Irish dancing lessons, that's in the church hall around the corner and across the parking lot. But you're a wee bit early I'm afraid. It doesn't start for another hour."

"Were not here for that." Becca stepped forward. "We've come to ask you some questions."

"Have you now?"

"About Willow Farm."

"I see." The priest narrowed his eyes. "And why would you be interested in that old place?"

"Because I live there." Sarah spoke up. "You came to see my father a couple of days ago."

"I did. It's true." Father Bertram nodded in agreement. He sighed, a cloud passing over his face. "But I'm not sure I should be discussing things of that nature with girls such as yourselves."

"We're big girls. We can handle it," Becca said, a scowl on her face.

"Please?" Sarah intervened before Becca could say anything else. "It would mean a lot to us."

"Does your father know you're here?" The priest asked.

"Of course," Sarah felt bad for lying to a priest, but it was the only way. "He thought it would be a good idea to know the history of our new house, get to know it better."

"Did he now." The priest didn't look convinced, but even so, he motioned for the girls to take a seat on one of the benches. He settled on the bench in front and turned to them. "You didn't hear any of this from me, understand?"

"Yes." Sarah nodded her agreement. "Of course."

"Very well," Father Bertram said. But still, he hesitated.

"Why did you go to Willow Farm?" Becca chimed in. "What did you tell Sarah's dad?"

"I came to see your father because I thought he should know the things that happened in his house, why it was empty so long."

"And?"

"I arrived at this church many years ago. It was the mid-eighties and I didn't know a sole. Of course, that changed pretty quick, what with the congregation eager to acquaint themselves with the new priest, but one family in particular opened their arms, and their house, to me."

"The people that lived in Willow Farm," Sarah said.

"Exactly. The Stevenson family. They purchased the house at about the same time I came to town, and they seemed happy there, at least at first. Then one day Mr. Stevenson, Andy, came to me for advice. It was a few weeks before Thanksgiving. He said he'd been seeing things late at night, hearing noises. He claimed that his wife had seen stuff too, that she refused to go into the cellar, and sometimes slept with the lights on.

"He asked me to do a blessing, and of course I obliged. After that he said the house quieted down, that everything was calm. And then one cold winter's day, he loaded his wife and the kids into the family car, and pointed it straight toward the oak tree at the entrance to the property."

"That's horrible." Sarah looked on with wide eyes. "We're they-"

"Killed?" Bertram wiped a bead of sweat from his forehead, even though it was chilly in the church. "I'm afraid so. The girl hung on for a little while, hovering at the threshold of death, but soon she was gone too. It was a dreadful affair, and there was no logical reason why it happened. Except…"

"What, Father?" Becca leaned forward. "There's more, isn't there."

"I'm afraid so. The police ruled it an accident, and even though they could find no evidence for it, decided that the car must have suffered a malfunction, that Andy lost control and hit the tree before he could do anything to stop it."

"But you don't think that's what happened?" Becca said.

"No." The priest swallowed, moistened his lips. "Andy said some troubling things the day he sought my help. He spoke of hearing voices in the walls, of seeing a figure lurking late at night, skulking in the darkness, even though all the family members were accounted for. He had formed the impression that the nocturnal visitor was a female, said she came to him when everyone else was sleeping, whispered to him, told him to do things, horrible things."

"You think she told him to drive into that tree?"

"I think Andy wasn't in his right mind when he got behind the wheel that night. As for the cause of his mental state, I really don't know," The priest said. "When I went up to the house to give the blessing, I thought he was exaggerating his experiences, much to my eternal shame. It was later, after the accident, that I found out I wasn't the first priest to have dealings with that house. It had a history already, and not a good one."

"I'm not sure I want to hear this," Sarah said, feeling a little nauseous.

"You don't have to, if you don't want to," Bertram said.

"I really don't want to hear it, but I think I need to hear it." Sarah looked to Becca for support, feeling better when her friend put a hand out, touched her shoulder. "Please, go on."

"Very well." The priest drew in a long, measured breath, and then started again. "Back in the late Fifties the parish priest here was a man named Christopher Halloran. He was beloved by all accounts, a soft spoken Irishman with a heart of gold. One night, with the snow coming down in a frenzy, and the ground frozen hard, he got it into his head to drive up to Willow Farm, right there and then. He told his housekeeper that he had a bad feeling something was very wrong up at the farm. She tried to dissuade him, pleaded with him not to go out on such a night, that it wasn't safe to be on the road, but he was adamant. That was the last time anyone saw him. At least, still alive."

"What happened to him?" Becca was engrossed.

"That's where things get weird. When he didn't return by morning the housekeeper put a call in to the sheriff, reported the priest missing. They drove up to the farm, found his Plymouth parked out front, and everything quiet as could be. At first they thought he must have decided to stay over rather than risk the drive back in a blizzard, but then, on the ground at the side of the house they came upon his broken body, frozen hard as an icicle.

"The glass and shattered window frame strewn about gave them a fair clue as to his cause of death, but not how it had come to pass. They assumed, naturally, that the Walker family, the owners of Willow Farm back then, would be able to enlighten them. Sadly they were a little late on that score."

"Why?" Sarah felt butterflies writhing in her stomach. She dreaded what she was about to hear, but knew she must know the rest of the story.

"When the sheriff went to the front door, he found it unlocked, slightly ajar. But still he went inside, searched the house. It wasn't until he went upstairs that he discovered the family, at least two of the three. Thomas, the Walker's ten year old son, was tied to his bed. I'll spare you the gory details, but suffice to say he was no longer alive. Mrs. Walker was in her room, laying on her bed. She too was dead. She had poisoned herself.

"Mr. Walker was found in the cow barn, his head caved in. He'd been dead for at least three days, much longer than the others. The assumption was that Mrs. Walker killed her husband, then tied young Thomas to the bed and tortured him for days, until Father Halloran paid them a visit. That appears to have been the tipping point. She killed Father Halloran, swiftly followed by Thomas, and then joined them by downing the poison. There was a note on her nightstand, the only clue to her motive, in which she wrote that the house had made her do it."

"I think I'm going to be sick." Sarah leaned over, cupped her head in her hands. "I'm living in a murder house."

"Perhaps I shouldn't have said anything," Father Bertram said, a concerned look on his face. "You have to understand, all of this happened a very long time ago."

"Why didn't you tell my father about the Walker family when you had the chance?" Sarah looked up at the priest.

"I wanted to. That's the reason I went there. But when I saw the amount of pain already in his eyes, I couldn't do it."

"And yet you were okay with telling me."

"You wanted to know the truth." Bertram clasped his

hands together. "And I wanted you to know, so that you can make sure your family stays safe."

"Are you saying they won't?"

"No." The priest narrowed his eyes. "I'm not saying anything of the sort, but I am saying that Willow Farm has seen a lot of grief, and I would rather it not see any more."

Chapter 40

ANDREW WAS SITTING in the den, at his computer, when the email came through. He reached down, clicked his mouse and opened it.

The message was from his realtor in Boston.

There was an offer on the house.

He read the message once then read it again, a strange feeling overcoming him. He sat for a while contemplating the news. Things seemed real now. Up until this point there was the possibility they could go back. The brownstone was a safety net. Now there was nothing.

It felt strange, knowing he would never see the Boston house again. He and Jennifer had spent many happy days there. Jake was a baby when they bought it, and he thought of it like another member of the family. In some ways selling it felt like a betrayal, even though he knew that Jennifer would have wanted them to start afresh.

But times changed, and Jennifer was gone. Keeping the old place would be more sentiment than practicality.

That didn't make him feel any better, and for a while he wondered if they were doing the right thing. But then he remembered Sarah, and the suicide attempt. Boston was too raw for her, and he worried about Jake too.

No, this was the way it must be.

In a few weeks the house would belong to someone else, and that would be the end of the matter. In the meantime he decided to put the issue out of his mind. There were better things to worry about anyway, like the book. If he didn't finish that it wouldn't matter where they lived, they would be broke.

He closed the email and switched to the manuscript. The bare, white page glared out at him from the screen.

Little by little, he started to type.

Chapter 41

"WELL, THAT WAS DEPRESSING." Becca said as they strolled back toward the car. "Do you believe any of it?"

"What's not to believe?" Sarah was glum. She felt numb. No wonder there was such an oppressive atmosphere in the house. "I live in the house of death."

"Don't be so dramatic," Becca chided. "We don't even know if half of what the priest said actually happened. Most of it sounds like hearsay to me."

"Except that he knew the last family who lived there. That isn't hearsay."

"So what," Becca said. "It was a long time ago. Forget about it."

"How can I?" Sarah felt like crying. "I'm stuck in that place. You saw what happened with the Ouija board. You saw the grave."

"I know." Becca sighed. "I just think you need to relax. If the ghost really is there, it might feed off negative energy."

"I suppose." Sarah wasn't convinced. "Do we have to go home yet? I don't think I can stand seeing that house right now."

"We could get ice cream," Becca said. "I know an awesome stand where the Creemee's are wicked big."

"I don't think so."

"Come on. You said you wanted to stay out."

"I know," Sarah said as they reached the car. "I'm not in the mood for ice cream. Something else."

"The movies." Becca opened the car door and climbed in, then waited for Sarah before continuing. "We haven't been to the movies for ages."

"Fine." Sarah really wasn't in the mood to watch a film either, but it would kill a few hours, and she wouldn't have to talk.

"The movies it is then." Becca turned the key in the ignition. The engine sprang to life. "Here we go."

Chapter 42

ANDREW WAS STILL in the den when Sarah and Becca returned from town. After several hours of writing he didn't feel he'd achieved a damn thing. There were words on the page for sure, but they weren't good, and he knew it. In fact, they were more that that. They stank.

He selected the three new pages, six hundred dreadful words. His finger hovered over the delete key.

What the hell, he thought. It isn't like anyone would publish this drivel. He stabs his finger down. The words disappeared.

So much for that.

He stood up, stretched.

It was already getting dark, the sun dropping low over the trees and turning everything a magnificent shade of gold.

From the window, high on the second floor, he watched their car pull up the dirt track and park near the ramshackle barn. A few seconds later there was a thud as the girls came through he front door, then the sound of footsteps on the stairs.

He stayed at the window even as the footsteps moved down the hall and faded. By now his daughter and her friend would be in the attic room above. He wondered if he should go up there, but decided against it.

The phone rang, the sound harsh and loud in the broken silence. He started, his heart quickening before he realized what it was.

He looked down, saw the name on the caller ID – Harvey Nolan. It was his agent.

For a moment he considered letting it go to voicemail. His eyes flicked to the bottle of vodka sitting to the left of the laptop. Next to it, a gift from the celestial bartender, a full shot glass. He considered slamming the shot, letting good old Harvey wait. He could talk to him when he was good and ready. The problem was, he would never be ready. He'd let it go to voicemail three times in the past two weeks. Each message sounded a little more irritated. This time Harvey might actually explode.

With a groan, Andrew picked up the phone.

"Hello."

"Andrew. My man. Glad that you answered. Sorry to call you so late." Harvey's nasal New York accent did him no favors. "I hope I'm not disturbing you."

"Nope." Andrew wondered if he could end the call, claim the line dropped, decided against it.

"Good to hear," Harvey said. "How have you been?"

"Surviving." Andrew stole a look at the shot glass. "You?"

"I'd be better if my favorite author did me the service of returning my calls."

"Favorite author. What a bunch of bull. You hate me and you know it." Andrew was in no mood for false platitudes.

"I only hate you because you make my life a living hell," Harvey said. "I quite liked you when we were making money together."

"The book. I know." Like there was anything else Harvey would be calling about. He wasn't calling because he wanted to shoot the breeze. "I'm going to need a bit more time."

"Time is the one thing we don't have, Andrew, my boy." There was a hard edge to Harvey's voice. "The publisher wants their pound of flesh."

"I hear you. But they can't have what I haven't written." Andrew went to the desk, sat down.

"Then write," Harvey said. "I don't care if it's the worst thing you've ever produced. At this point, it can be a steaming pile of horse manure for all I care, but I need something to give to them. Anything."

"A few more weeks."

"That's what you said a month ago, and the month before that." Harvey cleared his throat. "It's been almost a year, Andrew."

"I know that." Like he needed reminding.

"Let me be honest with you," Harvey said. "The publisher is threatening to pull if we don't come up with a manuscript soon. They took a big risk with this three book deal, and they want to make their money back."

"They already have, ten times over." The first two books had been bestsellers, far outstripping expectations. "And they can't have the advance money back because I'm living in it."

"Whoa, don't jump the gun there my boy. No one is asking for any money back," Harvey said. "But think of this. If you get dropped, it will be impossible to sell your next book, assuming you actually bother to write one. No other publisher will want to know. You will be damaged goods. New York might be big, but it ain't that big."

"So what do you want me to do?" Andrew said, defeated.

"Come down here. There's a convention at the Midtown Hilton. Show up, sign a few books, and smile for the fans. You know, play nice. Afterward, we'll go to dinner with the powers that be, let them see that you are still with the program, reassure them."

"I can't," Andrew said. "There's too much to do here."

"You can't, or you won't?"

"Does it matter?"

"Hell yes, it matters," Harvey said, his voice raising a notch. "Can I be frank with you?"

"Can I stop you?"

"Not so much." Harvey paused. When he spoke again his voice carried an air of gravitas. "It's been a year, Andrew, a whole year. We were all very sorry to hear about Jennifer, truly we were. But this can't go on. I've given you the benefit of the doubt. The publisher has gone above and beyond, allowed you the time to grieve. But here's the thing. When it comes down to it, they don't really give a rat's ass about your situation."

"Well that's-"

"It's the truth. I know you don't want to hear it, but at the end of the day, they are a business selling a product. They gave you some leeway because they believe in you, but that only goes so far. They want their book."

"Alright. You've made your point."

"Then you'll fly down here?"

"I never said that." Andrew drummed his fingers on the desk. The vodka was looking better and better with each passing moment. "Give me two more weeks, three tops. I'll work all night if I have too."

"No dice," Harvey said. "If I go back to them with another delay, it might be the last. You're not the only one with something to lose you know."

"Oh, right. I get it. Your ten percent."

"You are a cynical man, Andrew."

"I'm a realist."

"You know what? Screw it. Who cares. You want to get drunk every night, that's up to you." Harvey's voice trembled. "But you have a chance to rescue your career here, I'm throwing you a lifeline, but if you're too stupid to grab hold…"

"Okay, I'm sorry." Andrew was alarmed at the outburst. It

was unlike Harvey. "Listen, I can't knock the book out in a week, but I can come to New York. When do you want me there."

"Tomorrow."

"Jesus, Harvey. Talk about short notice."

"If you'd been writing the book, like you were supposed to, I wouldn't have to ask. This was the only way I could convince the publishers not to cut their losses right now. You should be thanking me."

"How am I going to get a flight? I don't even have internet yet."

"I'd suggest you use the browser on your phone," Harvey said. "You have data, right?"

"Why do I even need to be there? You're the one that's supposed to handle this stuff."

"Yeah, right. That only works if you hold up your end of the deal. I'm your agent, not your mother. Book a ticket, pay whatever you have to, and we'll expense it. I'll deduct it from your next royalty check."

"It's not the money."

"Then quit complaining and get down here. If this goes well, it will buy you enough time to finish the book."

"Fine. I'll make the reservation and email it over to you."

"Good man. You're making the right decision." Andrew could hear the relief in Harvey's voice. "I'll see you tomorrow, earlier the better."

"Sure thing."

"Oh, and Andrew?"

"What?"

"Make sure to book a coach ticket. No premium upgrades, not if you want me to expense it. You hear?"

"Sure," Andrew said. "Coach it is."

"Fabulous." Harvey sounded relieved. "Until the morrow."

"Yeah. Tomorrow." Andrew pulled the phone away from

his ear, hit the button to end the call, and placed it on the desk.

He sat there for a long while, staring at the empty laptop screen. The last thing he wanted to do was leave the house, leave Sarah and Jake, and fly to New York. But he didn't have a choice. Harvey had made that crystal clear. It was either New York, or end up broke. Another burned out author left by the wayside.

Damn.

But at least he had the vodka, the magic elixir that got rid of his troubles, for a while at least. That counted for something. He leaned over, took the shot glass, raised it, and downed the contents in one. He placed the glass back on the desk, sat back, and waited for the celestial bartender to do his job.

Chapter 43

SARAH WAS quiet for much of the journey back to Willow Farm. She sat in the passenger seat, huddled down, staring out of the window even though it was already dark. Try as she might, she could not get the priests words out of her head, and the closer they got to home, the more morose she became.

When they arrived at the house, Sarah went straight upstairs. Becca followed.

"You want to talk about it?" Becca said as they entered the attic bedroom.

"Not really." Sarah flopped onto the bed, buried her head in the pillows.

"Okay. I'm here if you want to talk." Becca moved a pile of clothes from the chair near the window, sat down.

"I can't believe all that stuff happened here, in this house. Our house." Sarah's vice was muffled through the pillows. She turned over, looked a Becca. "How can I go on living here?"

"I don't think you have much choice." Becca shrugged. "Unless you want to tell your dad what you found out today, see if he'll move back to Boston."

"He won't," Sarah said. "I know it."

"You don't know that."

"I know one thing. We'd have to admit we lied about where we went today, tell him we went to see the priest. Besides, it would be a waste of time. My dad wouldn't listen anyway. He'd just think I was causing trouble, trying to get him to move back to the city."

"Aren't you?"

"Yes, but this isn't about that. This house, the farm, there's something very wrong. I felt it the day I was trapped in the cellar, and the night I heard footsteps in my room. We both saw it at the grave in the woods. This place has a bad energy."

"So what do we do about it?"

"I don't know. I don't want to think about it right now," Sarah said, her eyes glistening wet in the dim light from the lamp on the nightstand. She rolled over, slipped under the covers, pulled them almost all the way up over her head. "I'm tired. I'm going to get an early night."

"Like that?" Becca asked. "You're not even undressed."

"I can't be bothered." Sarah's voice sounded a million miles away. "I'll put my nightgown on in a while."

"An early night does sound good." Becca glanced at her watch. It was almost ten. "Mind if I take the shower first?"

"Knock yourself out." Sarah waved a hand above the covers. "But leave the light on when you go downstairs. I don't want to be in the dark."

"Sure." Becca scooped up her nightgown and walked to the door. From behind her, on the bed, she heard a gentle snore. Sarah was already asleep.

Chapter 44

BECCA DESCENDED the stairs and padded along the corridor to the bathroom. The wood floor was cold on her bare feet, and she soon wished she'd slipped her sandals back on.

A thin sliver of pale yellow light eked out from under the door opposite the bathroom. This was Andrew's den. She hadn't been inside, but he seemed to spend most of his time in there. She wondered what he did, since Sarah said he wasn't writing anymore.

The bathroom was even colder than the corridor. She closed the door, turned on the heater, and hurried to get her bare feet onto the bathmat. She reached in past the shower curtain, turned the shower on, and waited for the water to heat up before undressing.

When she stepped into the tub under the jet of piping hot water, a shiver of satisfaction raced through her. She pulled the plastic curtain closed to stop any stray wetness escaping onto the floor, and stood there, letting the steamy spray cascade down her body. It felt so good that she didn't want to move. She dipped her head into the water, her scalp tingling as the droplets massaged it, and squirted a handful of shampoo into her hand, before applying it to her hair. She was about to rinse when the light flickered and went out.

Becca let out a startled whimper.

The blackness was absolute. She couldn't even see her own hands. If she was back home in Boston the darkness would be diluted by the street lamps outside, but here the small bathroom window did nothing to help her situation.

A knot of fear twisted inside of her when she remembered Sarah's story about the basement. Was this nothing more than a blown bulb, or was it something worse?

Whichever it might be, Becca didn't want to be here anymore. But first she must rinse her hair. The shampoo was already running down her forehead. But she had no desire to do that in the inky blackness. If she could get to the door, open it, there would be enough light to sooth her panicked nerves while she finished up.

She extended a shaking hand, fumbled around until she found the edge of the shower curtain, and pulled it wide enough to pass through.

The tub was high, an old claw foot that was charming enough to have escaped replacement over the years. Now it presented a hazard as she attempted to step out. On the first try her toe contacted the rim, causing her to curse in pain. She reached down, rubbed her aching digit, her hair falling over her shoulders as she did so, wet and cold. She was about to make a second attempt when the light snapped back on.

Becca squinted and shielded her eyes from the sudden flare. For a few moments everything was dazzling and white, but then the bathroom swam back into view.

She breathed a sigh of relief.

It wasn't some vengeful spirit setting a trap for her in the darkness, just bad wiring.

The shampoo was dripping from her hair and onto her arms. She could feel it creeping down her forehead, threatening her eyes. She pulled the shower curtain across once more, then stepped back under the water and started to rinse, massaging her scalp, washing away the day's grime.

She closed her eyes, letting the shower douse her face, relishing the warmth that spread through her body.

And then she heard it.

A light shuffle.

Becca froze, her breath catching in her throat.

She opened her eyes, wiped the water away.

"Is someone there?"

She received no answer, just the sound of the shower drumming on the metal floor of the tub, and the steady thrum of the small, outmatched heater set high upon the wall.

She listened.

Whatever had caused the sound was gone now. The bathroom was still, quiet. She wondered if it was Andrew leaving his den, or Jake needing to use the bathroom, finding it occupied already.

But then there was the short blackout.

It seemed like too much of a coincidence that both things would happen at the same time.

Becca stood there, frozen with indecision. She wanted to hop from the shower, run back to the safety of the attic bedroom, but at the same time, she feared what waited for her on the other side of the shower curtain.

As if to answer, the shuffling repeated.

It was louder than before, and closer. Becca gave a quick intake of breath, her eyes wide.

It came again, like feet dragging across the floor. This wasn't Sarah, or anyone else in the house. This was something different. And it was right there, on the other side of the curtain.

Waiting.

Becca shrank back, her shoulders hitting the tiled wall.

She raised a hand to cover her mouth as her breath came in sharp, rapid quivers.

And then, to her horror, the shower curtain moved.

It rippled, as if there was a body stirring the air close by, and then it started to press inward, ever so gradually.

The curtain bowed in the middle, the hem inching up the side of the tub, scrapping.

A dent appeared, pushing inward toward her.

The curtain wrinkled, formed around something that looked very much like...

A face.

The realization hit Becca right around the same time that the countenance in the curtain opened its mouth, the fabric falling into the space between the lips, which moved up and down, silently miming a single word.

Rebecca.

This was too much.

Becca let out a shriek, her stomach tightening in fear, and lunged forward. She gripped the edge of the curtain, threw it back in one sweep, several eyelets ripping from their hooks as she did so.

The grotesque face vanished as the curtain flew aside, the fabric relaxing and slouching on one side under the weight of the unsupported material.

The room was empty.

There was no demon lurking beyond the tub, waiting for her. Everything was as it should be.

Becca let out a sobbing breath, her nerves tingling, the memory of those lips, silently mouthing her name, burned into her mind.

She slumped back against the wall, the cascading shower water, now tepid, splashing over her body. She drew in a long, measured breath, her heartbeat returning to normal.

At that moment the bathroom boor burst inward, slamming back on its hinges.

Becca let out a scream, expecting to see the ghastly, misshapen form of Martha Ward lurching toward her. But it was just Andrew, standing in the doorway, a concerned look on his face.

"What's going on?" He stepped into the room. "Are you alright?"

"I'm fine," Becca said, but the tremble in her voice betrayed her. "I just got spooked, that's all."

"Oh. I see." Andrew looked relieved. But then his face changed. A look of shy awkwardness came upon him, and he back peddled. "I'm sorry. I didn't mean to..."

At first Becca didn't comprehend what he was talking about, but then she followed his gaze, glanced down, and remembered that she was naked.

"Oh my god." She reached out, pulled the shower curtain toward her, sheltered behind it, her face a burning shade of crimson.

"You're sure you are okay?" Andrew was looking away now.

"I'm good. Thanks." She wished that the floor would collapse and swallow her up.

"Okay." Andrew nodded. "I'll leave you to it then. I'm across the hall if you need me."

"Thanks." Becca watched him leave, pulling the door closed as he went. She let the curtain fall away and turned off the water, stepping from the tub. She grabbed a towel, dried off as fast as she could. There was no way she was staying in this room a moment longer than necessary. She slipped the nightgown over her head, scooped up her clothes and went to the door, checking to make sure the coast was clear before she entered the hallway and scurried toward the attic stairs. By the time she reached the bedroom, her heart was pounding. She slipped inside, pushed the door closed.

A few feet away Sarah still snored, although her clothes now lay in a crumpled heap on the floor.

Becca scooted down into the sleeping bag and lay there, her cheeks still flushed from the naked encounter with Sarah's dad, her stomach churning at the memory of the face in the shower curtain. When she finally fell asleep the two merged, and she dreamed of Andrew, his face mashed into the curtain, watching her while she bathed.

Chapter 45

ANDREW ENTERED his den and closed the door, leaning heavily on it. He felt embarrassed, foolish. He should have knocked instead of barging into the bathroom like that, but when he heard Becca's scream he hadn't stopped to think.

What if it had been Sarah? What if she had hurt herself, tried something again. He couldn't bear the thought of losing her too. Only it wasn't his daughter, it was her friend. An image of the girl cowering in the shower, the water dripping off her, forced its way into his mind. He pushed the memory away. She was mortified, no doubt. Heaven alone knew why she had let out that scream, but she certainly hadn't expected him to come flying to her rescue, barreling through the door, of that he was sure.

Now he was glad to be going to New York. By the time he got back she might be gone already, and if not, at least the incident would have faded.

From the corridor he heard a faint click, and soft feet hurrying away.

This would be Becca, hightailing it back to the attic.

He stepped away from the door, went over to the desk.

The laptop was awake, its screen glaringly white and empty, the cursor blinking at him.

When are you going to write again, it said. *What's up, can't think of anything?*

That much was obvious.

If he could come up with a single line worth a damn he wouldn't be flying to New York in the morning to pander to a bunch of slick suited shysters with nothing but dollar signs in their eyes.

Andrew glanced sideways to the shot glass, ready and waiting, full to the brim as always. How many had he consumed tonight? It didn't matter. One more wouldn't hurt.

He picked it up, knocked it back in one gulp.

The liquor burned a path down to his stomach, where it sat, warming him.

He leaned back in the chair, the alcohol making him drowsy. He fought to keep his eyes open, but lost the battle. A few minutes, nothing more, he told himself as tiredness washed over him. But he knew it would be more than that. This wasn't the first time he'd fallen asleep at his desk. He had a feeling it would not be the last.

Chapter 46

BECCA'S EYES SNAPPED OPEN.

She lay for a minute, unmoving, almost as if she was taking stock of her surroundings, then squirmed free of the sleeping bag and stood.

In the bed Sarah was curled up, only her head visible above the sheets.

Becca extended a hand, her fingers grazing Sarah's forehead, teasing a stray curl of hair.

Sarah moaned and rolled over, turning away.

Becca went to the door, eased it open. She crept down the stairs and walked along the corridor toward the chink of light that still glowed under the furthest door.

When she reached Andrew's writing room she tapped on the door and waited.

Chapter 47

ANDREW AWOKE to a quiet rapping on his writing room door. He opened his eyes, finding first the vodka bottle, the always full shot glass. How long had he been sleeping? It was still dark outside, so it wasn't morning yet. He sat up, found his phone, and checked the time.

Almost one o'clock in the morning.

The tapping came again, urgent and quick.

Andrew stood, felt his legs wobble a little under the fading influence of the booze, staggered to the door.

He pulled it open a crack, peered out.

Becca stood there. She wore a knee length nightgown, and not much else. Despite everything, his mind wandered back to the shower.

"What's wrong?" His mouth was dry, like someone had poured rocks down his throat.

"Nothing." Becca looked up at him, wide eyed. "Why would you think there was something wrong?"

"Why else are you knocking on my door at this hour?"

"I feel bad about earlier," She said. "The shower."

"If anything, I should be the one apologizing."

"Can I come in?" Becca ran a hand through her hair.

"What?" Andrew was taken off guard. "Why?"

"I've never been in the new writing room. I want to see where the magic happens." She smiled. "Besides, it's freezing out here in the corridor."

"I suppose." Despite the alarm bells going off in his head he pulled the door wide and stepped aside. "Maybe you should have put something a bit warmer on if you're cold, a sweater or something."

"Don't you like this?" Becca stepped into the room, pushed the door closed. She looked down at her nightgown. "I think it looks nice."

"I don't think it's entirely appropriate for the situation."

"What situation is that?" Becca inched closer. She looked up at him.

"This." Andrew waved an arm. "You being here in the middle of the night."

"I see." Becca bit her bottom lip. "Can I let you onto a secret, Mr. Whelan?"

"Sure." Andrew wondered if he was still sleeping. Something about this encounter felt weird, like a dream.

"I like you." She snaked an arm around his neck. "I've liked you for a long time. I've thought about this moment so often."

"This isn't a moment, Rebecca." Andrew fought the rising tide of desire. He took her by the shoulders, pushed her back. "This is wrong on so many levels."

"So what?" Becca played with the top of her nightgown. "Are you telling me that you didn't like what you saw in the bathroom?"

"That was a mistake." Andrew shook his head. "I should have knocked. I'm sorry."

"You still haven't said if you liked it," She said, a smile lifting the corners of her mouth. "I think you did."

"For heaven's sake." Andrew felt the conflicting urges battle inside him. "You're my daughter's friend. You are still in high school."

"I turned eighteen last month," she said, her voice not much more than a whisper. "You don't need to worry."

"That's not the point."

"Then what is?" Becca cooed. She closed the gap between them again. "I won't tell Sarah. I promise."

"It's not just that." Andrew felt her body pressing against him, felt the hot tickle of her breath on his neck.

"Jennifer?"

He didn't need to speak that time. The look on his face said it all.

Becca slipped an arm under his, her hand resting in the small of his back. "You don't have to keep everyone at arms length. She would want you to be happy. She would want this."

"No."

"Yes." Becca snaked her other arm back around his neck. "You deserve this."

"I…" He struggled to find the words. His mind raced.

"Hush." She lifted herself on tiptoe, found his lips with hers.

Andrew closed his eyes, felt his whole body tremble. Becca tasted like cherries. Her mouth was soft and inviting. He could feel her breasts against his chest, could hear the blood rushing in his ears. He slipped an arm around her, caressed her back, let his fingers trail down her spine until they couldn't go any lower. He felt the desire surge inside of him. He pulled her in, his other hand finding the back of her neck and holding it tight as he returned the kiss, his fingers in her hair.

And then it was over.

When she pulled her lips away he felt a pang of longing.

"See, I knew you wanted it as much as me," she whispered in his ear. "Why don't we go to the bedroom."

"No." It hit him all of a sudden. No matter how much he wanted this, no matter how alluring and manipulative Becca was being, he could not let it happen. It was wrong. Worse, if Sarah ever found out she would never forgive him. "This has gone too far already."

"Don't worry…"

"Enough." He pushed her away. "This can't happen. Ever."

"Maybe this will change your mind." She reached down, took hold of the nightgown, and lifted it up over her head in a quick, fluid movement, discarding it on the floor.

"I said no." Andrew wanted to look away, couldn't.

"You're really turning me down?" Her voice carried an incredulous tone. "I don't believe it."

"Believe it." Andrew snapped, averting his eyes from her nakedness. When he spoke again his voice was hard, angry. "Now go back to bed."

"If that's what you really want." She bent over, picked up the nightgown, and walked to the door. When she got there she lingered, turned back to him. "The bedroom's right there. It's not too late."

"Just go." Andrew felt drained, defeated. Any desire he'd harbored was gone, sapped by the realization of what could have happened.

"Alright then. You're the boss." She pulled the door open and stepped through.

He thought she had gone, felt a wave of relief, but then she was back, the nightgown draped over one arm.

"One more thing, before I go."

"Yes?" He felt a tingle of dread. Something in the tone of her voice told him she wasn't going to apologize.

"Your family. Jake and Sarah."

"What about them?"

"They're both going to die, just like your wife." A cruel grin forced the sides of her mouth high to her cheeks. It looked like her face was about to crack in half. "And so are you."

Chapter 48

ANDREW AWOKE before nine the next morning, the alarm on his phone reminding him that he couldn't sleep in. There was a flight to catch. He rose and went to the bathroom, splashed water on his face and brushed his teeth. His stomach churned, a leftover from the over indulgence the night before. He leaned over the sink, waited until the feeling passed.

After that he dressed and went downstairs.

He was in the middle of preparing a breakfast of bacon and eggs when the rest of the occupants of Willow Farm showed up. Jake arrived first, rubbing sleep from his eyes. He sat at the table and watched his father crack eggs and butter toast. A few minutes later Sarah and Becca appeared.

"Good morning." He flipped the bacon in the pan, doing his best to avoid eye contact with Becca. "How did you guys sleep?"

"Fine." Sarah leaned against the wall near the pantry.

"How about you, Becca?" Andrew met her gaze as he spoke, his eyes searching for any sign that she was as uncomfortable as him. "Did you get a good night's sleep?"

"Of course, Mr. Whelan." Becca smiled and went to the table. She took a seat next to Jake. "It's so quiet here."

"That it is." An image of Becca, her mouth bent by a twisted smile, entered his head. Her words lingered in his mind, fresh as the moment she'd spoken them.

He looked at Jake, then Sarah.

They're both going to die, just like your wife.

Why would Becca have said such a thing, and how could she breeze in here now like nothing happened. He would need to have a chat with her later, when Sarah wasn't around. For now though, there was a more pressing matter.

"I have something to tell you guys, actually a couple of things." Andrew shimmied the bacon out of the pan, dolled it between four plates, and then turned his attention to the eggs.

"What, dad?" Jake asked.

"Well, you know we put the house in Boston up for sale."

"Yes." Sarah narrowed her eyes.

"We have an offer. Full asking price."

"Don't accept. Please?" Sarah looked frantic. "We can move back after the summer, sell this place."

"That's not going to happen. I've already accepted. I just thought you guys should know."

"So we're stuck here," Sarah said. "Great."

"Come on, it's not that bad."

"For you maybe." Sarah glared at him. "What's the other thing?"

"I have to go on a trip." He watched Sarah's face, hoped she wasn't going to pitch a fit about that too. "Harvey wants me to take care of some business in New York."

"What?" Her eyes brimmed with indignation. "When?"

"This afternoon. I'm booked on the 1pm shuttle from Logan."

"You're leaving me here alone?" A look of panic flashed across Sarah's face. "You can't do that."

"I don't have a choice. It's that, or look for another job." He served the eggs, took two plates to the table. "Besides, you won't be alone. Jake will be here, and you have Becca to keep you company."

"Please don't go," Sarah begged. "Tell them you're sick or something."

"I'm not a liar, Sarah." His eyes flicked to Becca. If she caught the look she didn't react. "I gave my word."

"Who's going to be in charge?" Jake asked, before stuffing a piece of bacon in his mouth with his fingers.

"Your sister," Andrew replied. "And I want you to be good, do what she says."

"Why can't I be in charge?" He was working up to a second rasher of bacon.

"Because you are ten years old." Andrew deposited the remaining plates on the table, pulled out a chair, glanced back at Sarah.

She still lingered in the doorway, her face dark and stoic.

"Are you coming to eat?" Andrew asked her. "It'll be cold."

"How long will you be gone?" Sarah took a grudging step forward, then another, squeezed in between Jake and Becca. She picked up a fork and poked at her eggs.

"One night. I'll be back tomorrow night. Think you can handle things until then?"

"Not really."

"Why do you have to make this difficult?" Andrew felt the familiar frustration that always surfaced when dealing with his daughter. "Most teenagers would be happy to get the house to themselves for a night."

"Don't worry, Mr. Whelan," Becca said. "I'll make sure Jake is looked after. I've done my share of babysitting."

"I'm not a baby." Jake scowled.

"Sorry, I didn't mean it like that." Becca slid a piece of her bacon over onto his plate. He grinned and snatched it up, all thought of the perceived insult forgotten. She turned her attention back to Andrew. "See?"

"Alright." A picture of Becca naked, inciting him to join her in the bedroom, wormed its way into his head. He looked down, suddenly ashamed. The eggs and bacon starred right back up at him, and he realized he wasn't hungry anymore. He pushed the plate away, stood up.

"What's wrong, Mr. Whelan?" Becca asked. "Aren't you going to eat your breakfast?"

"I don't think so." He shook his head.

"Can I have it?" Jake asked.

"Sure. Knock yourself out." He turned and hurried from the room. When he reached the den, he closed the door and stood there. The image of Becca was still in his head, only now he could not shake her chilling prediction, and he wondered if he was doing the right thing letting her stay at the house while he was gone. But in the end, what choice did he have?

Chapter 49

"I CAN'T BELIEVE dad's going to New York." Sarah was cleaning away the breakfast dishes, stacking them in the new dishwasher Andrew had installed a few weeks before they moved in.

"Why?" Becca hovered near the table, watching Jake finish up the last of the food. "What's the big deal?"

"After everything you heard that priest say yesterday you want to be alone here, in this house?"

"I won't be alone, will I?" Becca said. "You will be here, and so will Jake."

"What did you hear yesterday?" Jake asked between mouthfuls of egg.

"Nothing. Grown up stuff, that's all," Sarah replied. "Now hurry up and finish your food so that I can wash the plates."

"I don't see why you have to be the boss." Jake pulled a face. "Mom could be in charge."

"Mom's dead Jake." Sarah turned and leaned her back on the counter. "Surely you didn't forget."

"I know she's dead."

"Then how can she be in charge, dummy?" Sarah asked.

"I speak to her."

224 • ANTHONY M. STRONG

"We all do, Jake. I talk to her every night before I go to sleep," Sarah said. She felt overcome with a sudden pang of sadness. Her throat tightened and she turned away so that the others wouldn't see the tear that meandered down her cheek.

"I don't mean inside my head," Jake said, pushing his empty plate away. "I talk to her on the telephone."

"You don't have a phone." Sarah scooped up the last plate from the table, deposited it in the dishwasher.

"I do too." Jake pouted his lips, scrunching them up. "I found it when we moved in."

"Ah, I see." The old rotary dial. Sarah wondered if it was healthy for him to be pretending their mother was on the other end of a phone that probably hadn't worked in thirty years. It didn't seem right, but if it helped Jake deal with the loss, who was she to judge. After all, it wasn't long ago that she was laying in a hospital bed with a belly full of pills. This seemed like a tame coping mechanism in contrast. "Well next time you speak to her on the telephone, make sure she knows I'm in charge, okay."

"I don't think she'll like that." Jake wriggled off the chair. He walked to the door, paused. "She isn't like she was before."

Chapter 50

ANDREW SLIPPED his laptop into the small carry on bag he'd packed the night before with the essentials for his trip - underwear, a clean pair of pants, two shirts. He coiled the power cable, pushing it into the front pocket along with his phone charger. As he did so his eyes skipped to the bottle of vodka sitting on the desk. He couldn't leave that out in the open. If Sarah were to come in to the den for any reason she would see it, assume he was drinking again. Not that it wasn't true, but she could never understand the magic bottle, would not believe it to be the same one she'd poured away, the same one he had tried to pour down the drain even before that.

He slung his bag over his shoulder and picked up the bottle, then left the room, closing the door behind him, and hurrying down to the first floor hallway.

The girls were still in the kitchen, he could hear them moving about, talking. It sounded like Sarah was loading the dishwasher, which surprised him. She didn't normally take responsibility for anything.

He had intended to hide the bottle in the cabinet under the sink, a place his daughter was most unlikely to ever look, but now he must modify his plan. The basement was right there. It would be a perfect place to deposit the bottle until he returned. Even better, there was no way Sarah would set foot in it after the last time. Finally her over active imagination had worked in his favor.

He put the bag down near the front entry, went to the basement door, eased it open as quietly as he could, and flicked the light switch. The darkness receded below him as the light came on. He stepped inside and walked down the steps, his footfalls making the old wood groan and complain. It sounded loud enough that Sarah might hear it from the kitchen, but he knew that was unlikely. Still, he breathed a sigh of relief when he reached the bottom.

He stood for a moment, eyes scanning the filthy space. Cobwebs hung from low rafters, and here and there he saw a spider waiting for some hapless insect to drift too near.

The basement was mostly empty, save for a large rack near the stairs that was cluttered with all sorts of paint cans and boxes, and the washer and dryer. But in the far corner stood a battered old hutch, its wood chipped and dark with age. He made his way over to it, pulled on the brass handles attached to the double doors. At first nothing happened, and he wondered if it was locked, but he didn't see a keyhole. So the hinges must be seized. No surprise there, it had been under the house, untouched for thirty years.

He gave it another tug, harder this time. The hutch rocked on uneven legs, and Andrew briefly wondered if it was going to come crashing forward on top of him, but then the doors gave way with a sharp crack, the decades old seal broken, and swung wide.

He stepped back as a gust of foul air, reeking of chemicals and rot, belched from the cabinet's interior. When he stepped close again he saw three shelves lined with an assortment of old cans, mostly paint, and a few bottles, their labels browned and unreadable. One bottle oozed a thick gelatinous gunk through a broken cap. This would all need cleaning out, but right now it provided a perfect hiding place.

He pushed aside the contents of the top shelf, shuddering as a fat spider, belly bloated and bulbous, scuttled back out of sight. When he returned he would be coming down here with a can of insect killer, but right now he had more pressing matters to attend to.

He reached up and tucked the vodka bottle almost to the rear of the shelf, then slid the rusted cans back across to hide it.

Job done, he made his way back across the basement, and climbed the stairs. As he reached the top there was a faint clink from down below. He turned, his eyes scouring the empty basement, but there was no clue to the origin of the noise. Deciding it was a bottle shifting in the newly disturbed cabinet, he switched off the light and stepped back into the hallway, closing the door.

He glanced at his watch.

It was time to leave for the airport, but there was enough time to say goodbye to the kids first. He could still hear Sarah and Becca in the kitchen, talking in hushed tones, which they did a lot. Jake was, no doubt, already upstairs in his room.

Andrew climbed to the second floor and hurried along the corridor. When he opened Jake's door his son was sitting in the middle of the floor, the old phone up to his ear.

Andrew watched for a moment, befuddled that Jake found the antiquated device so fascinating, and then caught his son's attention.

"I'm off to the airport," he said. "Behave for your sister."

Jake nodded, never taking the phone from his ear.

"Love you, son." He waited for a response, but Jake had turned his attention back to the phone, was now listening intently to something only he could hear in the receiver. Andrew wondered if he should take the phone away, it was unhealthy to be so fixated. Imaginary friends were fine, but something about the way Jake listened to what could only be silence, made Andrew shudder. He took a step into the room, thought better of it, and beat a hasty retreat. There would be time to deal with Jake's weird obsession after the trip. The last thing he wanted was a tantrum right when he needed to leave.

Downstairs, Andrew went to the kitchen. Sarah, near the sink, looked up when he entered.

"I'm off," Andrew said. "Try to stay out of trouble while I'm gone, and no boys in the house, understand?"

"Where are we going to find boys out here?" Sarah pulled a face.

"Don't worry Mr. Whelan, we're just going to hang out and watch TV, maybe go to the mall."

"Make sure Jake sits in the back and wears a seatbelt if you go out."

"We will." Becca grinned. "Have a good trip."

"I'll try." Andrew said. "Call me if you need anything."

"I know." Sarah nodded. "I'll see you tomorrow."

"Tomorrow." Andrew turned and walked to the front door. It was windy outside, a line of dark clouds gathering beyond the tree line. He went to the car, popped open the trunk, and heaved his bag inside. He pulled the drivers side door open, was about to climb in, when Becca appeared at the front door.

"You forgot this." She waved a wallet in the air, jogged over to him.

"Thanks." He took the wallet and pushed it into his pocket. "Wouldn't have gotten far without that."

"My pleasure." She spun around, started back to the house.

"Wait." Andrew followed her. "Can I have a moment?"

"Sure, Mr. Whelan." Becca came to a halt. "You don't need to worry. We'll take good care of Jake, and I promise we won't get into any trouble."

"It's not that." He rubbed his hands together. "About last night…"

"Forget about it," Becca said, her face flushing. "It was an accident, totally my fault, I shouldn't have screamed."

"No, I mean afterward."

"Afterward?" Becca looked perplexed. "I'm not sure I know what you mean."

"In the den. I shouldn't have let things go as far as they did." Andrew felt a bead of sweat push down the back of his neck. "I don't want you to think-"

"Mr. Whelan, I have no idea what you are talking about." Becca interrupted. "The den?"

"The den. You came to see me later on, after the shower incident."

"No, I didn't." She shook her head.

"Becca, you came to me, offered me… things."

"Are you feeling alright Mr. Whelan?" Becca said. "You look a little flushed, and you aren't making any sense."

"Look, if you want to pretend it didn't happen, that's fine, but…"

"I swear, I don't know what you are talking about." Becca shook her head. "What am I supposed to have done?"

"I'm sorry. Forget I said anything." Andrew didn't know why, but he had the feeling that Becca really had no recollection of coming to him, seducing him. "Don't worry about it. Not important."

"Sure, no problem." Becca threw him a quizzical look, then turned and walked back to the house.

Andrew waited until she disappeared inside, and then climbed into the car, but even then he sat there a while, going over the events of the previous evening in his head. Eventually, unable to make any sense of it, he pushed the key into the ignition. Whatever was going on with Becca, he would figure it out after the trip.

Chapter 51

SARAH STOOD at the dining room window and looked out. Her dad was talking to Becca on the driveway. She couldn't figure out why, but at breakfast she had sensed a weird vibe between the two of them. She felt it again now, as they conversed.

When Becca turned back toward the house Sarah stepped away from the window. "What was all that about?" She asked when Becca appeared through the door.

"What?" Becca replied. "Your dad forgot his wallet, left it on the counter."

"I know that." Sarah hesitated, then pressed on. "Dad was acting weird around you today."

"No he wasn't," Becca said. "You're imagining things."

"I don't think so."

"Well I do think so." Becca took Sarah's arm, tugged. "We have the house to ourselves for two days. Aren't there better things to do then talk about your dad?"

"We don't have it completely to ourselves. There's Jake." Sarah countered, but even so the realization hit her all at once. They were free from adult supervision for almost forty-eight hours. They could do whatever they wanted. And then another thought struck her. They would be alone in the house all night, defenseless if whatever was hiding in the shadows, and Sarah was pretty sure it was Martha Ward, decided to play tricks. This filled her with a cold dread.

"So what?" Becca was steering Sarah toward the stairs now. "He's a good enough kid. As long as we make sure to feed him three times a day he'll be fine."

"He's not a cat." Sarah raised her eyebrows. "You do know that, right?"

"All I'm saying is that he isn't going to have any interest in hanging out with us. He won't care what we do as long as we let him do his thing."

"I shudder to think what his *thing* might be," Sarah said, although she suspected that he would be playing with that creepy phone again. He was obsessed with it these days. She shuddered, thinking of him sitting there, the phone between his crossed legs, the earpiece thrust up against the side of his head as he whispered into it, just quiet enough that no one could hear what he was saying. She forced her mind from the thought, changed the subject. "So what do you suggest we do?"

"We could have a sleepover." Becca grinned.

"You're already staying here."

"Not me, stupid." Becca glanced around, made sure Jake was nowhere in sight. "Tyler."

"No way." Sarah shook her head. "That is such a bad idea."

"Why?" Becca met Sarah's gaze. "You said he came to see you the other day. He still likes you."

"We're not together anymore," Sarah said. "Besides, dad would kill me if he knew we had a boy over."

"Who's going to tell him?"

"Well, Jake for one."

"Please. We can handle that squirt," Becca snorted.

"Surely you know something he doesn't want your dad to find out about."

"Not really." Sarah shook her head. "I don't pay that much attention to him."

"Shame." Becca thought for a moment, then her face lit up. "I know, we can sneak Tyler in after Jake goes to sleep."

"I don't know."

"Come on, it'll be fun," Becca pleaded. "Besides, if anything happens, there will be someone else here to protect us."

"What would happen?" Sarah asked. "You think someone is going to break in here or something? We're in the middle of nowhere."

"No, I mean with the ghost."

"We don't even know that there is a ghost," Sarah said.

"I know that some weird crap has been happening. What about the cellar? The woods?"

"There could be…"

"Please don't say there could be a reasonable explanation," Becca said. "You saw that strange wind, we both did, and I swear, there was someone out there with us. And how do you explain the Ouija board?"

"I don't know, okay?" Sarah didn't want to talk about it. She was scared enough, without Becca pushing the point home. If she didn't think about it she could pretend that nothing strange was happening, but only if Becca cooperated. "Can we talk about something else?"

"Fine. But first, tell me you will call Tyler."

"I'm not calling Tyler."

"Why not?" Becca pleaded. "It'll be fun."

"For who?"

"Please, I know you still like him, and he is crazy about you."

"So?"

"So tell him to come here tonight."

"Alright. Anything to shut you up." Sarah threw her arms up. "But on one condition."

"What is it?" Becca leaned against the wall, her arms folded.

"You have to invite Logan." Sarah grinned. There was no way Becca would ask the boy she'd pined for the whole of her junior year, especially since they'd only went on one real date, at least as far as she knew.

"I can't. Come on, not fair." Becca shook her head.

"Hey, if you want me to invite Tyler, you have to invite Logan."

"Sarah…"

"Three's a crowd."

"And four is even more of a crowd," Becca replied.

"That's the deal, take it or leave it."

"Fine. I'm texting him now." Becca pulled out her phone. She tapped out a message on the screen, then glared at Sarah. "Happy?"

"Yep." Sarah took her own phone out and found Tyler's number. As she typed, her fingers flying over the virtual keyboard, she felt a sudden tingle of anticipation. Maybe their night alone wouldn't be so bad after all.

Chapter 52

AT EIGHT O'CLOCK that evening Tyler's blue Mustang pulled off the road and drove up to the house, followed by a light colored Toyota that Sarah assumed must be Logan. As instructed, they pulled to the far side of the building and parked up under a stand of birch trees, far away from Jake's bedroom window, where the young boy might see the cars and start asking awkward questions.

Sarah met them at the door, ushering them in with a whispered warning to keep quiet until they got to the attic bedroom. Jake was nowhere to be found, having already scoffed down a plate of chicken nuggets Becca had found in the freezer and heated up in the microwave. After that he scurried from the room, feet stomping as he ran up to the second floor. A final thud announced the fact that he was back in his room. Sarah would have to make sure he went to bed at a reasonable time, but first there was Tyler to take care of.

"This place is even creepier from the inside," Tyler whispered as they made their way up to Sarah's room.

"It's much better than it was a few months ago," Sarah replied as they reached the attic. "You should have seen the state it was in. There was even a hole in the roof."

Becca was sprawled across the bed on her stomach, one legged hooked in the air, her bare foot angled toward the ceiling. When they entered she looked up from the cell phone clutched in her hand, a slight smile upon her lips. "Hi, Tyler."

"Hey." Tyler looked toward her, then back at Sarah.

"Hi Logan. Why don't you come over here." Becca scooted sideways, making room on the bed.

"Sure." Logan was a tall, lanky kid with a mop of curly blonde hair. He picked his way past the inflatable mattress and perched on the edge of the bed, looking a little uncomfortable.

Becca swung her legs off the bed and sat up, exchanging a look with Sarah as she did so.

Tyler turned to Sarah. "I hoped to hear from you again after the other day."

"I would have texted sooner, but we were busy," Sarah felt a flutter of excitement deep inside. Now that he was here, she was pleased Becca had talked her into inviting him. "I wasn't sure you would come."

"Why?"

"I don't know. Things have been so weird between us," Sarah said. "I know we kissed, but..."

"I still feel the same about you." Tyler walked to the window, looked out. "I didn't want to break up, remember."

"I was in a bad place." Sarah watched him gaze out over the landscape, his back to her. "I wasn't thinking straight."

"Forget about it." Tyler glanced back over his shoulder, then returned his attention to the window. "Is that the woods where we found the grave?"

"Yes." Sarah glanced at Becca, who shot her a knowing look. "It is."

"There's a grave behind your house?" Logan's eyes flew wide, his interest piqued.

"Creepy, huh?" Becca said. "The woman buried there is a

witch. She was hung from the tree near the road, the big old dead oak."

"No way," Logan said.

"For real?" Tyler turned away from the window. "Neat."

"Not really," Sarah said. She didn't bother to mention the second trip to the grave, the one she took with Becca a few nights before, or the strange winds. It was as if telling another person would somehow make it all the more real. "It's pretty gross actually."

"We should go take another look at it." Tyler's eyes glinted with excitement.

"Hell yes." Logan jumped up.

"No." Both girls spoke at the same time.

"I don't think that would be a good idea." Sarah added. "Besides, it's getting dark. The woods won't be safe."

"What, are you scared?" Tyler said. He looked at Becca. "I thought you liked this kind of thing. You're always the one dragging us into stuff."

"Not tonight." Becca shuddered.

Tyler looked between them, confusion on his face. "Okay, fine. So what do you want to do?"

"I don't know," Sarah said. She remembered her brother downstairs. It was almost nine o'clock, and she didn't want to get in trouble with her dad for not looking after him. "Why don't you two think of something while I make sure Jake goes to bed. The last thing we want is that squirt discovering you guys and making a fuss."

Chapter 53

JAKE WAS FLICKING through the pages of a coloring book, looking for a picture that he hadn't filled in yet, when the phone rang. He got up, went to the dresser where the phone sat when he wasn't using it, and plucked it down.

He perched on the bed and lifted the receiver.

A familiar voice filled his ear, scratchy and faint, as if it was talking from a very long way off.

He listened.

The voice spoke, telling him what it wanted him to do.

Jake nodded.

He didn't need to vocally confirm that he understood. It was as if his mother – because that was who Jake was sure he was talking too – could somehow see him.

The voice faded, the line filling for a moment with a hiss of static, and then there was no sound at all.

His mother had gone back to wherever she came from, at least until the next time the phone rang. A couple of times he had wondered where she was, why she only talked through the phone, and did not visit him in person. When he'd asked that very question the voice had replied without hesitation.

Heaven.

Apparently one could not just leave heaven, it wasn't allowed, which was why they must talk over the phone. But, the voice promised, if Jake was very good, he would come to heaven and be with her soon. All he had to do was follow her instructions. Even if those instructions seemed to contradict what he'd been told to do previously, which they did.

It didn't matter.

All that was important was that he was a good boy, and then he would be with her again and everything would be back to the way it should be.

He slid from the bed, picked up the phone, and placed it back upon the dresser.

Next he went to the closet and pulled the door wide. Reaching as far in as he could, he fumbled around, pushing stuff aside until he found the planchette hidden there a few days before. He pulled it out and inspected his prize, feeling no small measure of satisfaction.

When the knock at the door came, he was ready.

Chapter 54

SARAH MADE her way to Jake's room.

She knocked on the door, waited a moment, then gripped the handle and opened it just enough to poke her head in.

"Time for bed," she said, a second before her eyes fell on Jake, standing in the middle of the room, something small and familiar clutched in his outstretched hands.

"I think this is yours." Jake took a step forward, then another.

Sarah opened the door wide and met him half way. She looked at the object, recognizing it. "Where did you get that?"

"I..." Jake hesitated. His eyes grew wide. "I found it."

"This was in my bedroom." Sarah snatched the planchette out of her brother's hand. "Where did you find it?"

He shrugged, said nothing.

"Talk to me, you little creep." She felt the anger rising. Had he been up in the attic — her attic - snooping around when she wasn't there? Had he stolen this? What else had he looked at, her journal? Probably not. She hardly wrote in the diary that sat in a drawer next to her bed. Most of the time she wrote online, venting her frustrations anonymously, blogging about boys, shoes, and everything else a teenage girl cares about. Except that she hadn't even done much of that during the last year. Encountering violent, unexpected death at an early age had a habit of making such things seem trivial. "Well?"

"I don't know." Jake glanced down, avoiding eye contact.

"Damn it. You stole this from my bedroom, didn't you."

"No." Jake looked up at her, and something in his eyes gave her pause. Instead of the usual glint of mischief, there was something else. Something dark and brooding. For a fleeting second she imagined she was looking into the eyes of a complete stranger.

"Forget about it." Sarah took a step back, uncomfortable. "It's time for bed."

"Okay." Jake made no attempt to move.

"You should go brush your teeth," Sarah said. "And then you can get into your pajama's. I want you in bed within ten minutes, understand?"

"Sure." Jake shuffled his feet.

"I'm waiting." Sarah wondered if this was what it was going to be like when she had kids, or rather, if she had kids.

"Alright. Stop nagging me." Jake pushed past her and went to the bathroom. When he reached the door he stopped, turned back. "Sarah?"

"Yes?"

"Why are there boys upstairs?" His unblinking eyes searched her face. "Why is Tyler here?"

"What?" Sarah felt herself floundering. How could he possibly know that Tyler and Logan were here? She had been so careful, and there was no way he saw them sneaking up to the attic. Jake's bedroom door had been closed the whole time.

"I know that Tyler is upstairs." Jake lingered at the bathroom door, half in, and half out. "There's another boy up there too. I don't know who he is."

"It's no one. A friend of Becca's." Sarah could feel the

anxiety wadding up in her stomach, a hard ball of fear that refused to settle. "I suppose you're going to tell dad?"

"Why are they here?"

"We didn't want to be alone while dad's gone, that's all."

"I don't like Tyler." Jake spoke the words in a low, matter-of-fact voice. "He shouldn't be here."

"You get on great with Tyler." Sarah said, confused. "He used to play with you all the time, you used to go to Boston Common and chuck footballs."

"I don't like him now."

"Why not?"

"He's ruining things. They both are."

"I don't understand," Sarah said, a creeping unease coming over her. "Why do you think he's ruining things?"

"Mom told me so." Jake glared at Sarah, his eyes narrow slits.

"Mom told you." Sarah repeated the words. "What are you talking about. Mom's dead Jake. How many more times do we have to go over this."

"I told you, she talks to me on the phone."

"You need to grow up." Sarah did her best to keep her voice level, but even so it cracked. "If you want to play with imaginary friends that's fine, but you have to understand that the dead don't come back and talk to you on the telephone."

"Yes they do," Jake said.

"No, they don't," Sarah said. Only She didn't truly believe that. Not after the events in the cellar, the other stuff that had happened. Maybe there were such things as ghosts, and maybe there was even a ghost in Willow house, but the telephone in Jake's room was absolutely not a hotline to heaven. Of that she was certain.

"I won't tell dad," Jake said. "Mom told me not to tell him. It's our secret."

"Well, aren't I lucky," Sarah said, and even though she felt a wave of relief that Jake wasn't going to rat them out, she still felt uneasy. There was one good thing though. They wouldn't need to creep around anymore, since Jake already knew the boys were in the house.

"I'm going to get ready for bed now." Jake turned and disappeared into the bathroom. Soon the sound of water running reached Sarah's ears.

She stood there, looking at the empty corridor a while longer, and then retreated back to the attic stairs. Jake could get himself into bed. She no longer cared if he stayed up all night. She sensed something strange in him, a subtle change, cold and dark. And even though she didn't want to admit it, deep down she knew the truth. Jake's newfound friend frightened her, because maybe, just maybe, there really was someone, or something, on the other end of that phone.

Chapter 55

BECCA TURNED toward the door when Sarah entered the attic. Her eyes alighted on the planchette cradled in her friend's hand. "You found it."

"My little crap of a brother had it in his room." Sarah closed the door. "He claimed he found it. I bet he snuck up here when we were out and stole it. What a creep."

"I hope you gave him hell."

"I wish," Sarah said. "He knows we snuck Tyler and Logan in."

"Great." Tyler looked crestfallen. "Your dad's going to ban me from seeing you after this. You'll be grounded for like, a million years."

"He's not going to find out," Sarah replied. Jakes words stuck in her head. *Mom told me not to tell him. It's our secret.* She shuddered, overcome with a sudden sense of foreboding. "He said he wouldn't tell anyone."

"Why?" Becca looked up in disbelief. "That doesn't sound like Jake."

"Beats me. I have no idea," Sarah lied. "At least we don't have to sneak around anymore."

"So what did he steal?" Logan asked, peering at the planchette. "Looks like some kind of weird mouse."

"It's a pointer," Becca said. "For an Ouija board."

"No way." Logan jumped up. "Let's do it."

"Absolutely not." Sarah stepped in. "We're not playing with that thing again. Not after last time."

"Last time?" Tyler raised an eyebrow.

"Forget I said anything." Sarah didn't want to talk about it, especially to Tyler. He must already think she was half crazy after the whole pill incident, and then shutting him out for months, blaming him. But to tell him that they had spoken to a spirit she suspected was a seventeenth century witch, and that she thought the witch was haunting their house, that would seal the deal. He would never want to see her again, and she couldn't have that, not now when things were finally starting to go well between them again.

"Come on, tell us," Tyler persisted. "You can't leave us in suspense like that."

"Yes, I can." Sarah went to the bed, sat down.

"I'm with Tyler," Logan said. "Something must have happened or you wouldn't be so secretive."

"Nothing happened." Becca came to Sarah's defense. "We just played around for a while and it spelled out some stuff. It's a game, that's all. No big deal."

"I still think we should do it tonight." Logan glanced between Sarah and Becca, a grin on his face. "It'll be fun."

"I agree." Tyler jumped in, but when he saw the look on Sarah's face he backpedaled. "I mean, if everyone wants to. I don't really care."

"You said it was just a game," Logan said. "What are you afraid of?"

"I'm not afraid of anything," Sarah shot back. "I just don't want to do it, is all."

"So don't. The rest of us can still do it." Logan looked around, his eyes searching the room. "Where's the board."

"It's there, on top of the dresser." Tyler pointed.

Sarah let out an annoyed snort.

Tyler turned to her. "Sorry."

"It's fine," Sarah replied. "Do the stupid board if it makes you happy."

"Everyone needs to do it or it won't work." Becca stood up, retrieved the board and opened it on the floor between the bed and the air mattress. "There can't be any distractions."

"Whatever." Sarah sighed. "I'll do it with you, but I don't like it one bit."

"Really?" Tyler slid to the floor, sitting cross legged. He motioned for Sarah to join him. "Awesome."

"Yeah, so awesome," Sarah said, a sarcastic tone to her voice, as she slid off the bed.

"Are we all ready?" Becca took her place at the fourth side of the board, and glanced across at Sarah.

"Get on with it already," Tyler said.

"Don't be so impatient." Becca held her hand out, waiting until Sarah gave her the planchette. She placed it on the board, just as she had done the first time, and touched a finger to it. "Come on, everyone else do the same."

One by one the two boys reached over and placed fingers on the pointer. Sarah hesitated, but then, with a sigh, did the same. Maybe it wouldn't be too bad, she reasoned. After all, it was only a game. Except that she didn't believe that, not after the last time. But it was too late to back out now, especially since she didn't want to seem any worse in Tyler's eyes.

"Good." Becca studied the small group, making eye contact with each before speaking again. "Now remember, don't push down. Touch the pointer, but don't influence it."

"What now?" Logan asked. "Do we just wait?"

"I have to invite the spirits to come to us." Becca cleared her throat, and then, as she had before, she spoke to the air above the gathered group. "Is there an entity that wants to converse with us?"

Sarah watched the planchette, expecting it to remain still. The first time they had done this the pointer seemed reluctant to remove at the beginning, but not so this time. It shot sideways so fast that she lost contact with it for a moment before it settled over the word *YES*. She let out a gasp and resisted the urge to pull her had back.

"Holy crap," Tyler said. "Did one of you do that?"

"Not me." Logan replied, shaking his head.

"She's here." Becca's face had drained of color. There was a tremble in her voice. "It must be her."

"Who?" Tyler looked confused.

"The witch." Sarah felt sick. Her hand shook, but she didn't have the nerve to remove it from the pointer. "We should close the connection right now."

"What? No way," Logan said. "Isn't this why we're playing with this thing?"

"I agree with Sarah," Becca said. "We shouldn't have done this again. It was stupid. I'm closing the connection."

Sarah felt a rush of relief, but then, before any of them could say another word the planchette quivered, as if it were trying to shake itself free of the fingers resting upon it.

They froze, four sets of eyes on the pointer.

It slowed, stopped, and for a moment nothing happened. Then it rushed sideways in the other direction with such force that the feet left thin scratch marks on the surface of the board.

It stopped above the word *NO*.

As it came to rest there was a buzz, and the lights flickered, plunging the room into momentary darkness before coming back on.

"Oh crap," Sarah breathed. "She's not going to let us, is she."

"Okay. One of you might be pushing the pointer, but how the hell did you make the lights go out?" Tyler looked shaken. "Please tell me this is a joke?"

"It's not," Becca said. "This is the real deal. I have to close the session before anything else happens."

"How?" Tyler asked.

"We drag the pointer to the word *GOODBYE*."

"So let's do it," Sarah said. She pressed down, tried to force the planchette upward.

It didn't move.

"Is anyone holding it in place?" Becca looked around the group.

"No." Tyler shook his head.

"Absolutely not," Logan said. "It seems to be stuck."

"That's impossible." Sarah pushed again, but still the pointer refused to move.

"I've had enough of this." Tyler pulled his hand away.

"No," Becca shrieked. "Don't do that."

"Fine." He reached out again, but at that moment the planchette moved to the center of the board. It sat there, as if it was waiting, and then, all of a sudden, spun counter clockwise so fast that all four drew their hands away instinctively.

"Dammit." Becca tried to catch the unfettered pointer, but before she could grab it, the triangular piece of wood was off again. It careened across the board, picking out letters so fast that it was hard to keep track.

"What's it spelling?" Tyler was watching the pointer, his eyes wide.

"I have no idea," Becca said. "But this is bad. Really bad."

"Close the board," Sarah said. She had no idea what the repercussions might be if they did not end the session, but she also knew they couldn't let the pointer keep going on its own. "Do it now."

"No," Becca said. "I don't know what will happen if we do that. "

"We have to do something," Sarah reached toward the still moving pointer, then changed her mind and drew her hand back. "We can't let it carry on like this."

"Get me a pen and paper," Becca said. "Quickly."

Sarah jumped up, went to her nightstand, and pulled out her diary, the one she never wrote in. There was a pen laying next to it. She snatched that up too. "Here, how about this."

"Perfect." Becca took the proffered items and pulled the cap off the pen. She opened the diary and started to jot down letters. "Someone call these out to me. It's moving too fast for me to watch the pointer and write at the same time."

"I'll do it." Tyler shifted forward, his eyes following the planchette. "The first one's a W. Then an E. L. C."

"Keep going." Becca scrawled the letters down in quick succession.

"O. M. E."

"Welcome." Becca stared at the word.

"Doesn't sound like a very frightening spirit to me," Logan said.

"We're not done yet." Tyler was still following the pointer as it scurried across the board. "Y.O.U.A.R.E." He shot a glance at Becca. "You getting all of this?"

"Yes."

"N.O.T."

"Welcome you are not?" Logan raised an eyebrow. "That's an odd turn of phrase."

Tyler hadn't taken his eyes from the board. "It's still going. W.E.L.C.O.-"

"The board is repeating the same phrase over and over." Sarah felt a shudder run through her. "You are not welcome."

Chapter 56

THE PLANCHETTE STOPPED.

All four teens drew back a little, as if they expected something worse to fill the sudden void of activity.

"Is it done?" Sarah said, her eyes focused on the pointer.

"I don't know." Becca shrugged, her face pale.

"Put the board away," Tyler said. "Quick, before something else happens."

But even as his words dissipated into the ether something did happen. The planchette started up again, scrapping across the board, slower now, until it reached the letter T.

"Not again." Sarah pushed herself backward until her back contacted the side of the bed, trying to get as far away from the unruly board as possible.

The pointer slid sideways, stopped at Y.

It moved again, the motion erratic and jerky. L.

"It's spelling my name." Tyler watched in horror as the planchette picked out the final two letters, and then started to repeat the word. "It's not the group that isn't welcome. It's me."

"Ask it something," Becca said.

"No way." Tyler shook his head.

"Then I will."

"No, don't." Tyler's eyes were wild. "We might make things worse."

"Worse than the board just spelling out whatever it wants?" Becca said, then cleared her throat before talking in a slow, calm voice. "Why don't you like Tyler?"

The pointer, which was still spelling out his name over and over again, came to a juddering halt.

"Why don't you like Tyler?" Becca repeated, louder this time.

The pointer crept forward, stopped, moved again. It crawled to a letter and hovered there a moment before moving off.

The four friends watched as the pointer meandered around slowly, until it completed its answer.

R-E-M-I-N-D-S M-E.

Becca starred down at the phrase she had jotted down as the pointer moved. "Reminds you of what?"

The planchette started up again, spelling another answer.

B-A-D M-A-N.

"Bad man?" Sarah said, doing her best to keep the fear from showing in her voice. "What does that mean?"

"Beats me." Becca shrugged. To the board she said, "what bad man?"

H-A-N-G-M-A-N.

"The man who hung you?" Becca asked.

Y-E-S.

"Tyler isn't that person."

R-E-M-I-N-D-S M-E.

"He's sorry about that, but he really isn't to blame."

"I've had enough of this," Tyler blurted.

Becca shot him a glance, silencing him just as the planchette moved again.

W-A-N-T H-I-M G-O-N-E.

"You want Tyler to leave?"

N-O.

"I don't understand," Becca said. "You said you wanted him to go, but you don't want him to leave?"

N-O.

"So what do you want?"

Sarah felt her gut tighten at this question. She wished Becca hadn't asked, but it was too late now, the pointer was off again, spelling out one more message.

W-A-N-T H-I-M T-O D-I-E.

There was a hushed silence, as each of them let the message sink in, and then Tyler stood up, his face dark and angry.

"This is a bunch of crap." He snatched up the board, the pointer toppling and falling to the floor. He turned toward the window.

"Tyler, don't." Becca warned, realizing what he intended to do.

"Why not?" He was at the window now, prying the bottom pane upward.

"Because we don't know what will happen. We haven't closed the session. Things could get out of hand."

"More than they already are?" Tyler countered. "The board is talking to us on its own."

"Becca's right." Sarah didn't want to see anymore either, but she was also afraid of what might happen if the connection with the other side was left open. She didn't want to provoke Martha Ward any more than they already had. "Please, come and sit down. Give us the board back."

"Hell no." Tyler stood silhouetted in the open window, the wind ruffling his hair, tugging at his clothes. He took the board, twisting until the small brass hinges along the fold gave way. And then, holding the ruined pieces like some vanquished enemy, he tossed the board out into the night.

"What have you done?" Becca screamed, her face contorted with fear and rage. She leaped to her feet, running to the window and pushing past Tyler, but the board was lost in the darkness. After a moment she turned toward him, her eyes two narrow slits. "I can't believe you just did that."

"What were you going to do?" Tyler replied. "Let the damn thing keep talking all on its own?"

"Well I wasn't going to destroy it."

"I'm sorry." He turned and walked back to the others, sliding down next to Sarah. "It freaked me out, that's all."

"It freaked all of us out, Tyler." Becca advanced on him. "But the rest of us had the good sense not to do anything stupid."

"I didn't-" Tyler had barely gotten two words out when Sarah stood up.

"That's enough." She shot a look at Tyler, then turned her glare upon Becca. "Don't you see, this is what Martha wants, to make us turn on each other."

"Sorry." Tyler dropped his head, staring at the ground. "I'll go out and get the board. I can probably screw it back together."

"Don't bother." The anger fell away from Becca's face. "It's been nothing but trouble. We should never have used the board tonight. We should have known better."

"What's done is done." Sarah breathed a sigh of relief. For a while she had thought neither of them would let the matter drop.

"Well this has been fun and all," Logan said, climbing to his feet and glancing at his watch. "But I have to be home by midnight or my dad will make Martha the witch look like a nun."

"You're leaving?" Becca looked disappointed.

"Yeah." Logan nodded, his hair flopping over his forehead as he did so. "But I'd like to call you when you're back in Boston, if that's okay?"

"I'd like that."

"Awesome." Their eyes met, sharing a silent moment, and

then, sensing that Sarah and Tyler were watching them, Logan dropped his eyes and turned toward the door.

And then he froze.

Sarah, sensing the shift in mood, followed his gaze, and when she did, a prickle of fear crept down her spine.

There, standing at the top of the stairs, blocking the doorway, was Jake. His face was tense, jaw set forward as if he was angry. His eyes, cold and hard, found her, drilling into her very soul.

She gasped and took an involuntary step back.

Jake watched them, unblinking, arms placed at his sides. His pajamas, blue with white cartoon elephants parading over them, added to the creepiness, despite the almost comical nature of their subject matter.

He swallowed, opened his mouth to speak.

Sarah held her breath, terrified of what he might say.

"You shouldn't have done that." Jake turned his attention to Tyler, still sitting next to the bed. "She wasn't finished."

"Sorry," Tyler mumbled. He drew his knees up as if he wanted to make himself as small as possible.

"Mommy's very mad," Jake said, his eyes once more finding his sister. "She doesn't like to be interrupted."

Sarah wanted to say something, but stayed silent. Her legs felt like jelly, but she managed to stay on her feet.

Jake took one look around the room, his gaze coming to rest on each of the four teenagers. And then, without uttering another word, he turned and walked back down the stairs.

Only after she heard her brother's bedroom door slam on the floor below was Sarah able to let herself sink to the ground, relieved that the confrontation was over, scared for what might happen next.

Chapter 57

"ARE you sure you have to leave already?" Becca stood on the driveway and watched Logan fish his car keys from his pocket, wishing she could convince him to stay.

"My dad will go berserk if I'm home late." Logan gave an apologetic smile. "You don't know what he's like."

"Can't you call him, ask him if you can stay longer?"

"No chance." Logan took a step toward his car. "But I'll call you next week, I promise. Maybe we can go out to the movies or something."

Becca followed behind, doing her best to quell the disappointment that she felt. "Next week is so far away."

"Then you will miss me that much more." Logan grinned, climbing into his car. He rolled the window down and leaned out. "Besides, it's not like we could do anything, not here."

"Logan." Becca felt her face redden. Thankfully they were out of earshot, but even so, she glanced back toward the others to make sure they hadn't heard.

"What?" He shrugged. "I'm just saying."

"I think you should get out of here." Becca leaned through the window, gave Logan a peck on the cheek.

"Are you sure you will be okay up here?" He looked up at her. "That was pretty scary back there."

"I'll be fine." She glanced over her shoulder toward Tyler and Sarah. "I'm not alone, and I have my phone if anything happens."

"I wish you'd come back with me." Logan started the engine.

"I can't." Becca shook her head. "Sarah needs me. Don't worry."

"Well-"

"You'd better get going before you are late." Becca took a step backward. "Go on."

"Next week." Logan blew her a kiss and pushed the car into reverse, then steered it backward until he could turn around.

Becca watched him pull away before turning back to her friend. Her eyes fell upon Tyler. "What time do you have to be home?"

"I don't." Tyler weaved an arm around Sarah's waist and pulled her toward him. Becca noticed her stiffen for a moment, unsure of herself, but then she relaxed. "I told my mom that I was staying over at my friend Pete's. It's all good."

"You told your parents you were staying at Pete's?" Sarah said. "What if they find out you aren't there?"

"How are they going to find out?" Tyler replied. "If they want to check to make sure I'm alright they can always call my cell phone, and Pete will cover for me if they call him. Don't worry about it."

"Sounds like you've done this before." Sarah pulled away. "Have you snuck out to meet other girls?"

"No." Tyler sounded indignant. "Pete owes me one. I covered for him a few weeks ago, that's all."

"You'd better not be planning to sleep upstairs with us," Becca said. "I don't want to listen to you two making out all night."

"That's not why I'm staying," Tyler said. "I don't think you girls should be alone tonight. Not after what happened."

"A knight in shinning armor," Becca replied.

"You're welcome." Tyler gave an exaggerated bow.

"Except that you arranged all this with Pete beforehand."

"Look, I was hoping Sarah would ask me to stay over. I admit that. But when things got out of hand I decided to stay even if she didn't invite me. I meant what I said, you shouldn't be by yourselves in this house right now."

"You're still not sleeping in the same room as me."

"Fine. I'll take the couch," Tyler reassured her. "Just give me a blanket and a couple of pillows."

"Come on Becca, ease up a bit." Sarah took Tyler's hand on hers. "This whole thing was your idea, remember?"

"I know that." Becca wished that Logan had planned things with as much forethought as Tyler. If so, she would have had no problem with the boys sleeping in the attic bedroom. She wondered if she was being petty, acting out of jealousy, but came to the conclusion that she was not. It didn't feel right to have Tyler up there with them without Logan, and besides, Sarah would not let Tyler fool around with her there anyway, so what was the harm?

"Can we go back inside now?" Tyler shivered. "It's getting really cold out here."

"It is cold." Becca hadn't noticed before, but it seemed more like December than the middle of summer. The sudden chill had come out of nowhere. She shivered and moved toward the door, following the others inside. As she stepped across the threshold she caught a flicker of movement out of the corner of her eye, back where Tyler's car was parked. She turned her head, and for a split second thought she saw the dark outline of a large crow circle up into the night, but then it was gone. She lingered, staring out into the black void above the tree line, her eyes searching for any sign of movement, but whatever had drawn her attention was gone now, swallowed up by the blackness.

"Are you coming in?"

Becca turned to find Sarah looking at her, a quizzical expression on her face.

"Of course." She backed up and closed the front door. "Sorry."

"What were you looking at?" Sarah asked.

"Nothing," Becca replied. Had she really seen a crow? It was unlikely. She was sure birds didn't fly around at night. Maybe it was a bat she'd seen, or maybe it was nothing at all. Just a figment of her over stimulated imagination. That must be it, she told herself. It was simply her mind playing tricks. But even so, as she followed Sarah and Tyler up the stairs, she couldn't quite shake the feeling that there really had been a crow out there, watching them. Worse, she couldn't quell the nagging thought that it was the same bird that had been at the attic window a few days before.

Chapter 58

ANDREW WAS in the hotel bar, on his third scotch of the evening. The book signing had been long and boring, the dinner that followed, a disaster.

Despite Harvey's reassurance that the publishers could be placated by a personal appearance and some well chosen words, that was not the case.

Four weeks.

If the manuscript was not on the table of Bob Knowles, the Editor in Chief, when that deadline expired, he was done. Within days every major publisher, and most of the smaller ones, would view him as a liability. A washed up writer not worth the trouble. Andrew would be persona non grata in New York.

Not that he minded so much. He hated the editorial meetings, the long wait while the book weaved its way through everything from typesetting to marketing. He loathed the business side of things. The writing was the thing that gave him joy, the artistic expression. At least until the well dried up and the words stopped coming.

What he did mind was that without a publisher, the writing

was useless, even assuming he did ever manage another manuscript. There would be no more hefty advances, no more book tours or interviews. He would sink into obscurity until even the royalty checks from his previous books dried up.

And then what?

Take work teaching English at some inner city high school? Farm himself out as an editor? Neither of those jobs sounded appealing, and there were no guarantees that he would succeed at either one.

There was only one thing he could do.

Finish the book.

Even if it sucked. Even if the publishers hated it.

So that was what he would do.

But not before he had another drink.

He signaled the bartender, a gruff looking individual with dragon tattoos snaking down both muscular arms. While he waited for his drink he pulled out his cell phone and tapped out a brief text message to Sarah.

How are things going? Is everything fine at home?

He waited for the reply, wondering if he should have called, not wanting to hear the disdain in Sarah's voice when she realized he was checking up on her.

Better to send the text message.

The drink arrived.

He picked it up, peered into its amber depths.

At that moment the phone buzzed. Two curt words appeared on the screen.

We're fine.

So much for pleasantries. She hadn't even bothered to ask how he was, if his trip was going well. Not that he expected her to. Since Jennifer's death Sarah had become a different person. Dark. Brooding. The once happy teen had turned inward, losing herself inside her own head. There were occasional flashes of the old Sarah, just enough to remind him of all that he had lost, but those moments were few and far between. Islands amid a sea of despair.

The worst thing was he couldn't blame her.

He knew how she felt, because he felt it too.

Andrew took the phone, slid it back into his pocket, and lifted the scotch to his lips, slamming it back in one fluid movement. Then he placed the empty glass back on the bar, and caught the eye of the bartender once more.

Tomorrow he would fly home and try to finish the book, but tonight all he wanted to do was forget.

Chapter 59

THE BEDROOM WAS dark save for the dull glow of the nightlight affixed to the far wall. The only sound came from the nearby bed, the gentle in and out of Sarah's breathing.

Becca rose, her movements stiff at first, as if she were getting used to her own body. She paused near the bed, but Sarah didn't stir. She was deep in slumber.

Next, Becca turned toward the door, her footfalls barely audible as she slipped out of the room and descended the stairs. She padded along the corridor and made her way to the ground floor, before turning toward the living room.

Tyler was asleep on the sofa, his body nothing more than a vague lump under the blankets, his head nestled into two soft pillows propped against the side of the couch.

Becca moved toward him, hovered for a while, watching him sleep, his arm above the blanket, holding it close. She reached down and ran a hand down the exposed arm, her fingers lingering upon his skin, the touch light and gentle.

He stirred, mumbled something.

Becca touched his hair, weaved her fingers through it.

He opened his eyes, looked up.

The surprise on his face was evident.

"What are you doing here?" He asked. "Is something wrong?"

"Nothing is wrong." Becca kept her voice low, barely more than a whisper.

"Where's Sarah?"

"Sleeping."

"So why are you down here?" Tyler sat up, holding the blanket to his bare chest.

"Don't you know?" Becca took a step back, her mouth curving into a tight smile. She never took her eyes from him.

"No, I don't," Tyler said. He paused, then spoke again. "Your voice, it sounds funny."

"How so?" Becca reached up and played with the collar of her nightgown.

"Just different." He shook his head. "I mean, it's you, but somehow it doesn't sound like you. Are you alright?"

"Shhh." Becca put her finger to her lips. Her eyes travelled toward the corridor. "Come with me."

"Why?" There was a trace of suspicion in Tyler's voice.

"I've seen the way you look at me."

"What?" Tyler shrank back. "I don't know what you are talking about."

"Of course you do." Becca moved close. "You want me. You always have. You only dated Sarah to get to me."

"That's not true." Tyler started to rise, looking for an escape route.

"Yes, it is." Becca pushed him back down. Her hands fell to the hem of the nightgown. She lifted it up, the fabric bunching as it came free. She discarded the garment and stood there, wearing nothing but a pair of white panties. She reached out her hand. "Come with me."

"This is so messed up," Tyler said, but his eyes were fixed on Becca's body. "What if Sarah finds out?"

"She won't."

"I can't."

"Yes, you can." She took his hand, pulled him to his feet. "I've wanted to do this for so long."

"Becca-"

"Hush." She turned, walked toward the hallway, with Tyler following behind.

Chapter 60

SARAH WENT from sound asleep to wide awake in an instant. At first, before her consciousness snapped back into place, she wasn't sure why. But then she felt the pair of eyes looking at her in the darkness.

She sat upright, a crawling feeling of dread overtaking her. And then she heard the noise. It was light, just a small shuffle of feet, but it was enough to draw her attention.

Jake stood in the open bedroom doorway, still wearing the elephant pajamas. His arms at his side, face expressionless, he looked like he was standing to attention, a ten year old soldier dressed in bedroom fatigues.

"Jake?" She spoke his name before she even comprehended the oddness of the situation.

He didn't move.

His unblinking eyes fixed her with a deadpan stare that sent another shiver of fear up her spine.

"You should be in bed." She did her best to keep the apprehension from her voice, tried to sound authoritative, but knew the moment the words escaped her mouth that she had failed.

"They're in the barn," Jake said, his eyes never straying from his sister.

"There's someone in the barn?" A barrage of thoughts cascaded through her mind, as if a mental floodgate had opened. Who was in the barn? Were they in danger? Should she call the police? No, better to wake Tyler and make sure there was actually something to worry about before jumping to conclusions based on the information of an imaginative ten year old boy.

"They're in the barn." Jake repeated the words in the same bland monotone as before.

"Who, Jake?" She tried again. "Who do you think is in the barn?"

But Jake didn't answer. Instead he turned and started to descend the stairs without even a backward glance.

Sarah sat there, watching as he disappeared into the gloom, and then she noticed something.

Becca was gone.

Her bed was empty, the covers pushed back off the air mattress.

With a growing sense of unease, Sarah slipped out from under the covers and found her shoes. She grabbed her robe and pulled it on, then hurried to the door, taking the narrow stairs as fast as she dared. She reached the second floor landing in time to see Jake's bedroom door swing shut. At first she considered following him into the room, asking him what was going on, but she knew it would do no good. Jake was different now, odd and a little frightening. She knew something else too, he was getting worse every day. The move to the country, the new house, was affecting him.

Not to mention the old telephone.

She shuddered when she thought of that. There was something unnatural about his obsession with it.

No, it was better to keep going.

She moved down the hallway, made her way to the first

floor. A few feet away, in the living, Tyler would be sleeping. Maybe he could help her find Becca, figure out what was happening.

Only when she reached the couch he wasn't there.

She swiveled, a dreadful fear overcoming her.

They're in the barn.

The words echoed in her mind and all at once she knew that Jake wasn't talking about some random intruders. He was talking about Tyler and Becca.

But why would they be there?

THERE WAS ONLY one way to find out.

She navigated the entrance hall, went to the kitchen, was surprised to find the back door wide open. Without a second thought she passed through it into the night, the sudden chill air making her wrap her arms around her chest as she crossed the patch of grass behind the house.

There were three barns on the property. The one her dad had wanted to turn into a garage, which stood to the side of the house, and then there were the twin cow barns further away. Instinctively she knew that this was where Becca and Tyler had gone.

She passed the swing set off to her left, the weathered seat rocking back and forth in the breeze, the twin chains emitting languid, drawn out squeaks with each slow pass. She shivered at the eerie sound.

Up ahead loomed the barns, a pair of ominous sentinels stark against the backdrop of the Milky Way as it spiraled across the clear night sky.

She reached the barns and paused.

Which one were they in?

She glanced between the buildings.

The one on the left was dark, the double doors shut tight.

But from the one on the right she saw a faint glimmer of light escaping through a crack between the doors.

She had her answer.

A part of her didn't want to go on. It was as if she sensed that some things were best left unseen. But a bigger part, that which had drawn her from the comfort of her bed and brought her out here, needed to know. Even so, she took the last few steps to the barn with a trepidation she had seldom felt before.

Chapter 61

SARAH PEERED through the crack between the barn doors, her heart thudding in her chest. At first she didn't see anything, but then her eyes focused on the two silhouetted shapes half way back, between the cow stalls.

A flashlight was propped up against one stall, the beam piercing the darkness. It wasn't much, but it provided enough illumination for Sarah to recognize Tyler and Becca.

They were locked in an embrace, their arms entwined around each other, their faces together in a passionate kiss.

Sarah let out a startled gasp.

Tyler's head whipped in her direction.

When he saw her, his eyes grew wide, and he staggered backward, leaving Becca alone in the center of the barn.

"This isn't what it looks like." His face was a picture of anguish.

"Then what is it?" Sarah pulled the door open and stepped into the barn. It smelled like old wood and stagnant water, but she ignored the odor.

"She came to me, I swear." He stepped around Becca, who still stood motionless, and approached Sarah. His bare chest stood out a pale white. Below that his jeans were unbuttoned, his belt hanging lose from the loops. "I would never do anything to hurt you."

"You already have." Sarah wondered what would have happened if she hadn't interrupted them. She could feel the tears welling at the corners of her eyes. She brushed them away with the back of her hand, angry that he should see her distress.

"I made a mistake. I don't know what I was thinking. It was like I couldn't help myself." He turned his head toward Becca, as if he was looking for some help, but she remained mute. "She seduced me."

"That's a lame excuse." Sarah walked past him, toward Becca. For the first time she realized that her friend was practically naked. A sudden surge of anger flared up within her. She closed the distance, intent upon unleashing her fury, but at that moment Becca moved.

Slowly at first, she lifted her arms, touched her hands to her face. She stumbled forward, as if surprised to be standing up. Her arms fell back to her side. Her mouth opened, but then she closed it again. Her eyes, which had seemed dull and lifeless before, now widened and came into focus.

She took a shuddering breath, then another, before the comprehension of her surroundings dawned upon her.

"What's going on?" Becca turned her head, her gaze shifting between Sarah and Tyler. She looked confused. "Where are we?"

"Really?" Sarah said, but even so she stopped short. There was something about the look on Becca's face that caused her to falter.

"Where are we?" She repeated the question.

"Like you don't know." Sarah kept an eye on Tyler, who was standing off to one side, a sheepish look upon his face.

"I don't." Becca looked genuinely confused.

"The barn," Sarah answered, a hard edge to her voice.

"How did I get out here?" Becca took a step forward,

glanced down, suddenly aware of her state of undress. A look of horror passed across her face. Her arms flew up to cover her chest. She paused, her eyes darting between Sarah and Tyler, and then, not waiting for an answer to her question, she fled toward the barn door, in the direction of the house.

Sarah, surprised by her sudden flight, stepped out of the way instinctively. She watched her friend disappear into the night, a strange mix of anger and sadness descending upon her. And then she turned to Tyler, fixing him with a glowering stare. "I think it's time you left."

Chapter 62

IT WAS after 4AM when Tyler reversed his Mustang in the driveway, turned around, and made his way down the narrow lane toward the road.

As he passed by the old barn nestled next to the house he tilted his head upward, overcome with the sudden feeling that he was being watched. There, framed in a second floor window, he caught sight of Jake, the boys face pale and emotionless, but soon he was beyond the house and all he could see was a vast expanse of black sky curving toward the distant tree line that marked the edge of the woods.

Tyler turned his gaze forward once more. He focused on the road ahead, avoiding the worst of the potholes that punctuated the driveway, not wanting to hit one in the darkness. Behind him, lingering near the front door, he knew that Sarah waited, unwilling to venture back inside until she was sure he had actually gone.

He couldn't blame her. The events in the barn still seemed bizarre, even to him. Becca had been alluring, intoxicating. It was as if she willed him to follow her, to engage in...

He forced himself to stop thinking about it.

Rehashing his mistake would do no good. He couldn't go

back in time and change things. What he could do was hope that Sarah forgave him after she cooled off.

Up ahead a shape loomed, the blackness falling away as he drew closer to reveal the gnarled, misshapen oak that marked the boundary between the farm and the road. It looked old, its contorted branches reaching out like bony fingers, grotesque and otherworldly.

He slowed, easing the car up to the intersection, even though he knew there would be no traffic. There were barely any other vehicles on the road during the day, let alone at this time of night. He flicked the indicator on anyway, out of habit, then nosed the car forward, turning onto the hard asphalt. As he did so, his eyes flicked up to the rearview mirror, another habit. To begin with he saw nothing but empty road stretching away from him, but then, at the corner of the reflection, his eye picked out a movement.

It was slight.

Nothing more than a quick, darting shadow.

His breath quickened.

A shape broke away from the oak tree, small and nimble, flitting out from the branches. He watched it rise into the sky, following along behind the car.

At first he wondered what it could be, his heart pounding, but then, when it drew closer, he almost laughed out loud.

It was a bird.

A big ugly crow, its wings a flurry of movement as it swooped toward the car.

He turned his attention forward again, pressing down on the accelerator. The engine surged under his foot, and the Mustang shot forward, putting some distance between himself and the bird. When he glanced back again it was gone, lost to the gloom.

Tyler let out a relieved sigh, unsure why the bird had spooked him so much, but glad that it was gone. He let up on the gas, the speedometer needle falling back, and settled into the seat.

And then he realized how cold the car was. He could see his breath on the air. It was weird, because he didn't remember it being cold when he climbed in. It was the middle of summer. The night was warm.

He reached for the heater, was about to turn it on.

At that moment he had the overwhelming sense that he was not alone.

He glanced sideways.

A lump of fear caught in his throat.

The passenger seat was not empty.

A figure sat there, features obscured by the dark cabin. Even so, Tyler knew it was a woman. He also knew she was not real, at least in the living sense.

She turned her head, empty eye sockets coming to bear upon him, and in that moment he felt a wave of malice so strong it made his gut churn.

Too late he realized that in his moment of shock he'd let the steering wheel go slack.

The car swerved across the road, careening toward the verge, and the woods beyond.

Tyler's foot flew to the brake.

It wasn't enough.

The car left the road, jumped over the grass, and took a nosedive into the drainage ditch running alongside the blacktop.

Tyler's body slammed forward with the sudden impact, his seatbelt cutting across his chest, drawing taut.

The car pivoted sideways toward a large maple tree.

There was a sickening thud.

Glass rained down as the window shattered inward.

Tyler's head jerked sideways and hit the doorframe. Searing pain exploded in his skull and down his spine. He felt blood in his mouth.

The car came to an abrupt halt with the back wheels in the air, the front of the vehicle submerged in a thick muck.

Jake fought to stay awake, fought against the blackness that closed in on his vision, but soon the world shrank to a dull pinprick, and then even that blinked out.

Chapter 63

FOR THE SECOND time in twelve hours, Sarah stood on the driveway and watched a friend depart Willow Farm.

This time it was Becca.

If it were up to her, Becca would have been gone hours earlier when Tyler drove away, but her friend had refused to go, saying it was a bad idea for Sarah and Jake to be alone in the house. Sarah hadn't argued. The truth was that she didn't relish the thought of spending the rest of the night alone either, and despite the feelings of betrayal, Sarah could not shake the thought that there was more going on than met the eye.

Becca had said as much, pleading for forgiveness. She claimed to have no memory of leading Tyler out to the barn, of seducing him, and seemed so genuinely distraught at the situation, and her circumstance, that Sarah didn't have the heart to demand she leave.

Now though, as the sun warmed the dew laden fields, and the air hummed with the happy chirp of birds, there was no reason to delay the inevitable. Becca might not have any memory of the previous nights events, but that didn't make it any better, or any easier for Sarah to deal with.

"It wasn't me." Becca had said as they sat in the attic room after Tyler left.

"It looked like you." Sarah was still seething with anger.

"I went to bed, the next thing I knew I was out in the barn, half naked, with Tyler." Becca had wiped tears from her eyes, her face a burning shade of crimson. "I still can't believe it."

"So what are you trying to say?" Sarah asked the question even though she suspected what the answer would be.

"The witch." Becca almost spat the words. "It must have been Martha Ward."

"So you were possessed?" The incredulity in Sarah's voice would have been hard to miss at the best of times. "Come on, is that even possible?"

"It's the only explanation I have." Becca shrugged, her face somber. "I never sleepwalk, and I certainly don't hit on boys in my sleep."

"It doesn't change anything."

"I know. You're hurting. That's what she wants. Martha Ward, or whoever she is, is trying to drive a wedge between us, don't you see?"

"What I saw was you and Tyler, together."

"I'm sorry about that. If I could go back and change it I would." Becca took a deep breath, her eyes meeting Sarah's. "I think I should leave tomorrow. Your dad will be back so you and Jake won't be alone in the house."

Sarah nodded, mute.

"I don't want this to ruin our friendship."

Again, Sarah nodded.

"So it's settled. I'll leave tomorrow."

And that was the end of the conversation. Sarah crawled into bed, pulled the covers up, and lay there, unable to sleep until dawn.

Now they were on the driveway and Becca was leaving for

Boston. It didn't feel real. It felt like a horrid dream, but Sarah knew it was not.

"Will you be okay until tonight, when your dad gets back?" Becca asked as she heaved her bag into the Toyota's trunk.

"Of course."

"Well then-" Becca let the words trail off, unsure what to say next.

"Go." Sarah forced a weak smile despite the fear and disappointment writhing in her stomach.

"Call me if you need anything at all." Becca was at the driver's side door. She opened it. "I will turn around and be back here before you know it."

"I will." Sarah watched her friend climb into the car, start the engine. And then the yellow Toyota was crunching gravel as it made a turn and moved away from the house.

Sarah kept her eyes on the car until it reached the old oak and turned onto the main road. Soon it was lost amid the trees lining the highway. Only the engine noise remained, and that too soon faded.

Sarah was alone.

Except for Jake.

That thought didn't give her much comfort.

Chapter 64

WHILE SARAH WAS OUTSIDE, watching Becca depart, a small figure eased itself out of the furthest room on the second floor and padded toward the bathroom. There came the sound of running water, and soon the figure emerged again, a drinking glass grasped in one hand.

The landing, as always, was dark and brooding. With all the doors closed, there were no windows to provide direct sunlight to the interior of the house. This also accounted for the musty smell that permeated the deepest parts of the building, but the boy did not care about that. In fact, he hardly noticed the odor at all as he made his way to the third floor staircase.

Moments later, the glass of water still cradled like a precious cargo, Jake slipped past the mostly closed door into the attic space that had been turned into Sarah's bedroom.

He paused, his eyes flitting from one surface to the next, looking for something. When he saw it, Sarah's most prized possession, her cellphone, he padded quickly forward.

The phone was on the bed, sitting atop the thin comforter with a pattern of interlocking blue circles. He took the device from the bed and held it, before positioning it a few inches above the glass.

He opened his fingers.

The phone plunked into the water with a small splash, only the top third poking above the rim of the glass.

The screen lit up, a brief flare of brightness, and then flickered a couple of times before turning black once more.

He plucked the lifeless cell phone out of the glass, holding it between his thumb and forefinger, and waited for the last of the water to drain from the device, then wiped it on his pajamas and dropped it on the floor.

From below came the sound of a car starting, the low rumble of the engine an indication that his time was limited.

With a flick of his ankle he kicked the sodden phone into the dark space under the bed, making sure that it was out of sight. He turned and retraced his steps back to his own room. He barely made it back before he heard Sarah enter the house, the front door slamming closed as the breeze caught it. Moments later she passed by his room on her way to the top floor.

He placed the glass on the nightstand and settled on the bed. He leaned back, a smile touching his lips. He had done well, followed his instructions to the letter.

His eyes lifted to the old rotary dial telephone perched on the far edge of the bed. He extended an arm, pulled it toward him, and waited for it to ring.

Chapter 65

BECCA PULLED out onto the main road.

Behind her the gnarled oak, and the sprawling fields of Willow Farm, receded into the distance. She passed a sign stenciled with the number 60 in a bold black font. The car's speedometer needle hovered a hair above 40. She was driving twenty miles under the speed limit. Beside her, on the passenger seat, her cellphone lay silent and dark. She had harbored a small hope that Sarah would change her mind. That she would call and ask her to come back. But the further she drove, the less likely that seemed. A pang of regret, tinged with disappointment, flowed through her.

Things were well and truly messed up.

The incident with Tyler had left her shocked and mortified. It also raised another, more disturbing, question. Had she done a similar thing to Sarah's dad? Was that why he had acted in such a strange way the previous day when she took him the forgotten wallet? The thought disturbed her, but short of confronting him, asking him what actually happened, she would never know the answer. She wasn't willing to broach the subject with him, partly for fear of what he would say, and partly because if nothing had happened she would look like a fool.

Better not to know.

At least, that was what she told herself.

Still, she could not shake the conviction that something bad was happening at Willow Farm, and the house in particular. Her thoughts turned to the Ouija board, and the terrifying way the planchette had spelled out words with a life of its own. It was easy to believe that the girls were subconsciously moving it when they were in contact with the pointer, but last night it had moved of its own volition, devoid of any human contact. Given everything that happened in the short time Becca had been in the house, it was obvious that things were not right. Should she call Becca's dad and tell him what they had witnessed? Would he believe her even if she did? Unlikely. She wouldn't have believed it herself if she had not witnessed it all first hand. Which meant she would have to keep quiet and hope the situation didn't get worse. And if it did, she hoped Sarah had the good sense to call her.

Chapter 66

IT WAS after 8PM when Andrew arrived home. The sun was setting low on the horizon, the trees throwing long shadows across the golden landscape.

He pulled up the driveway, parking under the shadow of the old barn, and walked to the house, his overnight bag in one hand, front door keys in the other.

There was no sign of Becca's yellow Toyota. He felt a flash of anger, assuming that the girls had taken off somewhere without telling him, but when he stepped inside he heard footsteps on the landing above, and then Sarah came into view.

"Hey there." He dropped the overnight bag, forced a smile. "where's Becca? Her car is gone."

"She went home."

"Oh." Sarah's tone was icy, and he got the feeling there was something she was not telling him. When she didn't volunteer any further information he spoke again. "Did you guys have a fight?"

"No."

"Is there anything you want to tell me?" Andrew sensed something was wrong, but Sarah was cold and distant, as usual. "You can talk to me you know, I'm your dad."

"I know," Sarah said, her voice flat. "There's nothing."

"How's Jake?" There was no sign of his son, which was unusual. Normally the boy would have come running when Andrew got home.

"He's in his room." Sarah cast a glance back along the hallway. "He's hardly come out since you left, except to eat. All he cares about is that old phone. He's obsessed with it."

"It's just a phone, Sarah." Andrew felt a wave of tiredness sweep over him. He'd hardly slept the night before, despite the copious amounts of whisky in his system, and even on the flight he'd found it hard to relax.

"Whatever." Sarah shrugged and turned, disappearing back the way she had come. After a few seconds he heard her bedroom door slam, and he was alone again.

He picked up the overnight bag and started up the stairs. He made his way to Jake's room, knocked, and opened the door wide enough to peer inside. The boy was on the bed, sitting cross legged, the phone in his lap.

Andrew suppressed an involuntary shudder.

The phone thing certainly was creepy.

Sarah had a point.

He made a note to talk to his son about it tomorrow. Tonight though, he didn't have the energy.

"I'm back." Andrew edged into the room, feeling a little like an intruder in his own home.

Jake glanced his way, unblinking eyes observing him before he turned away again.

The silence was unnerving.

"Did you have a good time while I was gone?" Andrew made another attempt at conversation, hoping for something, anything, to indicate that his son was pleased to see him. "I hope Sarah and Becca did a good job looking after you."

Jake nodded, his gaze cast downward, to the phone.

"Well, good." Andrew shuffled his feet, uncomfortable. "Half an hour and I want you in bed, understand?"

Again Jake nodded a silent reply.

"I'll be back to check on you later."

This time there was no reply, verbal or otherwise.

Andrew lingered in the doorway a while longer, hoping for something more, some flash of the old, happy Jake. But it soon became obvious that the conversation was over, that nothing more would be forthcoming.

He withdrew, pulling the door closed behind him, and turned to his own bedroom, throwing the overnight bag on a chair near the door. He took his jacket off, placed his phone on the nightstand, and sat on the edge of the bed wondering what to do next.

As if in answer, his stomach growled.

How long had it been since he'd last eaten. Ten, maybe twelve hours?

He glanced at his watch.

It was at least that long.

With a sigh he pulled himself up and made his way to the door, then along the landing. He was exhausted, wanted to do nothing more than sleep, but he also knew that if he didn't eat something he wouldn't be able to sleep.

He descended the stairs and went to the kitchen, opened the fridge and pulled out some cold cuts, cheese, and lettuce, made himself a sandwich.

He went to the living room, sank down to the couch, and began to eat. He was surprised at just how ravenous he was, and polished off the makeshift meal in no time at all. He leaned back into the soft, warm cushions and closed his eyes. It felt good and he didn't want to move. Moments later he was asleep.

Chapter 67

BECCA WAS in a deep and dreamless sleep when the text message came in.

The loud chirp awoke her with a jolt.

She lay in the darkness, looking up at her bedroom ceiling, and didn't know what had roused her, but then the phone chirped again.

She sat up, rubbed the sleep from her eyes, and grabbed the phone from her nightstand. As she did so her eyes fell on the alarm clock.

It was gone 10PM.

Who would be texting her at this hour?

She glanced down, but the screen had gone dark already.

A sudden, terrible thought entered her head. What if it was Sarah, and something bad had happened at Willow Farm? A lump caught in her throat. Sarah was the only person who ever texted her this late, and they were hardly on speaking terms, so if the message was from her friend, it couldn't be good.

With shaking hands Becca typed in her passcode and opened the text app.

A flood of relief washed over her when she saw the message.

It wasn't from Sarah. It was Tyler.

She almost didn't open it. After the events of the prior evening there could be nothing good that would come from conversing with him, and if Sarah found out she might never talk to Becca again.

Even so, she had to know what the message said, and eventually she opened it, reading the message quickly, and then reading it again to make sure she understood what it said.

THE WITCH IS REAL BECCA. I saw her. She tried to kill me. Forced me off the road. I'm fine, a concussion and some cuts and bruises. Spent all day at the hospital. The car is totaled and my dad's grounded me. I've sent this to Sarah too. I'm scared. Please make sure she reads it − T.

BECCA COULDN'T RIP her eyes away from the screen. She held the phone in her lap, a creeping tingle of fear edging up her spine. For a while she didn't move, her mind a whir of conflicting emotions. Up until now the spirit of Martha Ward had not done anything to outright harm any of them. It was frightening, but amounted to nothing more than the kind of haunting that the ghost hunter type reality shows on cable TV liked to feature. If the witch really had forced Tyler to crash his car that meant things had crossed a line. They were in unknown territory. It meant that the spirit was much more powerful, and dangerous, than any of them had thought. It also meant that Sarah and her family were in real peril. This was not some mischievous ghost out to wreak a little havoc, but the non-corporeal consciousness of a hate filled woman. What that woman wanted was anybody's guess, but it seemed more and more likely that she was out to do harm. She remembered the priest, and the story he had told them. She didn't want Sarah's family to end up like that. There was only one thing to do. She had to warn them.

She dialed Sarah's number, lifted the phone to her ear.

It took a moment to connect.

The phone rang.

She waited for Sarah to pick up.

Instead, the call went to voicemail.

She ended the call and tried again but once more it clicked over to voicemail.

Perplexed, Becca left a message, then hung up. Sarah was never far from her phone, and even if she was still mad, she would answer, given the circumstances.

Wouldn't she?

Becca wasn't sure.

What she did know was that Sarah would call her back after hearing the message. Except that the phone remained silent.

She called again, three more times.

No answer.

Frustrated, she rattled off a text message. Surely Sarah would see this.

But there was no reply.

The time on her phone said it was 11PM. Almost an hour had passed since Tyler's text message.

Becca felt a stab of fear. There must be something she could do. Sarah's dad owned a cell phone of course, but she didn't know the number. It was dumb that she had never bothered to enter it into her address book, but she hadn't thought a situation would arise where she needed it. Now she wished she had.

And then she remembered the priest. He had given her a card the day they drove into town to speak with him. She pulled her bag close, rummaged around, finding the jeans she wore that day, and there, in the pocket, was the business card.

There were two phone numbers. One was for the church offices, the other was a private cell number. She tapped the second number into the phone and waited.

It wasn't long before a male voice answered.

"Hello?"

"Father Bertram?" Becca said.

"Yes. This is he." The priest cleared his throat. "How may I help you?"

"Father, this is Becca Wright. I came to see you a few days ago with my friend, Sarah."

"Ah. I remember. Willow Farm." There was a softness to his voice that she didn't remember from their previous meeting. It was almost soothing.

"Yes." She paused, wondering how to continue. "I'm back home in Boston. I've been trying to contact Sarah and I can't get through. I think she might be in danger. I need your help."

"I see," Bertram said. "Would this have anything to do with our conversation, with what I told you?"

"It's happening again Father. There's something up at Willow Farm. Something bad."

"Tell me everything you know." The priest's voice was low, but there was a graveness to it that eased any fears Becca had about being taken seriously. "Start at the beginning."

And so she did. She told him about all the things Sarah had told her. The cellar, Jake and the telephone, the incident with the nightlight. She also told him about the Ouija board, and the grave in the woods.

The old priest listened to it all without uttering a word, and then, when she was done he inhaled a long, deep breath, as if filtering the information, absorbing it. When finally he spoke, his tone had changed. Now the soothing bedside voice was back. "Oh my. This is bad. I had hoped that time and neglect might have dissipated whatever negative energies were present in that house. It appears I was wrong."

"So what do we do?" Becca was desperate. She felt helpless.

"You don't do anything, my dear. You stay right where you are," Bertram said. "I shall pay a visit to Willow Farm, make sure everything is fine."

"Okay, if you think that's best. Thank you Father." Becca felt a lump form in her throat. She felt nauseous.

"Keep your phone close at hand. I shall call you when I conclude my visit. Hopefully I will be able to allay your fears."

"Thank you." Becca's hand shook as she held the phone to her ear. The whole thing felt like a bad dream, but she knew it was not.

"You are welcome. Remember, keep your phone close." And with that Bertram hung up.

Becca took the phone from her ear, looked at the screen until it went blank. She felt useless, sitting there in her bedroom while the old priest drove out to Willow Farm. But what else could she do? She was much further away than Father Bertram. It made sense for him to check on things, and hopefully he would call back in half an hour with nothing out of the ordinary to report.

Even so, she couldn't shake the feeling that something was terribly wrong.

Chapter 68

IT HAD BEEN TOO LONG.

Becca cradled the phone in her lap, willing it to ring, but it stayed stubbornly silent. She checked the time every five minutes, wondering why the priest had not called like he promised. The drive from the church to Willow Farm was a short one, and by now he surely must have arrived there.

After forty-five minutes, unable to wait any longer, she dialed his number.

It range once, twice, three times, then went to voicemail. She left a message, fighting back the fear that threatened to choke her.

She called again, with no answer.

This was too much of a coincidence. First Sarah wasn't picking up, and now the priest.

She wasn't willing to sit idly by any longer. She would drive to the farm herself and find out what was going on first hand.

She pushed the covers back, climbed out of bed, careful not to make a sound. Across the hallway, too close for comfort, her parents would be in bed by now.

She found her jeans, slipped them on, and grabbed a t-shirt from the closet. At no point did she turn on a light. She could not afford to be discovered.

Pulling on a pair of old tennis shoes, mainly because they would be easy to sneak out in, she went to her bedroom door and opened it a crack.

The landing was dark. The gap under her parents bedroom door was nothing more than a black slit. Good. They had settled in for the night.

She held her breath, scared that even the tiniest sound would alert someone to her nocturnal excursion, and swung the door wide enough to pass through.

She crept through the house, along the landing and down to the first floor. She lifted her car keys from a hook near the front door and was soon outside.

She stood there for a while, hardly daring to believe that she had actually made it without waking anyone. Her yellow Toyota was parked half a block away, in a resident zone. It only took her a few minutes to walk the short distance and soon she was safely behind the wheel. She glanced at her phone, checking one more time, hoping against hope, but still there was call from Father Bertram, or Sarah. In the end, with a heavy heart, she started the car and eased out into the sporadic late night traffic.

Chapter 69

SARAH LAY ON HER BED, fully clothed despite the late hour. She knew she should undress, climb into bed, but she didn't feel tired.

What she did feel was angry, betrayed, humiliated.

No matter how hard she tried, her mind kept going back to the scene in the barn, Becca had Tyler locked in an embrace. It was a dreadful betrayal made worse by the fact that Becca was her oldest friend. They had known each other since second grade. Becca was like a sister. Even so, a lingering doubt remained. She knew what she had seen, but at the same time, it was so out of character for her friend, that it defied belief. Then there was Becca's claim that she didn't remember taking Tyler out to the barn, seducing him.

None of it made any sense.

The more she thought about it the more she was convinced that Becca was somehow possessed. That she was even entertaining such a notion showed just how much she had changed since moving to Willow Farm. Ghosts were not real, the spirit world was nothing more than the sad delusions of dimwitted people. Except that she no longer held that view.

She had seen, and felt, so many things in this house, that she could no longer ignore the obvious.

Willow Farm was haunted, and the brunt of that haunting appeared to be aimed at her.

She lay there for a little while longer, her mind churning the events of the past few days. She regretted asking Becca to leave, wished she was still there. Even though her dad was back Sarah felt vulnerable, lonely. She was also scared of what might happen next. It was at that moment that she made up her mind. She would call Becca, clear the air.

She rolled over, reached out for her phone, which was usually on the nightstand.

It wasn't there.

Puzzled, she sat up and checked the bed, wondering if it had gotten covered by the comforter, but there was no sign of it on the bed either.

That was odd.

She stood up, checked the dresser, her pockets, but still nothing. Had she left it downstairs? She didn't think so. So where was it?

Sarah checked the bed again, hoping that she had missed it the first time, but came up empty. And then a thought occurred to her. Maybe it had fallen on the floor. She knelt down, checked beside the nightstand, then lifted the bed skirt and peered under the bed.

At first she didn't see anything, but as her eyes adjusted to the gloom she picked out a shape, flat and oblong.

Her cell phone.

She reached under, but it was out of reach. How could it have ended up so far in? If the phone had fallen off the bed it should be right there, close to the edge, not almost in the middle. Maybe she had kicked it and not noticed.

She flattened herself on the floor, pushed her arm further under. Her shoulder came up against the bedframe, preventing her from reaching any further. She extended her fingers. They brushed against the phone but she could not grasp it. With a grunt she repositioned herself, sliding her shoulder down and straining as far into the gap between the bed and the floor as she could. Now she had enough reach to inch the phone forward with her fingers until she could get a grip.

With a triumphant exclamation she pulled the phone free, and sat on the floor with the device in her hands.

Only something wasn't right.

The phone would not turn on.

The career remained black and unresponsive no matter how many times she pressed the power button.

The battery must be dead.

She stood and went to her nightstand, plugged the phone in, waited for the familiar lightning bolt icon to appear on the screen to show it was charging, but still nothing happened.

She unplugged it, examined it.

She could see nothing wrong, except that when she turned it over to inspect the back casing, a few drops of water leaked from the small speaker slit above the screen.

She turned it frontward again, confused, and noticed something she had not seen before.

Inside the phone, clinging to the back of the screen, were hundreds of tiny beads that moved and ran in rivulets when she tilted the device. At first she wasn't sure what she was looking at, and then it dawned on her.

The phone was waterlogged.

That was why it wouldn't turn on. The electronics were fried, shorted out.

She held the useless phone in her hand and stared at it, wondering how it could have gotten wet. Not that it mattered. Either way she wasn't calling Becca.

Chapter 70

ANDREW OPENED HIS EYES, and at first he wondered where he was, and why his neck ached. But then he remembered. He was on the couch in the living room. He had sat down to eat a sandwich and must have dozed off. He glanced at his watch. It was almost midnight.

He sat up, rubbed the nape of his neck where a dull pain throbbed from being in such an awkward position for so long.

It would be worse tomorrow.

There were pain killers in the upstairs bathroom. He struggled to his feet, stretched, yawned, and made his way to the stairs. On the second floor he turned left, to the bathroom, but then he paused. Across the hallway his office door stood open a hair, and beyond that was something much better than Aspirin.

Andrew listened, but the house as silent. No doubt Sarah and Jake were both sleeping.

He crossed the hallway and entered the study, turning on the light. He turned to the desk, which was emptier than usual. His laptop was still in the overnight bag in his bedroom. He would get it later. It was the other object absent from the desk that Andrew was really interested in.

The bottle of vodka.

He wondered if Sarah had been in here, had found it and poured it away. That didn't seem right. Even if she had it would be back by now, reappearing as if by magic.

And then he remembered.

The bottle wasn't there because he had hidden it.

Damn.

He would have to go all the way back downstairs and retrieve it from the cellar where he'd stashed it the morning before. A part of him thought that was too much work, but another part, a bigger part, wanted to taste the liquor, to feel it sliding down, taking the pain away.

And not just the pain in his neck. No, it would ease the sense of hopelessness he'd felt since the meeting the previous evening.

Four weeks.

That was a ludicrous timeframe to complete a book.

Andrew felt the frustration rising again. He choked it down, forced it back, and turned to the door. A few moments later he was at the bottom of the stairs, on his way to the cellar, and the bottle of booze that waited there, patient and ready.

Chapter 71

JAKE STOOD at his bedroom door, which was cracked open an inch or two, and squinted through the narrow gap, oblivious of the darkened room behind him. A door opened along the corridor. His father emerged and turned to go downstairs. When the coast was clear he crept out into the corridor.

From down below he heard the creak of the basement door, the unoiled hinges protesting the work.

He stopped, waited to make sure his father had time to reach the bottom of the cellar steps, before continuing on.

It was all happening exactly as his mother had said it would. He wished he could have stayed in his room, talking to her on the old telephone, but she had been most insistent.

Jake didn't want to upset her, so he did what she asked.

Now he was at the head of the stairs, looking down. A tremor of apprehension gripped him. What if his dad came back and caught him before he could complete his task?

But that would not happen.

He must keep going and do as he was told like a good boy. Because deep down he was a good boy, and soon, very soon, he would see his mother again. She had promised him that.

She had asked him if he would like to come and join her,

live with her and never have to worry about anything, ever again. And he had said yes. But only if his dad and Sister could come too. He wanted them to be a family again. Whole. Complete.

She had agreed, like he knew she would. Of course they would be a family again. But first he had to do something, and it would take a lot of courage, and he must not let anyone stop him, not dad, not Sarah, because they didn't understand.

They would soon though.

And they would thank him for bringing everyone together again.

Jake smiled when he thought of that. A flutter of excitement filled his belly. This was going to make everything right, put things back to the way they used to be. It wouldn't be long now.

With a renewed sense of purpose, Jake took a step forward, careful not to make a sound, and kept going.

Chapter 72

SARAH WAS STILL CONTEMPLATING the unusual fate of her cell phone with a mixture of confusion and anger, when she heard the faint thud of a door closing.

A tiny vibration shook the windows facing the rear of the house.

This only happened when someone opened the back door.

She leapt to her feet, crossed the room and peered out, wondering who would be going outside at such a late hour.

It was pitch black in outside, and at first she couldn't see anything, but then the moon rolled from behind a high bank of clouds and the landscape was washed with a pale white glow.

It didn't take long for her to spot the diminutive figure crossing the open space between the house and the barns, moving with stealthy ease.

Jake.

What on earth was he up to now?

He had never been secretive, or moody, but since moving to Willow Farm her brother had changed. He had become introspective, quiet. Worse, there was a distinct shift in his interactions with the rest of the family. And then there was the odd obsession with that telephone. That he thought their mother was somehow on the other end of the line – the dead, unconnected line - was creepy enough. But there were other things. The disappearance of the Ouija board pointer, showing up later in his bedroom, and the way he appeared at odd times with cryptic messages. And then her mind made a connection. Had Jake tampered with her phone, broken it deliberately? She could not think of any other way that it would have gotten waterlogged, and his recent behavior seemed to point in that direction. She didn't believe for a moment that he had stumbled across the Ouija pointer. It had been in her room along with the board, and neither she nor Becca had moved it, so that left one unnerving possibility. Jake was mooching around her room when she wasn't there.

He had taken the pointer, hidden it, and then given it back to her at a later time. For what reason she was not sure. Who knew how many other times he had snuck up when she was not there, poking through her personal possessions.

She shuddered.

The more she thought about it, the more she was convinced that Jake had sabotaged the cell phone. And now he was up to some other mischief.

How he had managed to slip out without their father catching him was anyone's guess, but he hadn't been that clever. Letting the back door swing closed instead of stopping to ensure it didn't slam was a mistake. If not for that she would never have been drawn to the window, would not have noticed his furtive escape. No matter how clever he thought he was being, he was still a ten year old boy.

She watched him move past the swing set.

He was half way across the yard now, still heading toward the barns. What reason could he possibly have for going there at this time of night? It didn't make sense.

One thing was certain. There was no way he was up to any good, and besides, it wasn't safe for him to out there at night. Who knew what was in those barns. He might put his foot through a rotten board, or trip and fall in the darkness.

That left her with a dilemma. Should she alert her dad to Jake's odd nocturnal outing, or deal with the situation herself? She had no desire to get him into trouble, partly because she felt some small measure of sympathy for him. Like her, he was trapped out here, miles away from his friends, but it must be worse for him. At least she could escape to Salem or Danvers if she wanted, and most of her friends had cars. They could drive out here to visit her. Soon she would have a car of her own and then there would be total freedom. Jake wasn't old enough to look drive, or take off on his own, so he was a prisoner in this place, totally at the mercy of her father's schedule until school started in the fall.

She knew what she must do.

She would follow Jake, go out to the barn and put an end to whatever he was doing. Being caught by his sister would be enough to send him scurrying back to his bedroom for the rest of the night.

Problem solved.

If her dad appeared, if he caught her leaving the house, then she would tell him about Jake. She wanted to cover for her brother, but not enough to get into trouble for him.

She went to the closet, grabbed a coat, and crossed the room. She would have to be quiet. Her dad had a habit of staying up late and was, more than likely, still in his study. There was also a good chance that he was drunk, at least if recent events were anything to go by. She wondered if she should check on him, make sure he hadn't found another bottle of liquor. But that would derail her plan to retrieve Jake unnoticed.

She gripped the door handle and turned it, expecting the door to open.

It didn't budge.

Perplexed, she tugged again.

Still it didn't move.

Surprised, she stepped back. The door didn't have a lock, and even if it did, the lock should be on the inside, not the outside. Maybe it was stuck. This was an old house. Even in Boston her bedroom door would stick once in a while if there was a change in the weather. Except that the door wasn't sticking earlier in the night. In fact, she hadn't noticed it sticking at any time, even when it was raining.

Determined not to let it beat her, she tried one more time, putting all her might into it, but to no avail. It was as if someone had drawn a bolt on the other side, which she knew was impossible.

She let out a howl of frustration and tugged at the handle, desperate to get the door open, but all she succeeding in doing was to leave angry red marks on her palm where the handle dug in.

She stepped back, her breath coming in ragged gulps, and then pounded on the door with her fists, all thought of saving Jake from her father's wrath abandoned. Except that her father did not come running.

A tremor of fear coursed through her.

She retreated to the bed and sat on the edge, glaring at the stubborn door, wondering what to do next.

But try as she might, she could not think of a way out of her situation. She was a prisoner in her own room.

Chapter 73

ANDREW MADE his way across the cellar. Above him the lone light bulb flickered, creating shadows that leaped and danced across the floor.

He reached the hutch and opened the doors, moving the various cans and bottles, pushing them aside, and reached in.

His fingers closed over the neck of the vodka bottle, and he pulled it free. He held it up to the light, relieved to see that it was full, as always. The bar was open. A flood of satisfaction flowed through him. He felt a subtle anticipation. A few more minutes and everything would be alright for a while, thanks to the never ending stream of liquor. Maybe he should open a bar, he mused, stifling a bitter laugh. At least the booze would never run out. Of course, it would be a rather dull establishment, a one trick pony. If you didn't like vodka, you were out of luck.

He pushed the old tins back in place – he might need this hiding place again – and swung the cabinet doors shut, then turned away.

From somewhere up above he thought he heard a footstep, then the sound of a door closing. Sarah maybe?

He would have to be careful. He didn't want her to catch him with the bottle. She would throw a fit.

Just like Jennifer.

His wife always abhorred his habit of drinking when he wrote. Sarah was very much like her mother, and he saw more of Jennifer in her every day.

A pang of regret tugged at his heart. If only he had gone with her that day. Things would have been different. They might have left a few minutes earlier, or a few minutes later. He might have taken the keys and drove. One small change was all it would have taken to avoid the accident. Jennifer might still be here.

Now he needed that drink more than ever.

The irony was not lost on Andrew. Jennifer hated his drinking, and now he drank to ease the pain of her demise. Somewhere up above, she was surely frowning upon him, shaking her head. Not that it mattered. She wasn't around to stop him.

Only Sarah.

As long as he avoided her, made sure she didn't see him retreating back to the study, he would be in the clear. More to the point, he could finally slip a much-needed double down his throat.

He was at the stairs now. They rose above him, a rickety affair cobbled together with coarse wood and lacking even a railing. If it were not for the fact that they hugged the wall he wasn't sure the stairs would even stay upright. He wondered how old they were. The farmhouse itself was well over two hundred years, and the steps looked like they might be original. He made a mental note to replace them at some point, or at least shore them up so that they didn't give way.

Up ahead he could see the bright patch of yellow light from the hallway, the glow spilling down through the open door onto the first few treads.

He shivered.

The cellar was very cold all of a sudden, as if an arctic wind had invaded the space. He quickened his pace, climbing the last few stairs and reaching the top with a sigh of relief.

He stepped forward toward the door.

At that exact moment two things happened in unison.

The door moved, slowly at first but picking up steam, and slammed with a loud thump. At the same time there was a swift pop, followed by the tinkle of glass, and the cellar light went out.

Andrew, startled and blind, recoiled.

Too late he realized his mistake.

His heel teetered on the edge of the step, and he felt himself tipping backwards. He fought to regain his center of gravity, reached out for a handhold that wasn't there. As his foot slipped off the step he twisted, turning in an effort to stave off the inevitable. But there was nothing he could do, and soon he was airborne.

Not for long.

He hit the next step, half on his side. A jolt of pain shot up his arm. His breath burst out in one almighty whoosh. And then he was tumbling toward the hard packed earthen floor below. The vodka bottle, which had somehow remained wedged between his chest and arm, jarred lose and bounced off into the darkness. A second later it exploded somewhere far below.

Andrew clawed at the rough stairs, hoping to gain some purchase, but it was hopeless. His own momentum carried him down, each twist bringing a new stab of pain, until there were no more steps left.

He hit the ground hard, his head whipping back and smacking against the floor.

And then there was nothing.

Chapter 74

SARAH PACED BACK AND FORTH, a tight knot of fear twisting in her stomach. For a while she had banged on the door, but it was no use. Every few minutes she made another futile attempt to escape, tugging at the handle until she was sure it would come away in her hands.

She went to the window and looked out over the pitched roof, wondering if she could crawl out and climb down somehow. She soon realized the risk involved with that course of action. Even if she managed to navigate the sloped roof without tumbling off, there was still the matter of a two floor sheer drop, over twenty feet, to reach the ground. She could not remember if there was a drainpipe nearby, but even if there was, it might not hold her weight.

Her eyes found the darkened shapes of the barns. Somewhere inside one of them was Jake. She wondered what he was doing. If she opened a window she could call out, attract his attention. He could come up and open the door from the outside, or alert her father of the situation. However, somewhere deep inside, she had a feeling her brother would be no help, and although she could not explain it, a part of her was frightened of him.

If she were going to do anything, now would be the time. She watched the barn door open. Jake's small frame appeared. He was walking at a slower pace now, struggling with something that he held with both hands. His lumbering steps looked awkward. She leaned close to the glass, her breath causing a fog of condensation. She wiped it away and peered down, trying to see what he was holding.

As he drew closer she got a clear view, and the knot of fear turning into a writhing ball of terror.

A gas can.

Jake was carrying an old metal gasoline container, the type used to fill tractors and mowers. Judging by the way he shambled forward, almost stumbling under the weight, it was full.

Her mind raced. What was he doing? Why was he dragging the gas can back to the house? There was only one reason she could think of. She stepped away from the window, a rising surge of panic overwhelming her. When she reached the bedroom door, she starting pounding on it with a renewed sense of urgency, tugging with all her might. She screamed at the top of her lungs, aware that with each passing second Jake drew closer to the house with his deadly cargo. She stepped back, went to the window. There was no choice. The only way out, the only route to safety, was over the roof.

She released the latch, pulled up on the bottom pane.

The window didn't move. Like the door, it was stuck in place.

She howled in frustration, moved to the other window, pried at the frame, but that would not budge either.

And then she saw the chair, a pile of dirty clothing stacked upon it like some laundry tower of babel.

If the windows would not open, she would try a more direct approach.

She tossed the clothes aside, sweeping them onto the floor. She picked up the chair, struggling under the weight, and heaved it against the windowpane with all the strength she could muster.

It bounced off, useless.

She tried again.

The window shuddered but didn't break.

Terrified, she let the chair slip from her grasp and sank to the floor, sobs wracking her body. There would be no escape. That much was clear. She was powerless to stop Jake. All she could do was wait.

Chapter 75

IT DIDN'T TAKE Becca long to weave her way through Boston. Traffic was light, thanks in part to the late hour. She kept below the speed limit, despite the nagging fear that gnawed at her, but still she made good time.

After leaving the city behind she snapped on her full beams, and pushed the car a little faster. A few times she caught sight of deer grazing by the side of the road, their eyes glinting in the glare of her lights. As she flew by they turned and bolted back into the woods.

By the time she saw the turnoff for Willow Farm, her anxiety had reached a crescendo. She eased up on the gas ready to make the turn up the dirt trail leading to the house.

And then she was slamming on her brakes.

The car came to a juddering halt, half into the turn.

In front of her, blocking the driveway was a squat, dark shape with two glowering red eyes.

At first she couldn't tell what it was.

She leaned forward, peering though the windshield. Then it dawned on her.

A car.

Another vehicle was sitting there, unmoving. The red glow

was not a pair of eyes, but taillights. And now she could see the twin beams of headlamps piercing the darkness ahead of the motionless car.

Her mind raced.

There was not enough room to squeeze past the car, and it wasn't going anywhere. So that left one option.

She pulled over to the side of the road, parked up on a narrow strip of grass, and got out.

A new fear gripped her as she approached the stricken vehicle. The situation felt very wrong. She wasn't sure she wanted to know why the car was sitting motionless in the darkness. She prayed that Sarah was not inside. Her mind flew back to the priest's story about the last family to own the house.

She reached the driveway, rounded the car, coming up along the drivers side.

To her left the dead oak tree rose out of the night, even more sinister than she remembered, branches straining outward, contorted and misshapen. She shuddered and ignored the tree, focusing on the car.

She leaned in toward the driver's door, peering through the window.

Her heart skipped a beat.

There was someone inside. She couldn't see much in the darkened interior, but there was a shape slumped over the wheel.

She reached down, tugged at the door handle.

The shape was still. Unmoving.

"Hello?" Her voice sounded small. "Are you okay?"

There was no response.

She took a deep breath and leaned inside the car, took the prone form by the shoulders and heaved it from the wheel.

It was Father Bertram. A trickle of blood had crusted on his forehead. He must have slammed forward when the car came to a halt.

She put her hand to his chest, was relieved to find that he was still breathing.

And then she noticed the windshield.

It was caved in, a ragged hole in the middle where something had pierced it - A tree branch.

He must have been turning onto the trail when a branch came off the oak tree and struck the car. No wonder he hadn't answered his phone.

She took a step backwards, shocked.

Surely this was no accident.

What were the odds of a limb falling at the exact moment the priest was passing beneath? It wasn't very likely.

Martha Ward.

For some reason she didn't want the priest to reach the house.

That thought terrified Becca.

It meant that something was happening, something awful, just like all those years ago.

She glanced back at her car.

Could she move the priest's vehicle to the side of the road, give herself enough room to pass by? It seemed unlikely. She would have to move Father Bertram from the drivers seat, and then hope that the car started. Also, there was the matter of a heavy tree limb pinning the car down. It was hopeless. There was only one way she was going to reach the house, and there was no time to waste.

She checked the priest one more time, did her best to make him as comfortable as possible, and then she turned and began the long walk up the trail.

Chapter 76

ANDREW AWOKE to a wall of pain.

He groaned and reached up, touching his head, which felt like it had lost an argument with a sledgehammer. When his fingers found the lump on his crown he winced.

It was pitch black.

He fought to remember the moments before the fall. He was at the top of the stairs, stepping toward the hallway, and then the door was swinging closed in his face. After that there were a few seconds of gut wrenching terror as he struggled to stay on his feet. The next thing he knew he was hitting the ground, crashing into the metal shelving at the bottom of the stairs, feeling it start to topple.

The cellar light bulb had gone out too, right about the time the door slammed. He had heard the pop when it blew.

That was why he couldn't see anything now.

Andrew sat up, his head throbbing at the sudden movement. He would have given anything for an aspirin. Did he have a concussion?

It was hard to tell in the darkness.

Once he got out of the cellar he would check himself for damage, take a couple of pain killers, and make sure he wasn't seeing double. He extended an arm until his hand came in contact with the granite wall that formed the foundation of the house. Somewhere off to his right were the stairs.

He was sure he could find them, even in the darkness.

He extended an arm until his hand came in contact with the granite wall that formed the foundation of the house. Somewhere off to his right were the stairs.

He leaned on the wall and pushed upward, struggling to regain his feet.

A searing bolt of pain exploded in his ankle.

He let out a cry and leaned against the wall, his foot in the air. This was not good. He must have twisted it when he fell.

Or worse, it could even be broken.

That was not a pleasant thought. It would be almost impossible to mount the stairs with a broken ankle.

Regardless, he had to get out of the cellar.

Andrew took a deep breath, pushed off again, favoring the damaged ankle this time.

Standing on one foot, he let the other touch the ground, shifting his weight, testing it. No sooner had he done so than the pain flared up again.

He stifled a yelp, waited for the throbbing pain to recede to a manageable level, and then took a step forward, using the wall as a brace. He limped along, trying not to use his damaged ankle more than necessary, until his foot found the bottom step.

Relief washed over him. He was closer to escaping.

But now there was a new problem.

He would have to put more weight on the ankle in order to climb the stairs. There was a handrail, but it was old, rickety. He was sure it wouldn't provide much support.

Even so, he had no choice but to continue.

He put his foot on the first tread. Just as before, the ankle buckled under him, sending bolts of white-hot pain up his leg.

He waited for the pain to ebb away, then tried again. This

time he gripped the handrail, shifted some of the burden off his foot, and it was better.

Except that when he tried to climb to the second step, his shin banged into something large, blocking the stairway. He cursed and leaned forward, hands grasping in the dark for whatever was in his way.

It was the shelving he had crashed into when he fell. It must have toppled across the steps.

Andrew fumbled around, feeling for a way past, but there was none. He took hold of it, pulled. The shelf inched forward, but then stopped.

He tried again, balancing on his good foot, but the shelf would not move. It was stuck, and there was no way he was going to be able to climb over it with his injured ankle.

Worse, he could feel a sticky wetness on the treads. At least one of the paint cans stored on the shelving had burst open when it fell, which meant the stairs were also slippery.

He wasn't going anywhere.

Andrew slumped down onto the bottom step.

If only the light as still on, if the bulb hadn't blown, he might stand a chance of getting out, but the cellar was a void of swirling blackness.

It was cold too.

Freezing in fact.

This was new. He didn't think it had been cold when he came to. He wondered if it was a sign that he did indeed have a concussion.

But then, off to his left there was a sound that made his blood run cold. It was low, almost indiscernible, but he was sure he'd heard it.

A cackle.

Was someone in the cellar with him?

His mind flew back to the day Sarah had run, scared, from the cellar claiming that something was down here. At the time he'd dismissed it was nothing more that a teenage girl's over-active imagination. Now he wasn't so sure.

The laugh came again, closer this time.

There was no doubt this time. He was not alone in the cellar. A tight wad of fear balled in his throat. He struggled to pull a breath in. His eyes darted around, looking for the origin of the sound, but all he saw was inky darkness.

"Who's there?" He called out, hoping it would be Jake or Sarah fooling around, knowing deep down that it was not.

The only response was a light shuffling sound, off to his left.

Andrew recoiled.

The air was frigid now. Goosebumps covered his skin.

The shuffling came again, closer this time. He shuddered, something to come at him out of the blackness at any moment. He drew in a sharp breath, tried to control the surging panic. All he wanted to do was jump up and flee, get as far away from whatever was in the cellar as possible. Except that he was blind. He would kill himself trying to climb over the fallen rack and spilled paint cans, especially with the damaged ankle. That only left one place to go, and he had no desire to retreat further into the cellar. At least he had the illusion of a way out if he stayed where he was.

The shuffling was so close now that the hairs on the backs of his arms stood up.

He held his breath, afraid that even the slightest noise might attract the attention of whatever was out there in the blackness.

And then something grazed his cheek, and Andrew started to scream.

Chapter 77

JAKE ENTERED THE KITCHEN, letting the door slam behind him. There was no need for stealth now. In a few minutes everything would be different.

From beyond the hallway he heard muffled cries. Jake paused. It was his father, trapped in the cellar. Mom had said she would take care of everything, and she did. His dad would only have to wait a few minutes more, and then, when everything was done, when Jake had completed his task, his father would thank him, because they would all be together once more.

Jake felt a rush of anticipation.

Soon he would see mom, and she would hold him, and kiss him, wrap her arms around him in a big hug, like she used too.

But first there was the small matter of the gas can. It was heavy, the sloshing liquid making it hard to handle. He set it down on the floor and twisted the cap. It protested at first, but then moved, rust flakes falling away as he unscrewed it.

A waft of fumes escaped through the spout. He wrinkled his nose against the strong gasoline smell, and heaved the can again, tilting it forward until the liquid inside spurted out.

Then he started forward, letting the gasoline splash up the sides of cabinets, and over the floor until the can was empty.

He let it drop from his hand.

It hit the floor with a metallic thud and teetered briefly before coming to rest on its side.

He admired his handiwork, a slight smile touching his lips. But there was still more to be done. He went to the back door, and out into the night once more. There was a second gas can in the barn. He would retrieve it and make sure to give everything a thorough dousing, just to be sure.

And then came the fun part.

Chapter 78

BECCA HURRIED UP THE DRIVEWAY.

She ran as fast as she dared, ignoring the stich that stabbed at her right side. She reached the house, passing the barn, and Andrew's car, and raced up to the front door.

She was about to knock when she hesitated.

What if there was nothing wrong at all? She would look foolish. Worse than that, Sarah's dad would probably call her parents and then all hell would break loose. But on the other hand there was an unconscious man in a car at the end of the driveway, and no one from the house had bothered to investigate. Surely they must have seen the headlights.

No, something was wrong. She knew it.

Becca made up her mind.

She hammered on the door and waited.

Nobody came to answer.

She rapped again, louder this time.

The seconds ticked by, becoming a minute, then two. Still nothing. The house might as well be empty, except that she knew that it was not.

Pulling her phone out, she dialed Sarah's number again,

even though she didn't think it would do any good. She was right. It rang twice then went to voicemail.

Damn.

She gripped the door handle, jiggled it.

Locked.

There was only one thing left to do. The door featured a central frosted glass pane made up of several leaded panels. She would have to break it. The problem was, she didn't have anything that would do the job. There would be something in the car though. A tire iron would do the trick. Except that she would have to go all the way back to the road, and then return. It would take far too long. She needed something closer - But what?

Her eyes alighted on the flowerbeds on each side of the door. More precisely, on the rows of bricks, stuck half in the ground at forty-five degrees, that made up the edging. She bent over, selected a suitable brick, and pried it from the ground. At first it resisted, but then it came free, trailing dirt and grime.

She felt a brief sense of satisfaction, until she remembered what she had to do with the brick.

If there really as nothing wrong, this would be breaking and entering. She wasn't sure if Sarah's dad would call the cops, but she didn't want to find out. Regardless, she had to follow through, because the alternative, that the family was in trouble, was much worse.

She gripped the brick tight in one hand, heaved it back, and brought it down on the glass with all the strength she could muster.

The brick bounced back, jarring her wrist.

She leaned in.

The glass was chipped, with a spider web of fine cracks radiating out from the point of impact. Not bad for a first try.

She brought her arms back and swung again, letting out a grunt. This time the brick didn't bounce off. It kept going amid a hail of glass. She almost lost her grip, but managed to hang on. When she saw the ragged hole in the empty window she used the brick to knock the last shards of glass away, then threw it back toward the flower bed before reaching through. Her fingers found the latch, and then she was inside.

The smell hit her the moment she crossed the threshold. She stopped, gagged. It burned the back of her throat, lingered in her nostrils.

Gasoline.

Why did the house smell like gas?

She felt a stab of fear. This was so much worse than she had imagined.

"Sarah?" She called out, hoping to hear a response.

There was nothing.

She ran through the house, went to the kitchen. The smell was worse here, and she could see that the floor was slick and wet. This was where the odor was coming from.

The back door was wide open.

She went to close it, thought better of the idea. The open door would allow some of the fumes to dissipate.

She turned and raced from the room. By the time she reached the front of the house a faint cry reached her ears.

It was coming from the cellar.

She changed direction, opened the cellar door and peered into the darkness beyond. Seeing nothing, she pushed a hand into her pocket and pulled out her phone, activating the flashlight. When she shone the beam downward she gasped.

There, at the bottom of the stairs was Andrew. He sat on the bottom step, trapped behind a heavy metal shelf unit that had fallen across the steps. Paint cans and boxes were strewn all about.

He looked up at her, a mixture of surprise and relief registering on his face. "What are you doing here?"

"I couldn't reach Sarah on the phone. I was worried." She took a step into the cellar. "Are you alright?"

"I busted my ankle. I can't climb over this stuff." He nodded toward his leg. "I fell."

"What's going on? The back door is wide open, and there is gasoline all over the place. One spark and the whole house will go up in flames."

"What?" Andrew looked shocked.

"Hang on," Becca said, dragging a side table across the floor and wedging it against the cellar door to stop it from closing. "I'm coming down to get you."

"No." Andrew shook his head. "Find Sarah and Jake first. I can wait."

"But..."

"Don't argue with me," Andrew said, his voice hard, commanding. "Get them, then you can help me."

She looked at him, wavering between helping him anyway and doing as she was told.

"Go." Andrew shouted the word. "Now."

Becca jumped, startled.

She lingered a second longer, and then, seeing the look on Andrew's face, turned fled down the hall.

Chapter 79

SARAH HAD all but given up on trying to get out of the bedroom when she heard footsteps pounding up the stairs. To begin with she thought it must be her dad, but then, to her surprise, Becca's voice drifted through the door.

"Sarah?"

"Becca. I'm stuck I here. The door won't open." She wondered what her friend was doing back at the house, how she had known they were in trouble, but she could ask those questions later. There were more important things to worry about right now. "Please hurry."

"Hold on." There was a pause, then the door handle rattled. "I can't get it open either. I don't understand it. Are you sure you don't have it locked on your side?"

"No," Sarah replied. "There isn't even a lock on the door. Can you find something to break it down?"

"I don't know," Becca said. "I'd need something heavy, like a sledgehammer."

"I don't think we have one of those." Sarah paused. A sudden fear gripped her. "Where's my dad, is he alright?"

"The cellar," came the reply. "He took a fall down the stairs."

"Oh no. Is he-" She couldn't bring herself to finish the sentence. Her heart pounded in her chest.

"No. He hurt his ankle and the stairs are blocked. He told me to come find you and Jake before helping him. Your brother is nowhere to be found."

"Jake is outside. He's fetching gas cans from the shed. I'm so scared. I don't know what he's planning but it can't be good. Please hurry." Sarah felt her lip tremble. She fought back a sob.

"There's no way I'm going to get this door open. What about..." Becca stopped mid sentence. Then she spoke again, quicker now. "Hang on. I have an idea."

"What?" Sarah said, praying that Becca knew how to open the door. "Tell me."

"I have to go downstairs. Hang on." And then she was leaving, her footfalls receding as she hurried back down the stairs.

Sarah was alone again.

She waited.

It felt like forever, and then Becca was back. This time there was no timid rattling of doorknobs. Instead the door shuddered under a brutal blow, then another.

Sarah stepped back, alarmed.

The door shook again, only this time there was a cracking, splintering sound. And then the lights went out.

Sarah let out a shriek.

From the other side of the door she heard Becca swear.

"I can't see anything," Becca said. "Did the power go out?"

"No." Sarah glanced toward the nightstand. "My clock is still on. How is that possible?"

"I don't know." There was another thud, and more splintering. The door crashed back on its hinges. Becca stood there holding her phone up, the flashlight blazing. In her other hand was a baseball bat. "We need to get out of here."

"Where did you get that?" Sarah was looking at the bat.

"Your dad's office. I saw it when I was in there."

"You were in dad's den?" Sarah raised an eyebrow. "When?"

"Do you want to stand here talking all night or do you want to get out of here?"

That galvanized Sarah into action. Of course she wanted to get out. It was all she'd been thinking of since seeing Jake go to the barn. "Let's go." She marched past Becca, and started down the stairs.

"Wait up." Becca followed behind, hurrying to overtake her. "I have the light."

"We have to stop Jake," Sarah said, breathless. "I don't know what he's doing with gas cans, but he has been acting really odd lately."

"I know what he's doing," Becca said. "There's gasoline all over the kitchen."

"What?" Sarah was shocked. "Why would he do that?"

"Only one reason I can think of."

Sarah let that sink in. Was Jake really going to set the house on fire? It didn't seem possible, he was such a mild mannered boy, but then, he wasn't himself anymore. Even so, she found it hard to believe. "Are you sure?"

"You think I'm making this up?" They had reached the second floor landing. Becca kept the flashlight held aloft so that they could see where they were going.

"No." Sarah wished she did. She glanced toward Jake's room as they passed, peering through the open door. No sooner had she done so than the door started to move. It swung closed, slamming with a loud bang.

"Holy crap," Becca exclaimed. "Was that you?"

As if in answer the door opened again, then closed. Along the corridor the other doors started slamming, the chorus of thuds deafening. The lights flickered on, and then went off again.

"This is insane." Becca shouted over the noise.

"Keep moving. It's the witch. She doesn't want us to stop Jake," Sarah replied.

A picture flew off the wall, whizzed past Sarah's head. She screamed and ducked barely in time. It shattered on the far wall.

Another picture, a photograph of Andrew and Jennifer taken on their wedding day, hurled itself across the hall inches from Becca's face. It exploded across the floor ending shards of glass flying.

Sarah kept her eyes fixed upon the beam from Becca's light, ignoring the doors and the flying objects. They were almost at the main staircase.

Becca led the way a step ahead of Sarah.

Without warning she came to a halt.

"There's something here. I don't think we're alone." There was fear in Becca's voice.

"Please no." Sarah stopped next to her friend. Her voice trembled when she spoke. "What did you see?"

"I'm not sure." Becca lifted the cell phone, playing the light across the walls, the floor. "Something moved."

"There, near the stairs." Sarah could barely make out a shape, a darker black against the dark. "I see it."

Becca swung the light forward. The beam slanted across the floor, the wall, and something else. She let out a scream.

The witch stood motionless. Her black waistcoat and petticoat old, tattered. The shift that poked out around her neckline was stained and discolored. Her hair, pulled back in a tight bun, must once have been a lush dark brown, but now it looked faded and brittle.

She had been beautiful in life, but now her face was drawn, skeletal. Her lips, pressed into a grim sneer, were pale and thin. But it was her eyes that filled Sarah with dread, or rather, the deep, black sockets where her eyes should have been. Despite this, Sarah knew the witch was glaring at them.

She could feel the pain, the anguish, emanating from this sad figure. She could also feel the hate.

Sarah gripped Becca's arm. She fought the urge to run. It would do them no good. Instead, she stood her ground. "You don't scare me." The words were forceful, defiant. There was no way she was going to let Martha Ward terrorize her family the way she had done the previous residents of Willow Farm.

The witch observed her with cool indifference.

"This is *my* house." Sarah took a step forward. "My family."

"What are you doing?" Becca held her back.

"I'm not putting up with this any longer," Sarah said, all the while keeping her eyes on the apparition. "I'm done with being afraid."

"I don't think this is such a good idea," Becca said.

"I don't care." Sarah could feel the fear turning to anger. She shrugged off Becca's hand, inched down the corridor. When she spoke her voice was hard, commanding. "Get out of my house."

The witch lingered at the top of the stairs, her dead stare drilling into the teens, and then, as if Sarah's words had struck a nerve, she moved.

It was so fast the girls didn't have.

Martha Ward flew down the corridor, arms outstretched, face contorted into a twisted mask of rage.

The hallway lights flashed on and off, creating a strobe effect that made the advancing witch seem like she was in some old fashioned silent movie.

The doors flew back and forth in their frames, faster and faster, the loud cracks as the slammed over and over again a cacophony of noise that hurt Sarah's ears.

She let out a startled cry, threw her arms up. She stumbled backwards. Somewhere behind her Becca screamed. The flashlight bobbed around in crazy fashion, splashing over the walls and ceiling.

The air became ice cold, as if they had stepped into a freezer. It crackled with static energy that made the hairs on Sarah's arms stand up.

Then, just when She thought the witch's talons would find her, rip into her, the apparition faded as if it had never been there.

The doors ceased their banging. The lights flickered a couple of times more, and then came back on.

Sarah stood there, shaken and terrified.

Becca was the first to speak. "Do you think she's gone?"

"I don't know." Sarah could feel her heart pounding, the adrenalin rushing through her. "I doubt it."

"I'd really like to get out of here now."

"Me too." Sarah turned to her friend. "But not without my dad and Jake."

Chapter 80

ANDREW WAITED at the bottom of the stairs, praying that Becca would return soon with Sarah and Jake. He kept his eyes fixed upon the triangle of light from the hallway above, spilling down the first few steps. When the lights dimmed and went out he stayed that way, not daring to look into the cellar darkness for fear of what may lurk there.

It was warm again now.

Whatever was down in the Cellar with him had left and taken the sudden chill with it, and for that he was grateful. Even so, the memory of the fleeting touch, the unseen fingers raking his flesh, made him shudder. If it came back he was not sure he would be able to keep his sanity.

And then, without warning, the lights came back on, the glow from the hallway a comforting companion. Less than a minute later he heard footsteps, and Becca appeared at the head of the stairs, with Sarah close behind.

"Dad." Sarah took the phone from Becca, started down the stairs, the flashlight beam pushing away the darkness. "What happened? Why were you down here so late at night?"

"I fell." He didn't mention the vodka bottle, hoped she didn't smell the spilled alcohol. "The door slammed on me."

"I'm going to get you out of here."

"Thank god." Andrew felt a flood of relief. "Where's Jake? I don't see him."

"He's not with us." Sarah grunted and pulled at the fallen shelf unit. She struggled to move it until Becca, propping the cellar door open with the baseball bat, joined her. Together they heaved it off the steps.

It clattered away into the gloom.

"What do you mean, he's not with you?" Andrew felt his chest tighten. A tight wad of fear clenched his throat. "Where is he?"

"He went to the old cow barns." Sarah spoke the words fast, as if getting them out in a hurry would make things better. "He is dragging gasoline cans back to the house."

"Gas cans?" Andrew tried to stand, grimaced as a flaring pain shot from his damaged ankle. He remembered Becca's words from earlier. "You're saying that Jake is responsible for the gasoline in the kitchen?"

"Yes." Sarah took her father's arm and let him lean on her.

"Why ever would he do that?"

"He wants to burn the house down," Sarah said as they climbed the stairs, one agonizing step at a time. "He's convinced that mom is talking to him on that old telephone."

"Except it's not Mrs. Whelan," Becca said. "It's the witch."

"Witch?" Andrew's mind raced. "What are you talking about?"

"Martha Ward. She was hung from the old tree out front back in the 1690's. She's buried in the woods behind the house."

"And she's mad as hell about it," Sarah added. "She wants revenge for what was done to her."

"That's hard to believe," said Andrew. "A ghost?"

"So you think we're making it up?" Sarah asked. They were near the top of the stairs now.

"No. I don't." Andrew shook his head. "I think I had a run in with her. It sounds crazy, but there was someone in the cellar with me. I'm sure of it."

"We met her upstairs," Sarah said. A vision of the witch's face, the eyeless yet somehow starring sockets, sent a chill though her.

"I don't think I'll ever forget that sight as long as I live," Becca agreed, retrieving the baseball bat. She held it aloft. "I feel better with this though."

"I'm not sure that will do us any good of we run into her again," Sarah said.

"It can't hurt," Becca replied.

"We're wasting time." Andrew was impatient. Jake was out there somewhere, no doubt bringing another gas can back. They had to stop him before it was too late. He hopped forward, favoring the twisted ankle.

"Sorry." Sarah put her arm around him, supported him as they made their way through the dining room.

The smell of gas was stronger here. It burned the back of Andrew's throat. The knot of fear in his stomach twisted itself tighter. He hoped against hope that it was all a big mistake. He hat his son was not responsible for the foul odor drifting from the kitchen. When he got to the door though, he knew he was wrong.

Jake was there, a burning match in his hand.

A pair of discarded gas cans lay a few feet away.

"Jake?" Andrew moved past the door, into the kitchen. He made sure to keep his voice calm and level despite the roiling fear in his gut. "What are you doing there, son?"

Jake stayed mute.

The flame danced and weaved in the breeze from the open kitchen door to his rear.

From somewhere behind him, Andrew heard a sob. It sounded like Sarah.

"Why don't you blow that match out." Andrew made a quick mental calculation, debating whether he could reach his son and extinguish the burning match before Jake had a chance to drop it. He came to the conclusion that he could not. "What do you say?"

Jake stood motionless, with the match held between two fingers, his eyes locked on it as if hypnotized.

Andrew held his breath, watching the flame dwindle as it burned down. At first he thought it might actually go out, but then Jake brought his head up, looked at his father.

"We'll all be together again." And with that he let go of the match.

"No." Andrew lunged forward, but it was too late.

The match hit the floor.

A carpet of bright orange flame shot out in all directions.

The kitchen went up in flames.

Chapter 81

ANDREW TURNED HIS HEAD SIDEWAYS, shielding his face from the leaping flames, the scorching heat. At the same time he scooped Jake up into his arms and retreated. Sarah and Becca were frozen in the doorway, transfixed by the sudden blaze.

"Run." Andrew struggled to keep a hold of his son, who was flailing and twisting.

"Let go of me." Jake screamed the words, his voice full of anger.

"Not a chance." Andrew dragged his son backwards, away from the growing fire.

"You don't understand." Jake bucked against his father. Tears streamed down his face. "I want to be with mom."

"Whatever you've been talking to, it's not your mother." They were in the dining room now. Black acrid smoke billowed through the kitchen doorway. Andrew coughed and kept going. Sarah and Becca were already at the front door.

Sarah turned the handle, pulled. "I can't get it open." There was a flutter of panic in her voice.

"Is it locked?" Andrew fought to keep Jake from tearing free and running back toward the flames.

"No." Sarah tried again. "It's stuck, just like my bedroom door."

"The witch is trying to stop us leaving," Becca said. "We have to find another way out."

"The only other door is back in the kitchen, and we'll never make it through there." Sarah slammed her fist against the door. "Damn it."

Andrew glanced toward the advancing blaze. Flames were already curling around the kitchen door. It was only a matter of minutes before the dining room went up. They would succumb to the smoke before that though.

"The window," Sarah said. "We can break out the dining room window."

"Do it." Andrew was not sure how much longer he could hold on to his thrashing son. "Quickly."

"Good thing I kept this." Becca advanced with the bat. She positioned herself near the window and adjusted her stance, then swung with all her might.

The bat hit the window dead center.

There was a sharp crack and the windowpane exploded outward, sending shards of glass flying in all directions.

Life saving air rushed in, pushing back the fume-laden smoke.

"Go." Andrew motioned for Sarah and Becca to climb out and then followed behind, letting Sarah help him drag Jake to safety.

Once outside he glanced back through the empty window frame, to the burning kitchen.

There, surrounded by the hungry blaze, stood a solitary figure, a woman dressed in old-fashioned clothing, her hair in a bun. She looked at him, and even though there was nothing but two cold, skeletal pits where her eyes should have been, Andrew could feel the anger.

And then sudden a gust of wind blew up and howled through the opening, fanning the flames and sending them high in the air. When next they settled, the woman was gone, as if she had never been there at all.

Chapter 82

THEY WERE SAFE.

Their home was burning, and they had almost died, but somehow they had survived.

Sarah stood on the driveway and watched the flames lick at the downstairs windows, consuming the house. Next to her was Becca, her arms folded around her chest, a dazed look upon her face.

Andrew stood a few feet away, next to Jake, who had stopped struggling and seemed content to watch the house burn.

"Dad?" She glanced toward her father.

"Yes?" He looked tired. His face was stained with soot.

"I'm sorry."

"What for?" He looked at her, and she saw the concern in his eyes.

"Everything." Sarah fought back a sob. "If I hadn't done what I did, taken those pills, we would never have moved here. It's all my fault."

"No. It wasn't you." Andrew's voice was soft, gentle. "I'm the one who brought us here. I never should have bought this place."

"Do you think the witch is still in there?"

"I don't know, Sarah," Andrew said. "I have no idea."

"So it wasn't mom?" Jake spoke for the first time.

"No, son." Andrew held Jake close. "Whatever that thing was, whatever was talking to you on that telephone, it was definitely not your mother."

"I just wanted us to be with her." Jake was close to tears. "I miss her so much."

"We all do," Andrew said. "But I think its time we move on with our lives."

"What are we going to do now?" Sarah said. "Where are we going to go?"

"We go home."

"Back to Boston?" Sarah asked, a spark of hope igniting in her for the first time in weeks.

"Boston." Andrew nodded. "Where we should have been all along."

"But the house, it's been sold."

"Not quite yet," Andrew said. "The closing isn't for another couple of days. Plenty of time to pull out."

"I hope I never see this place again."

"Me too," Andrew said. "Me too."

Sarah stepped close, put her arms around her dad, just as a faint wail of sirens drifted on the breeze.

"Where did they come from?" Andrew asked, turning his head in time to see a flashing blue and red glow beyond the fields.

"I called them," Becca said. "When I first got here."

Sarah was about to ask why, but then she realized she didn't care. They were alive and that was all that mattered. Everything else could wait.

Epilogue

One Year Later.

"THIS IS A FANTASTIC OPPORTUNITY." Sandra Lawton said, adjusting the bright red blazer she wore over a crisp white shirt. An oval badge, affixed to her left lapel, bore her name, a small company logo, and three gold stars signifying the trio of times she had been awarded realtor of the month. "I don't think you will find anything better in this price range."

"I don't know." Jason Prince threw a glance toward his wife, Nora. "It's a little far out. I was hoping for something closer to the city."

"Houses like this don't come up very often," Sandra said. They were standing outside, under the shadow of the old stone building. They had already spent an hour inside, touring every room, and now it was up to her to close the deal. "And just look at the land. It will afford you plenty of privacy, which is what you said you are looking for."

"I love it," Nora proclaimed. "You're not going to walk away from this place just because it's a few miles further to the city are you, Jason?"

"Well-"

"Please?"

"I'm still a little confused about the price. It's almost too good to be true." Jason dug his heels in. "You said there was a fire here?"

"Yes, in the kitchen. It spread throughout much of the downstairs, but it has all been repaired to the highest standards as you can see, and everything is up to code, I assure you," Sandra paused, waiting for her clients to say something. When they didn't she continued. "I'll be honest with you, the seller is very motivated. I shouldn't tell you this, but it's the author, Andrew Whelan."

"Andrew Whelan?" Nora's eyes grew wide. "For real? I read his book. It was awesome. That settles it, we have to buy this place."

"You want to buy a house just because some famous author owned it?" Jason laughed.

"A bestselling author." Nora starred up at the house in wonder. "Is this the house in the book?"

"I believe it is" Sandra wondered if she'd done the right thing mentioning her client's name. For a moment she had forgotten what his book was about. "He didn't live here very long."

"So, is it true?" Nora asked. "Is the house haunted?"

"Funny you should ask that." Sandra took a deep breath. She hated this part. It had already scared away three prospective buyers. "My client requests that I impress upon you that the house is indeed haunted. If you've read his book I'm sure you are familiar with the details."

"But that was fiction, right?" Nora said. "It couldn't really have been that bad. Shame really. It might be fun to have a pet witch around. Still, to live in the house that inspired the book. How awesome is that?"

"I don't believe in ghosts." Jason stretched and glanced at his watch. "Or witches."

"So what do you say?" Sandra felt a glimmer of hope.

They hadn't said no, and the wife seemed genuinely enamored with the place. "If you put in a bid today, I can have the keys in your hands within two weeks, three at most."

"It is a great deal," Jason said. He turned to his wife. "What do you say?"

"I say we buy it." She hopped from foot to foot, excitement plastered over her face. "Let's do it."

Jason looked up once more at the old farmhouse, a smile touching his lips. "I may live to regret this, but to hell with it, we'll take the place."

The End.

Printed in Great Britain
by Amazon